JUST HIS PARTNER
A SWEET ROMANTIC COMEDY

SOUTHERN ROOTS SWEET ROMANTIC COMEDY
BOOK 4

ELANA JOHNSON

CHAPTER ONE

SABRINA

I GLANCE LEFT AND RIGHT AS I GET OFF THE elevator, trying to decide if the smell on this floor is the same as it was when I left for work. There's definitely a funk in the air, and I wrinkle my nose as I walk.

My new apartment sits near the end of the hall, with one more unit beside mine in the corner. I didn't mind the move, because I don't have a whole lot. I had to get out of that place with the blown-up egg bits everywhere, and no, I didn't get my cleaning deposit back. I'm lucky I didn't get an extra bill to redo texture and paint, in all honesty.

I *may* not have left a forwarding address and deleted my former landlord's contact information from my cell-phone. Since I only answer calls from numbers I know on my personal line, I suppose he could've called looking for me. I just don't know it.

With every step I take toward my new apartment—

where I don't want to be living, mind you—the scent intensifies. I glare at 4I as I pass, my goal 4K, which is where I
live. I want a farmhouse in the woods, where Archie—the
cat who came with this apartment—can chase mice and
birds to his heart's content.

I want to tear out a kitchen and put in a new one. I
want to soak in a really old tub, and then replace it with
something new. I'm not sure why, as I've never done much
remodeling or renovating. It just sounds fun. Plus, maybe
if I tear down old sheetrock and pull out defunct pipes, I'll
cleanse myself of the things that need replacing in my
life too.

Such a deep metaphor, I know. I am a lawyer, after all.

I reach 4K and fit my key into the lock, the smell as
strong as if I'm in the same room with it. Rodizio across the
hall must be making his mother's fajitas again. They put
off this decaying smell last time he tried, and I cast a look
at 4L across the hall from my place as the knob turns.

"M-row," Archie sings, running past my ankles.

"Hey, buddy," I say to him, but he's streaking down the
hall. He's kind of a community cat, though he stays in my
apartment, sleeps in my bed, and I feed and water him. So
he's kind of mine too. The previous renters of this apartment couldn't take him with them, and they'd asked with
such sad-kitty eyes if I'd take him that I couldn't say no.

I'm not sure why. I say no to plenty of other things.

Not Jason Finch, I think as I enter the apartment and

leave the front door open a crack so Archie can get back in. I sigh, reminding myself that Jason Finch—a man I work with at my firm—isn't asking me any yes/no questions. Certainly not if I'd like to go to dinner with him.

That would be a yes anyway, not a no.

I exhale and wipe my hand back across my forehead and into my hair as I drop my briefcase and jacket onto the armchair in the living room. The smell has gotten worse, and that takes my attention into the kitchen.

My mind is stuck on Jason, the wedding we attended together over two months ago, and our working relationship. That at least is working now, so it's probably best that he doesn't ask me out. In this day and age, I can probably ask him, but again, things are going so well at the firm that I don't dare jinx anything.

Not only that, but perhaps he didn't enjoy himself at his cousin's wedding as much as I did. Or maybe he decided it wasn't a date and that we'd simply gone together so he didn't have to go alone. Perhaps I'm just his partner, and that's just how he wants it. No matter what, I feel like I failed some sort of test I hadn't known I was taking.

And I'm a really good test-taker, so familiar frustration fills me as I enter my kitchen.

My eyes land on the slow cooker, and the world narrows to that appliance. The smell intensifies, as if I've been cooking squirrels—or human hands—on low for the past eight hours. Horror fills me, and I dash over to the counter and lift the lid on my "no-fail beef stew."

Oh, I've failed. Big time.

I gag as the full brunt of the scent hits me square in the face, wondering how in the world I ruined a dish that only has six ingredients. Six! Total.

Carrots, potatoes, broth, salt, pepper, and cubed beef.

"More like cubed barf," I say, slamming the lid down on the cooker. I have to get rid of this, stat. How am I the worst cook in America?

"Because you're Sabrina Shadows," I mutter to myself, lifting the heavy stoneware piece out of the cooking element. I look at the sink, which has a disposal, and veto that idea. Knowing me, the stew—and I use that term loosely—will get stuck in the drain and this smell will never go away.

The trash is also out, and I simply head for the door. This whole thing is going straight in the Dumpster behind the building, and I feel like a criminal dragging out a dead body as I enter the elevator, relieved I'm the only one inside the car on the way down.

I dash outside and heave the crock over the top lip of the Dumpster, my heart beating so fast. I just know crazy Mrs. Littleton is watching through her back window, and I glance up to the third floor where she lives. I swear the curtain in the third pane over flutters, and I tell myself I did nothing wrong.

Well, besides the crime against carrots, of course.

I'm going to have to move again. I *want* to move again, and I pull my phone out of my pocket as I march back toward the building entrance. Jessica Dunaway's line rings only twice before she chirps, "Hey, Sabrina."

"Jess," I practically shout. "Any progress on the house hunting?"

"Didn't you get my message?" she asks, causing my brow to furrow.

"No," I say.

"Hmm, strange," she says, and it sounds like she's distracted with something else. I know, because I sound like this all the time, and I'm constantly doing five hundred and eleven different things.

My phone makes a weird *bloopety-bloop* at me, and I pull it from my ear as Jess says she sent over some new listings for me to look at.

Jason Finch sits on the screen, his call coming in over Jess's. I drop my phone, my surprise too great to keep holding it. The device splats against the asphalt, and a terrible cracking noise fills the sky.

The phone tumbles away from me, and I go scampering after it. When I reach it and lift it up, I see a diagonal fissure running from the bottom left corner to the top right. "Great," I say, because the screen is completely black too.

No call connected to Jess. No line ringing in from Jason.

"Just great."

―――――

LATER THAT NIGHT, I pull into the parking lot at my building, my ire near its breaking point. I hadn't made it to the cell phone store before they'd closed. I can't get a new phone until tomorrow, and I seriously feel like Archie has gnawed off my arm and won't give it back.

I start to pull into my marked, covered, reserved spot and find a car already there. "Are you freaking kidding me?" I ask, wanting to go Fried Green Tomatoes on the fancy-pants SUV in my spot and floor the accelerator. See how they like their luxury vehicle then.

Instead of doing something that can get me arrested, I put my car in reverse and straighten out so I can swing into an unmarked, uncovered, and available parking space. Where that guy should've parked. I tell myself it doesn't snow in Charleston, that I'm not in Montana anymore, and it's fine.

Everything's fine.

I keep the mantra running through my head all the way to the fourth floor, where I step off the elevator, the hint of my beef stew fiasco still lingering in the air. Something else has masked it though, and I cock my head, familiarity running through me.

"Ah, there she is," a man says, and I know that voice.

Worlds collide as I turn toward the voice and my apartment and find Jason Finch himself standing there. He's still in his slacks and tie from work, but he's got

Archie in his arms, stroking the cat as if he's the original owner of him and has been searching for the feline for many long years.

My heartbeat goes wild, knocking against my ribcage like a crazed fish out of water. "What are you doing here?" I ask, walking toward him. Everything about this scenario is wrong. Jason Finch doesn't exist outside the walls of Farmer, Buhler, and Cason, Attorneys at Law.

And yet, there he stands, that gorgeous smile on his face and that traitorous cat in his arms.

"I called and left several messages," he says, those dark-as-danger eyes firing at me. "Saying I needed to come by so we could go over a case that's been called up in the morning."

"Tomorrow morning?"

"That would be morning," he says.

I glare at him, wishing his face would melt right off. Wait. No, I take that back. He's too handsome for such a thought. "Can you put down my cat?"

Jason looks down at Archie, and the animal is practically asleep, seemingly in complete bliss. I know if Jason held me like that, I would be.

He looks up at me. "Is he yours?"

"Yes," I say, taking Archie from him as I reach him. "How long have you been here?"

"A couple of minutes," he says.

"How did you figure out where I live?" I ask.

"Cheryl," he says, and I nod. She's my secretary, so I

suppose that makes sense. He's here about a case, and he stoops to pick up his briefcase. We've taken two steps down the hall toward my apartment when the elevator dings again, signaling the car has arrived.

I normally don't look to see who it is, but when a voice says, "There he is," in an indignant tone, I do. Mrs. Littleton stands there, pointing her crooked finger in my and Jason's direction. "He's been loitering around here for at least an hour."

Two police officers step off the elevator too, and I can't help but think of the body—er, crock pot—in the Dumpster out back. I blink, imagining a situation where they ask why it smells like death in my apartment and then haul me down to the station to ask me who I killed and then tried to cook slowly into a stew.

When my eyes focus again, the cops are nearly upon us, and one of them frowns at me. "I'm sorry," I say. "Did you say something?"

"He asked if you knew me," Jason says pointedly, to which I blink some more. "Why are you standing there like that?" He sighs and rolls his eyes. "We work together. She's my junior partner."

"Work together," one cop repeats. He's much bigger and beefier than his partner. I can't help but wonder what kind of stew he'd make since he is so beefy. Then my brain catches up to the pun, and I shake my head.

"You don't know him?" the skinnier cop asks. The

three of them stand there staring at me, and Archie goes, "Me-row," before jumping down from my arms.

I watch him do his cat-stalk into the apartment, wondering if he somehow did something to the stew. It was seriously six ingredients, and cats aren't exactly trustworthy. Sure, they look innocent, but—

"Bri," Jason barks at me, and I focus on the more immediate situation.

"Yes," I say to the cops, pulling myself all the way together. It's hard for this late in the day. "I know him. We work together at Farmer, Buhler, and Cason, and we have to go over a case that just got called into the grand jury tomorrow morning."

CHAPTER TWO

JASON

"Took you long enough," I say to Sabrina after the cops have gone, after they've assured the white-haired lady who'd accused me of loitering that I wasn't a stalker, and after we've gone into Bri's apartment and closed the door.

"I was thinking about something else," she says, hurrying into the kitchen to unplug something. It smells like overcooked leather mixed with Brussels sprouts in her apartment, and I really want to go home.

At the same time, the dark-haired beauty across the room holds me captive. I had a fantastic time with her at Tara and Alec's wedding, but I haven't asked her out again. I know how to do it, but I've held back. I want to get things right with Bri for some reason. I don't want her to be another woman in my long list of dates and acquaintances.

I've been trying out a bachelor lifestyle—a true bachelor lifestyle. The kind where I go to work, do a good job, and then go home. Where I don't flirt with every woman I meet, and I don't go out with three or four different women every week. In fact, I haven't gone out with anyone in the past six months, and that started before Tara's wedding.

Seeing her so blissfully happy with Alec changed a lot for me. I want her brand of happiness, and I know it doesn't come from having a different woman on my arm every evening. No matter what, I still go home alone.

I glance around Bri's apartment, taking in the mismatched furniture and the lack of pictures on the wall.

"I just moved in," she says, pulling my attention back to her. I don't see any boxes or anything else to indicate she's in the middle of unpacking, but I don't say anything about it. She opens the fridge and promptly closes it again. "I don't have any food here. Are you hungry?"

"I haven't eaten," I say coolly. "Do you want to get CarryEats or go out?"

She indicates my briefcase with her chin. "We better get CarryEats and get this ironed out." She sounds tired, and boy, do I understand that. Exhaustion pulls through my soul, and no one in law school tells you how tired you'll be some days. They should have an Utter Exhaustion 101 class simply as a way to weed out the strong from the weak.

Right now, I feel like I can't even stand for another second, so I move over to the couch and sit down.

"My phone broke," Bri says, moving to perch on the armrest on the end of the couch. "That's why I didn't get any of your calls or messages."

I look up at her, something quiet and powerful moving between us. I don't know how whatever that is can be both of those things at the same time, but it is. "I'm sorry about your phone."

"I was out trying to get a new one," she says. "You didn't have to wait an hour here."

Embarrassment floods me. That little old lady really sold me out. "It wasn't that long," I say, though it definitely was longer than a few minutes. "We need to go over the case, and I couldn't get in touch with you."

I actually have the case memorized, but Bri and I have been working it together, and I'd love to see her take the lead in court tomorrow. My throat goes dry, because I've never said that to her. Not once.

I pull out my phone and start swiping through the options at CarryEats. "What do you want?"

"Anything but stew," she says, which causes me to look up at her.

She shakes her head, displeasure in her dark eyes. "Don't ask. It's a long story." She pulls the band out of her hair, which causes it to tumble down over her shoulders. Oh, I can't stay here for much longer. Not with her dressing down like that, and not if we share dinner.

I'm going to say something I either mean or don't mean —both are really dangerous right now. I feel fragile, like I'm not sure who I am or what I'm doing. The truth is, I don't. I'm in a state of flux right now, and that is really bad news for me.

"No stew," I say, my voice only slightly pinched. "Not Your Momma's Noodles?"

"Sure," she says. "I like the firehouse mac and cheese there."

"You got it," I say, keeping my focus on the phone and not her. I have to. If I don't...well, I don't even want to think about what will happen if I don't.

She's just your partner, I tell myself. *You don't want to do anything to jeopardize your job.*

I've told myself these things before over the past couple of months. There's no rule at Farmer, Buhler, and Cason that would prevent Bri and I from seeing one another. There's a folder of paperwork though, and the relationship won't be kept secret if I start it.

I'm fairly certain I'm going to have to be the one to start it, as Bri hasn't said a single word about the wedding. She's so different from other women I'm usually attracted to, because she doesn't seem to like me. And that only makes me like her more, crazy as that sounds.

I finish with the order and look up again, sighing this time. "Twenty-four to thirty-four minutes."

She smiles at me and slips down onto the couch. "All right," she says. "Just enough time to lay everything out in order and then go over it while we eat." She pulls the coffee table closer to our knees.

"I want you to take lead," I blurt out, forgetting all of the tactful ways I was going to bring this up with her.

Her eyes widen. "You want me to do what?"

"You heard me." I reach for my briefcase. "So *you're* going to lay this out, and then you're going to present it to me while *I* eat."

"I haven't eaten either," she says, folding her arms and glaring at me. Seriously, that is so annoyingly-attractive, and I can't help grinning at her.

"You can eat when you get the case right."

"You're not my mother, Jason," she says, reaching for the first sheaf of papers I extract from my briefcase.

"Thank goodness for that," I mutter, because it would be super weird if her mother had the same feelings for Bri that I do. I've already fantasized about kissing her, and yeah. Super weird.

"What?" she asks.

"Nothing," I say, speaking up. "Now, that top paper is the list of witnesses the defense is going to call..."

———

BRI EXCHANGES A GLANCE with me while we sit at the prosecutor's table. I barely move my chin, and she pushes to her feet. "Mister Davenport," she says without leaving her spot at the table. "You were driving, correct?"

"Yes," the man in the witness chair says. People think court is so exciting, and it's really not. There's no flashy lights or big-name actors here. This isn't even truly court, but a grand jury to simply determine if we can take the case to court. It's a great way for Bri to get some experience with a witness, and she can consult with me any time she needs to.

"Driving your car, correct?" she asks, moving to the end of the table and leaning one hip into it. It was her idea to explore this idea of who the car and the weapon truly belong to, and honestly, it's a shot in the dark. There are so many witnesses, and so many perpetrators, and every single one of them has a different story.

We've combed over every police report and read every witness declaration, and even I don't know who was really the mastermind behind the United Methodist School robbery several months ago. Bri had the idea to question Derrick Davenport and see what he said about the gun and the car.

Right now, he glances toward the empty defense table and then to me. "Yes," he says.

"Who held your gun to your ribs?" Bri reaches down and shuffles some papers on the table, but I can tell she's not looking at them. She just doesn't want Mister Davenport to feel like she's studying him. There's no judge present today. No defendant is allowed to present his case.

The prosecution lays out the case, their evidence, and can question witnesses, and the members of the grand jury vote in secret as to whether there is enough to proceed with the case. With how convoluted everything in this particular case is, we'll be batting a thousand if we get it past the grand jury.

"Thomas," Mister Davenport says, and Bri lifts her head.

"Thomas Rowberry?" she asks.

Mister Davenport licks his lips. "I mean Teddy. Teddy Christopher."

"Was it Thomas Rowberry or Teddy Christopher?" Bri asks, taking a step toward the podium. She can't go past that, and I told her not to even use it. She stops after a single step, and I mentally cheer for her. She can be an intimidating woman, and Derrick Davenport certainly seems to be shaking in his boots right now.

"Teddy Christopher," he says.

Bri nods and turns back to the table. "And you drove your own car, with your own gun pressed to your ribs, into the river. Is that right?"

"Yes," he says. "Thomas said I had to. Then there'd be no prints."

Bri picks up the folder I slide forward on the table. "Yes, the prints." She holds up the folder. "Evidence for the United Methodist School," she says crisply. "Only Mister Davenport's prints were found on the gun and inside the car. He claims to have worn gloves, but no other DNA evidence was found either."

"Because the car went into the river," Mister Davenport says.

Bri hands the folder containing the print and DNA evidence—or lack thereof to the lead juror in the grand jury. There's twenty-one people here today, and Bri continues with, "You can speak freely, Mister Davenport. The purpose of this session is that you don't have to be afraid of anyone." She faces him again, and I see the fierceness on her face before she does.

"There's not going to be any retaliation from what you say," she says. "No one will know. Grand jury testimony is sealed." She migrates back to the table while Mister Davenport squirms and then coughs.

My word, she was right. He's the guilty party here, and we may have charged the wrong individual with being the mastermind behind the crime.

Our eyes meet, and I hope she gets the message I feel blazing in mine. *Ask him. Ask him now.* "Didn't you simply plan and carry out this robbery by yourself?" Bri asks, taking that step forward again.

Mister Davenport turns a shade of gray I haven't even seen on the sidewalk. "I—" He glances over to the jury.

"A yes or no," Bri prompts.

"No," he says. "It was Teddy Christopher."

"Not Thomas Rowberry?" she asks as if she doesn't really care. She's *good.*

"Teddy held the gun in the car. Thomas masterminded the whole thing."

"So Teddy is the same man who held your own gun to you and commanded you drive your car into the river," Bri says. "And whose prints were not found on either."

Mister Davenport clears his throat. "Right."

"Because Thomas told you both to." She sounds like my very disappointed fourth grade teacher, using a voice that indicates she doesn't believe Mister Davenport at all.

"Yes," he says.

"Very well," she says airily as if she's satisfied with the witness's testimony. She sits down next to me, and I keep my gaze on the notes in front of me while she closes with the evidence we do have, and how we'll be pursuing all leads to make sure the right person is charged and brought to justice in the robbing of a prestigious private school in the city.

"Even if that person is Mister Derrick Davenport," Bri says. "Thank you." We collect our things and prepare to leave the court-like conference room. Mister Davenport glares knives into Bri's face, but she acts like she doesn't even notice.

Out in the hallway, I finally take a breath that doesn't feel like oatmeal in my lungs. "That was great," I say, exhaling most of the words out.

Bri looks at me with hope in those pretty eyes. "Yeah? Really? I felt so...off. I really thought he was going to say he did it alone." She shakes her head, clearly disappointed.

"I think he did," I say. "And I've never thought that before you said it last night."

"I guess we'll see what the grand jury says. I really want to take this to trial. There's something not right with this case." She plops her bag down on a bench and rifles through it.

"You're going to read the brief again right now?"

"How long does the grand jury take?"

"Depends," I say. "Could be a while if they don't agree. Could be hours or tomorrow. Could be fast."

"Mister Finch?"

I turn toward the sound of Deputy Jones's voice. My eyebrows fly toward the sky. "They're back?" I ask, striding toward him. He hands me an envelope, and I flip it open as he returns to the room.

Bri presses in beside me, and I pull out the note. My whole body screams at me about the scent of Bri's perfume, and the way her arm is warming mine. I look up. "We can indict."

Her face splits into a grin, and she laughs. "We did it," she says.

I can't help smiling too, because a happy Bri is so much better than a growly one, and I've seen both. "No," I say. "*You* did it."

She grabs onto me and hugs me, and I try not to close my eyes in bliss. Yeah, that's a try and a fail. "Thank you, Jason," she says, so much sincerity in her voice. Maybe I'm imagining things, but I hear some emotion too.

She pulls back, and our eyes meet. She's maybe five inches from me, and I do what I usually do when a beautiful woman is in my arms. I lean down and touch my lips to hers. Fireworks and the National Anthem and entire choirs of angels sing down from above.

Wow, kissing Sabrina Shadows is *amazing*. Like life-changing-amazing.

She kisses me back, and while she might seem like the uptight, bun-in-her-hair, cardigan-wearing lawyer type, the woman has lips made of apples and honey.

My eyes are closed, and the next thing I know, she's ripped her lips away from mine. She says, "No, we're not doing this," and she shoves both palms against my chest.

I stumble backward, my eyes flying open. Surprise and humiliation swirl together in my chest, and all I can do is stand there as Bri marches away from me, collects her briefcase, and heads for the stairs.

"Wait," I say, but she's already gone. I push my hand through my hair and sigh. "Idiot," I tell myself as I collect the indictment paper and my own briefcase. "Stupid, stupid, stupid."

My phone rings, and my cousin's name sits there. How does Tara always know when I've made a complete and utter fool of myself? I won't be able to hide it from her. I'll say one word, and she'll be like, *What happened? Why do you sound like you've sucked down helium?*

If I don't answer, she'll stop by my house with dessert or a pan of lemon chicken and roast potatoes. I decide I better get something delicious out of telling her how I just made the worst mistake possible with my junior partner, and I swipe the call to voicemail.

Then I hurry after Bri, because she drove us over here. Because I have to make sure we're okay before we get back to the sixth floor of our office building.

Because she *kissed me back*, and I want to know why she did that if she doesn't want to "do this" with me.

CHAPTER THREE

BRI

I BURST OUT OF THE COURTHOUSE, MY HEART sprinting in my chest in a way it hasn't in a while. Once, I had to run in front of the school to get my little sister off the bus she'd gotten on accidentally.

I'm pretty sure that's the last time I did any sort of significant physical activity, and my chest had felt hollowed out like someone had scrubbed it with steel wool and then poured in bleach.

I feel just like that now.

Not only that, but my head has been superheated beyond belief, the origin point my mouth. The mouth that Jason just kissed.

I reach up and touch my lips as if they're now foreign objects that don't belong to me.

"Bri," he says behind me, panic in his tone, and that

spurs me to get moving again, despite the protesting in my muscles. "Wait."

I don't wait, but I can't outrun Jason Finch. The man probably puts in ten miles before dawn. A summer dawn, which is like four a.m. here, with no mountains.

I miss the mountains, I think, which is such a ridiculous thought. Every now and then, I miss my life in Montana, and the promise it held. As I stride down the sidewalk in front of the county courthouse, familiar feelings of that life surge forward.

Feelings of a future shared with someone with non-feline DNA. Dinner together, not alone. Someone to text when I have an amazing moment in court like I just had, and someone to talk to when the day goes wrong at every turn.

He'll make me tea or hot cocoa, despite the fact that we live in the South, and somehow by the time I'm done venting, my favorite cookies will be on a plate in front of me.

"Bri," Jason says as he reaches my side. He can walk just as fast as my mad march, and he's not afraid to look right at me. His confidence is astronomical, though he wears a look of extreme...fear? Maybe fear.

"I'm sorry," he says. "I just got caught up in the moment. You were *brilliant* in there."

"And you kiss women after their moments of brilliance?" Of course he does. The man's a player, and I'm a fool for thinking that just because he hasn't dated anyone in a few months he's changed.

"No," he shoots back at me. "Not usually...*their* brilliance."

"Oh my goodness," I say. "You need someone to tell you when to speak and when to just stay silent." I give him a glare and pull my keys from my bag. I tap the unlock button, because I have no idea where I parked my car.

I'm not even sure what my car looks like in this moment.

My body burns along my top lip, where Jason's had been. I hate that it's betraying me like this.

"Bri," he tries again, his voice much softer, more filled with pleading.

I stop suddenly, feeling all of my thorns rise to the surface. Since Max, I've kept everyone out of my life. Jason is just the next guy I need to prick a few times before he gets the hint that I'm not interested.

If only I truly wasn't interested.

"Can you bake?" I demand.

Jason comes to a complete stop, blinking all the while. "Bake...? What?"

"Your cousin is a chef," I say. "So I want to know if you can bake."

He blows out his breath and looks across the street. "I mean, I can feed myself. Usually boxed stuff or frozen things." He returns his gaze to mine, and our eyes lock. He smiles, and it looks like he's trying to be...kind. Trying to be himself.

I have no idea what to do with everything that's happened in the past hour. The hearing. This conversation. That kiss.

My *word*, that kiss...

"I'm a super-pro at those refrigerated cookie chubs." He wipes the smile from his face, but it comes right back. "Slice and bake? You know those?" He searches my face, and I realize I'm standing there staring at him.

At his mouth.

I yank my eyes back to his. "Yes," I clip out. "I think they taste like preservatives." I hit the unlock button again, but I still hear nothing.

"Tara taught me how to fix that," Jason says, falling into step with me again. It's easier and slower, and I'm glad I've calmed enough that I'm not running from him.

"They're always a little wet, you know? So she says to put in a little extra flour, and maybe more chips that aren't the same kind as the chub."

The word *chub* makes me smile, and I cut him a glance out of the corner of my eye. "That's a funny word."

"Chub?"

"Yeah," I say. "Is that really what it's called? Or are you making that up?"

"Making it up?" He shakes his head as if he's really wounded, but he's not. "That's what it's called. My brother used to have this dog. Well." He shrugs one shoulder, and all of my clarity comes back.

I know right where I parked my car now, and I head toward the lot down the block. I'd been nervous, and the two-block walk had helped with the nerves.

"I have the dog now, so he's still around."

"You don't sound super happy about that."

"I like dogs," Jason says. "My brother's been keeping my Great Dane for me." Work, my nightlife...it's kept me busy and not home, though I've given up all of my evening activities.

"Wow, a Great Dane." I look at him again, clearly getting that Jason would like to be a better dog-dad. "That's a big dog."

"He's *huge*." Jason keeps his eyes down the sidewalk, but the foot traffic isn't much at mid-morning. "But he thinks he's a small dog. He wants to sit right on my lap and lick my face, and yeah. I don't get much done at home, which is why I stay at the office or in the city."

I don't know what to say to him. Of course I know he's a real person; he's just so darn good-looking it's hard to remember that even handsome men have problems.

He's never given any indication that life isn't plated in gold. He sails into a partnership at a prestigious law firm, he wears the designer suits, and he's got the most charming farmhouse in the country. *And* it backs up right to the woods.

"How many brothers do you have?"

"Just the one." Jason swallows and says nothing more.

"And Tara," I say.

"Right," he says. "And if you want cookies, she can make anything. Just tell me your favorite kind, and I'll talk to her."

"I don't need your cousin to make me cookies," I say, though I certainly can't make them.

"She likes it," he assures me. "She does these little tea parties with her next-door neighbor. Mr. Reynolds? He's a widower, and he watches out for Tara when I can't, and she takes him treats. I get invited sometimes."

I catalog the invitation that he watches out for his cousin, and dang him, that makes him even more attractive. I don't know who I am when I say, "I like tea parties."

Jason chuckles, and he must know what that sound does to the double-X chromosome. "That surprises me a little," he says.

"Does it?"

"Yeah," he says. "I think you're more like a...five-star steakhouse."

"Well, there's nothing better than a good steak," I say, arriving at my car. I turn toward him and offer him a smile that fades almost the moment it fully forms. "I don't think any more...kissing would be wise." I swallow and clear my throat. "Unless you're going to go talk to Malcolm in HR."

Jason stares at me, blinks, and says, "I just lost my head for a minute."

I nod. Of course. He's so used to kissing the closest female. That's all this is.

"Unless you want to go to dinner with me," he says.

"What?"

His phone rings, and he looks at it. "It's Connor. I'll be right back." His eyes flick toward me and then he turns. He's walking away. He's gone, lost in a conversation with his brother about something I shouldn't care about.

I don't.

I get in my car, buckle up for safety—safety first—and head back to my office.

―――――

I STEP up to the line on the floor and then edge back about three inches. Not quite three, but my eye judges the distance easily.

The familiar weight of the hatchet in my hand triggers something in my head that allows me to find the exact right spot to stand. I don't have to throw hard to get the hatchet to stick in the target, something I learned during my first session at Hatchet Happy Hour. I've been coming here at least once a week since I moved to Charleston.

Today, I lift the weapon and let it fall behind my shoulder, then raise it again, all the movement coming from my elbow. I take a deep breath and blow out all the tension in my shoulders and upper back.

The worries of the day go with my oxygen, and I close

my eyes. In the moment my lungs are mostly empty, I launch the hatchet.

I don't open my eyes until I hear the satisfying *thunk* of the hatchet embedding into the wood platform in front of me.

Then, I expect to find it sticking in by the top tip of the blade, right in the middle of the green boards that criss-cross in the middle to make a square.

It's not there at all, but stuck in the outer white area, by the bottom tip of the blade. I don't care, because I threw it well enough to hit the board and embed. Good enough.

Compared to my court performance earlier today, this last throw can only be categorized as such.

I sigh as I check left and right to make sure no one has shown up while my eyes were closed. The last thing I need to add to my mental worries is getting impaled by a hatchet from another thrower, thus violating the number one rule in the facility. *Don't go retrieve your hatchet if anyone in your trio is throwing.*

No one else has shown up tonight, which isn't too surprising. It's early on a weekday still, and I grab my hatchet and lift it out.

Once all of the equipment is back at the front desk, I shoulder my giant alligator-skin patterned bag, and turn toward the door.

Someone is coming through it, and I dutifully step to the side to allow them to enter. The wind has been brutal this afternoon, and I'd hoped for someone to let me inside before they went out.

A man enters, and he looks vaguely familiar. My mind seizes onto him as another voice behind him speaks. I recognize him as a client at Farmer, Buhler, and Cason just before Jason says, "Bri."

My eyes fly to him—the second man who's entered the hatchet-throwing building. He wears pure surprise on his face, and my heartbeat thumps through my whole body like a thwapping dog tail.

"What are you doing here?" he asked, sweeping the check-in area for something or someone.

I don't know what to say. My lips tingle, thinking about his kiss from that morning. His head tilts slightly, and I wonder what he's thinking.

"Just leaving," I say, but I don't move.

"Do you want to join us?" the other man says, and I look at him. He has a fun, friendly face, and he's still wearing a dark, designer suit, although without his jacket. The vest, white shirt, and tie are still in place, his sleeves rolled to his elbow.

"Sure, join us," Jason says jovially. "Ben, this is Sabrina Shadows. She works at the firm with me."

Ben steps forward, his bright blue eyes sparkling with something. Mischief or delight, or...desire.

Oh boy.

I glance at Jason while I shake Ben's hand, my eyes

coming back to him easily. "It's great to meet you," I say, my smile now fixed firmly in place.

"You too." He holds my hand longer than necessary, his gaze sliding over to Jason's. "You said everyone was full." He looks back to me. "Is your client schedule full, Miss Shadows?" Ben actually grins and lifts my hand to his lips, giving it a delicate kiss.

My professional smile slips, and I too look at Jason for a way out of this.

He gives a chuckle that doesn't sound nervous or afraid. Not that happy either, but I don't know how well Ben knows him. Perhaps Ben won't catch that irritated undertone to Jason's laughter.

"Bri is my partner." He puts his arm around my shoulders and draws me back, which allows me to extract my hand from Ben's without seeming rude or forceful. "Trust me, her schedule is bursting at the seams." He nods at me and then the counter. "They don't look busy. I bet we can get a full trio of lanes beside one another."

Yeah, like the one I just left, I think.

"Unless you were here interviewing a witness." Jason's perfectly sculpted eyebrows lift, and I give him a slight nod.

He drops his arm and steps over to the desk. "Three, please."

Jasper behind the desk looks at me, and I beg him silently not to say anything. I see him every time I come here, but he obviously doesn't know how to speak my brand of silent begging yet.

Not that I truly expect him to. True, I know his birthday and I brought him a red velvet cupcake only a few weeks ago to celebrate it. I know the name of his girl-friend, and that his favorite food is a medium-rare steak with a huge baked potato. Butter, sour cream, bacon, cheese, and green onions on top.

"Can your wrist handle another hour, Bri?" he asks, turning to get the hatchets.

"*Another* hour?" Jason asks, cocking his hip into the counter.

I don't have a ton of work to do tonight. A brief to read for the sixth time. A coffee and a meal to get on the way home. The last half of my book to read.

"You know," I say, talking right to Jason. "I'm not sure I can. I was going to meet everyone for coffee at Legacy Brew."

"They'll still be there in an hour." Jason actually moves as if to block me from exiting. "I know, because Tara told me so." His eyes blaze with some sort of fire I don't understand.

"Great," Ben says, and this time, his arm goes around my shoulders, disrupting the lay of my denim jacket. I quickly pull it back into position, meeting his eyes as I do.

"Lane seven," Jasper says.

"We'll see you over there." Ben leads me away, his head already bent low to say something into my ear.

"So...are you seeing anyone, Bri?"

I glance back to Jason, and his eyes are slitted as he watches Ben and me walk away. I don't know why Jason's brought his client here, but it's probably important. And I know how to play important.

I put a less professional smile on my face and allow a giggle to come out of my mouth. "Not right now, Ben. You?"

"Not in this city."

My gaze jerks to his. "You mistake me for someone who has flings."

Ben only grins wider. "Just making sure you and Finch aren't anything," he says.

"Absolutely not," I say. "I'm just his partner. In fact, I've never known Jason to mix business and pleasure."

Not entirely true, as he did kiss me in the courthouse that morning. But like he said, he'd just gotten caught up in the moment.

We don't have anything outside of our business relationship, even if I've been thinking about him all afternoon. Or for a week. Weeks. Months.

Since I started at Farmer, Buhler, and Cason.

Whatever. We're nothing. Just caught up in little moments that don't matter.

CHAPTER FOUR

JASON

I DON'T LIKE BEN ARNOLD'S ARM AROUND BRI. NOT one little bit. The man is a bigger player than I am, and he doesn't even live here. I normally don't care what he does in his downtime between our meetings, and I always take him somewhere to entertain him after a long afternoon where we've been trapped in my office together.

I thought hatchet throwing would be a balm to my soul after today, which started in court and deviated all over from kissing the most interesting woman I've met in months, to a horrible veggie burger for lunch just to go along with Ben, and then arguing behind closed doors while I tell him to clean up his act.

He's clearly not going to do it tonight, and I follow him and Bri with three hatchets, already thinking about throwing one "on accident" in Ben's direction.

And Bri?

My surprise at seeing her continues to stream through me. With her cardigans and jackets and shawls, I have never pictured her in Hatchet Happy Hour, throwing sharp weapons at targets.

She stands in the end lane, and Ben works her hard, obviously trying to get a date with her. Bri shakes her head, her smile seemingly real and made for Ben. "My policy of dating out-of-town men stands. I'm sorry." She looks over to me and takes a hatchet from me. Her gaze locks onto mine, and I've been working with her long enough to get the gist of her thoughts.

I should've let her go get coffee with Tara and the others. Maybe I can call my cousin and she can rescue Bri.

I say, "Hey, did you get that email I sent you?"

She turns back to her alligator bag and plucks her phone from it. Meanwhile, I press the volume button on mine, which makes it chime. It gives me a good reason to look at it, and my fingers start moving at the speed of light.

I quickly send a text to Bri. *I'm sorry. How can I get you out of here?*

Her thumbs fly across the screen too, and her smile blinks onto her face. *I'm going to claim low blood sugar after my first throw. You better have a reason you and Ben can't take me to get something to eat.*

She looks up and tucks her phone into her bag.

"I got it," she says, returning to her lane. "You haven't thrown?" She indicates that Ben should go first.

"Have you done this before?" he asks.

"Yes," she says. "Do you want a lesson?"

"From you?" He actually slides his gaze down to her low heels and back to her eyes. "Yes, ma'am."

"Okay," she says, lifting the hatchet. "The key is in the grip, and then the wrist." She continues to instruct him on how to throw the hatchet—both one-handed and two. Since the man at the check-in desk knew her, I'm putting together a lot of pieces very quickly, and once Ben launches his hatchet, I nod at Bri.

She's more than I knew, and my attraction to her only grows as she steps up to the line, adjusts her feet, and then throws her hatchet like she comes here every evening after her day in the office. For all I know right now, she does. I'm more determined than ever to find out more about my junior partner, but as she turns from her target—where her hatchet has stuck very nearly in the middle of the green square—she stumbles.

"Whoa," I say, jumping forward before Ben can. "You okay, Bri?" I catch her around the waist, and dang, the lightning between us should be burning this building to the ground. If she can't feel that, I'm completely insane.

Our eyes meet, and Bri blinks a couple of times, several warring emotions running through her expression. "I—I—" she stammers.

"Have you eaten?" I prompt, glancing over to Ben. "You don't want to see her hangry, trust me."

"I haven't," Bri says. "And Mace texted to say she has only one lemon poppyseed muffin left."

"You better go then."

"I like muffins," Ben says.

I release Bri, my excuse ready. "Ben, we have reservations at Angelica's."

His face lights up, and I'm grateful my texting skills are so amazing. "Oh, right," he says. "I do love the baked beans there."

Bri stumbles out of the lane, and I lunge toward her again, wondering if she really is suffering from low blood sugar.

My foot catches on the slight outline of the lane, and the next thing I know, Bri and I are tumbling to the astroturf.

I've been trying to be a gentleman with her, but I'm not a superhero. I can't twist fast enough, and she hits the floor first. I land on top of her, causing another grunt to fly from her mouth.

My mind goes numb from the fall, pain moving through my knees and up my back. I sputter for breath, the same as Bri.

Somewhere outside of us, Ben laughs, and that breaks the film of idiocy that has enveloped my mind. "I'm sorry," I say, pushing myself up, my hand not quite meeting hard ground. It presses against Bri's arm instead, and she gripes at me.

"Jason," she says. "Get—off—me."

"I am," I gripe back, and I manage to roll away from her. I get to my feet, then turn back to help her up.

She gives me her trademark glare, but she takes my hand and accepts my help. I don't want to let go of her fingers, but I'm with a client, and I'm already in too deep with this woman as it is. Any more hand-holding, and I'll have to file paperwork with HR.

So I let go, and I say, "Go get your muffin, Bri. I'll call you later tonight about our case."

"Yes, sir," she says as if she needs my permission. She nods and then marches away in the tight, controlled steps I've seen her use lots of times.

I wish my blood didn't burn as hot as it does, and as I turn back to Ben, I know he's felt something.

"So she's off-limits," he says, his grin huge.

I choose to say nothing, because I'm trying not to lie anymore. Mama would be so proud.

———

WHEN I PULL up to my farmhouse, my brother gets out of his truck. This isn't good. I ease my luxury SUV past him and into the garage, annoyed he only gave me a couple of inches to do so. I take my time collecting my briefcase and suit coat, and everyone knows I can live out of my car for days if necessary, Connor included.

He has the patience of an elephant, because he stands right beside my window for ages while I pretend to answer someone Very Important on my phone. I really text Bri and ask her if she got her muffin and made it home okay.

She doesn't answer, which only sours my mood further. I have to get out of the car, so I do, and I meet Connor's eyes and blink as if I didn't know he was there. "Hey," I say, already heading for the steps that lead into the house. "What are you doing here?"

"One, I told you I was coming," Connor says, following me. His voice pitches higher than mine, but it always sounds lower when he's irritated—like he is now. "Two, I brought Timber back, just like I said I would."

I sigh as I go up the steps. "Fine. Is he in the backyard?"

"Yep." Connor comes into the farmhouse behind me. Everywhere I look, something needs tending to. Mama would never survive a night in this house, but I love it. It feels like it just needs someone to take care of it, and since I feel like that too, this house and I have a bond. Pathetic that I have more of a connection with a nearly dilapidated house than most humans, but whatever.

I love the house. I'm not selling the house. I also don't have quite the time I need to work on the house. But she knows I care, and I would fix her up if I could. And when I do get around to a project, our bond deepens.

"He's going to miss you." I put my briefcase on the built-in desk I installed last summer. It's shiny and new, and I drape my jacket over the bag with another sigh. "I'm starving. Have you eaten?"

"Joan is making burgers," he says.

I turn to look at him, my eyebrows up. "That sounds good."

"You're not invited," Connor says with a smile. "I've been waiting in your driveway for twenty minutes, and you wouldn't answer your phone."

I scoff. "So I don't get invited because I was driving home? It's not safe to text and drive, you know." I've done it loads of times, but I really have tried to do less and less of it lately. I need the downtime, and the last thing I need or want is a ticket, court appearance for personal reasons, and a meeting with my boss over any law delinquency.

Connor chuckles, and that's a good sign. "We're looking forward to a quiet night together," he says. "No dogs. No brothers. Nothing."

"Yeah." I turn toward my kitchen, which is cavernous and feels it. I can pour a bowl of cereal just fine. Tara hasn't texted about any special rendezvous with Mr. Reynolds, and she's done less and less of that since she and Alec got married a couple of months ago. I hate feeling alone and lonely, and my first instinct is to find a date and hit a good restaurant.

I don't reach for my phone. The woman I want to ask will just say no, and then I'll have to bask in my humiliation in my cavernous kitchen. No, thank you.

"Timber is going to be so lonely during the day," I say.

"Then find him a new home," Connor says, the sharpness back in his tone. "We're gonna have a baby in less than a week. I can't keep your dog for you anymore."

"I know." I face Connor again and offer him a smile. He's only a couple of years younger than me, and he has taken care of my Great Dane for a while now. I pay him, and for everything, but Timber is easily a hundred and thirty pounds if he's an ounce.

He takes me into a hug and slaps my back. "You look tired."

"I was in court early this morning," I say to his shoulder. "And I had a client who wanted to do everything around Charleston tonight. I only just managed to escape going to Hotel Ella for drinks."

Connor chuckles again and steps back. "You say that like drinks at the Ella is the worst thing that could happen to you." He quirks an eyebrow, because before he married Joan, we used to go to various hotels around the city to find dates.

He happened to find one, and they got along so spectacularly, he'd married her. I'm still waiting for that, and I've changed how I'm looking for my next date. I'm not just thinking a single date either, and that has provided a new perspective for me as well.

Because I'm not just looking for a good time. I'm looking for a wife.

Fear stabs through me, but I'm used to it after the past several months of reminding myself I'm ready to be serious. Settle down. Be a real person, with a real job, and a real house, and a real family life. I'm not in my mid-twenties anymore, and it's almost pathetic for me to be bumming around the bars with Ben on a weekday night.

I open the fridge and peer inside. "You brought food," I say, hope lifting my heart.

"It's a turkey and provolone sandwich," he says. "We had meetings today, and the contractor brought in lunch. It was extra."

"Thank you." I take out the brown box and open the lid. A sandwich wrapped in plastic sits there, as does a bag of dill pickle chips, and a small container of macaroni salad. It's a thing of beauty. Anything I can eat that I don't have to make is. I can cook; I just don't like to. It feels like such a waste of time to me.

"I have to get goin'," Connor says, his accent coming out strong now. He knocks on the desk a couple of times and turns around. "Timber's barking, so he probably wants to be let in."

I say, "Thanks, Connor," to his retreating back, then turn to the door that leads out onto the deck. I hadn't even heard my dog barking, but I do now. I cross through the cavern and open the door. It squeals into the night, and when I flip the light switch, nothing happens.

"Oh, right," I mutter to myself. "The bulbs are burnt out back here." I don't entertain on the back deck or anything. I can't even remember the last time I came out here. "Timber!" I yell. "Come on, bud. Come in the house."

The dog's nails clatter and scratch against the wood as

he leaps up the steps to the deck. It groans under his weight, and I should've braced myself before calling the dog. He barrels at me at top speed, and I say, "Whoa. Whoa! Slow down, buddy!"

He doesn't slow down, and I barely get out of the way before he charges through the door and into the house. He promptly hits the dining room chair as if he didn't see it, bounces off, and makes a turn—mid-air, mind you—and heads into the living room.

"Zoomies," I say as he jumps on my couch, dislodging the back cushions, then down, then zips down the hall toward the front door, then comes racing back. Around he goes again, and I yell, "Hey! Didn't you run enough in the back yard?"

He hits a lamp that crashes to the ground, and I see my whole house go up in flames and smoke. I dash over to it and right it, yelling at Timber to "Knock it off!"

The Great Dane finally comes to a stop, his sides heaving. He's pure muscle and stands almost to my chest. We face one another, and I have the very real feeling that he and I need to connect the way I have with the house. Only then will he do what I want him to—and maybe not chew my mattress to smithereens while I'm at work.

"Come here," I say, patting my thigh. He trots over, and he's made of power and grace now. "How are you, bud?" I stroke his head, flatten his ears, and scrub along his jaw. I swear he smiles at me. "Yeah, good? Glad to be home? I'm going to make you stay in the back yard, you know."

He barks, nearly deafening me. I cringe away from him, and he races toward the front door again. My phone rings, and it's the special tone I assigned to Bri. My heart catapults through my body, and I tell myself she only has a specific ringtone so I know I need to answer the phone. Lots of partners do that for their juniors. She's not special.

But when I say, "Hey," in a soft tone, some part of my mind knows she is. I just refuse to acknowledge it.

Then I hear the sirens.

CHAPTER FIVE

BRI

"Bri?" Jason asks again, and my mind thaws. Did I call Jason? I pull the phone away from my ear and look at it. Sure enough, the call is connected, the timer counting up, and my boss saying, "Are you home? Where are you? I can be on my way."

He sounds like he really cares, and I can't make sense of that. "I'm okay," I finally manage to say. My voice sounds like I've swallowed a handful of quarters and I'm trying to talk past them. "There's been a fire in my apartment building, and they asked if we could all stay somewhere else tonight."

And I called him.

My mind forms it into a question. *And I called Jason? My boss? My senior partner? The man who kissed me this morning—which feels like another lifetime—and then we agreed that would never happen again?*

Why didn't I call Tara? Or Callie? Or Macie? Or simply drive over to a hotel? Charleston has a billion of them.

"You can stay here," he says.

"No," I immediately say now that my brain is firing again. I honestly don't know where it went. I have no idea how long I've been sitting in my car either. The heat blows, and I'm suddenly too hot. I reach to turn it off. "I have Archie."

"I just got Timber back from my brother," he says.

"I called," I say, sitting up straighter. I clear my throat, trying to get the words to line up. "Because all of the case files are in my apartment, and they're not sure I'll be able to get them." I haven't called because I need a place to stay. I know where Jason lives, and his big, white farmhouse out in the country sounds really heavenly about now.

But no.

A hotel with a hot tub is what I need.

"You bought us time by winning the grand jury," he says. "It's not the end of the world."

"I'm waiting to see," I say, blinking myself back to reality. And in this reality, Jason and I don't kiss. I don't tell him personal things about my life, and he's not the friend I call when I'm in trouble.

He sighs and says, "Ben's calling. I have to take it."

"Sure, of course," I say, and the call ends. I stay in the car and watch the screen fade to black. I can never tell anyone that the fire started in my apartment, because I thought I could heat up my muffin in the microwave. Nothing dangerous about that, right?

In my defense, I have used a microwave oven successfully in the past. Tonight, I'd forgotten that I'd tossed a stack of dishes in there when I'd moved in, and I simply put the muffin on the top one. One of them had a metal ring around the edge of it, and boy, I've never seen flames jump so high.

"Ma'am," a man says through my window, and I press the button to roll it down. The Fire Chief stands there, and if I wasn't wearing the perfume Sooty Smoke, and I didn't entertain inappropriate thoughts about my partner, I'd find him handsome. I wouldn't do anything about it, but I'd at least think it.

"Everything's out," he says. "Nothing structural."

"Thank goodness," I say, though I fear I'll be asked to move out. Still, the relief moving through me cascades in powerful waves, and I catch sight of others going back into the building. "We can go back in?"

"They can," he says, turning to look too. "Your landlord wants to inspect the place before he lets you back in. Damages and such." The Chief wears a sympathetic look, and I nod.

"Okay."

"Do you have somewhere to go tonight?" He nods to the cat on the passenger seat. "With your cat?"

I look at Archie, my mind blanking again.

"Ma'am?"

I swing my attention back to the Fire Chief. "Yes," I say. "I'll be fine."

"I know there's a couple of hotels that allow pets," he says. "If you don't have a friend willing to let you couch surf."

"Can I go in and pack a bag or anything?" I ask.

"Sure," he says. "I'll have to go in with you, just to make sure everything is safe, but yeah. Let's go."

His firemen are packing up, and I quickly slide from my car. I'm not wearing a jacket, a cardigan, or a bulky sweater, and I feel naked. I cross my arms as if we live in Antarctica and it's the dead of winter, then jog across the lot to the apartment building entrance.

The Chief stands between me and the kitchen while I ask a couple of his men to load up my case files. Then I hurry into the bedroom and pack a few days' worth of clothes, add a few more jackets just in case, and stow a couple of my romance novels right on top. Zip, zip, zip, and I'm ready to go.

I lead the way, and before I know it, the firetrucks are moving out. The Chief rides in a big, red truck and he gestures for me to go first. I wonder if he'll follow me all the way to my destination—which I don't have—just to make sure I don't circle back here.

I'm not sure how I can ever show my face here again, and I pull out in front of him and start driving. "Okay, Archie," I say, trying to get a hold on my racing thoughts.

I've felt like this before, when I found out Max was married with kids. "We need somewhere to stay."

Back then, I'd driven from Butte to Billings, then to Casper, then Cheyenne, then Denver.

I push out the past, because it's a painful place to be. I don't know when the Fire Chief stops following me. I don't know how long I've been driving.

I pull to the side of the road and take a deep breath. "I left your cat food in the apartment," I say. "So we need that. Then we need a place to stay." I pick up my phone and start looking. All the while, I tell myself, *You're a competent woman. You can do this. Find a hot tub, Bri.*

Then I remember I didn't pack my swimming suit. Tears gather in my eyes, but I fight them. I will not cry over this.

In the end, everything on my screen is blurry, and I give up trying to find a hotel. I manage to go past Jason's name at the top of my text list and tap on Macie's name. I've stayed with her before, and she has felines of her own. There will be food for Archie, a bed for me, and no questions asked until I say it's okay.

"Bri," Macie says, her voice groggy. "What's up?"

"I'm so sorry," I say, my voice cracking. "I forgot you go to bed so early."

"It's fine." She sounds completely awake right now. "Where are you? Why are you crying?"

No tears have fallen yet, but I'm about to lose that battle. "I need somewhere to stay," I say, sniffling mightily.

I'm so glad I didn't call Jason. Sniffling is not sexy in any way. "There was a fire, and I have Archie, and I don't know for how long, but I swear it won't be for long. I just can't think tonight."

"A fire?" Macie sucks in a breath. "Yes, come here. I'll check the bedroom for you. You know the door code."

I did, once upon a time. "Text it to me anyway," I say, the rest of my words unspoken. Macie hears them though. *I'm a mess, Mace.*

"Do you know how far away you are?" she asks gently.

The first tears slither down my face when I shake my head. "No," I whisper.

"Then I'll just listen for you, Bri. It's going to be okay."

I accept her reassurance, though the lawyer in me wants to challenge her. Nothing has gone super okay since Montana, and I hate feeling cursed. The call ends, and I put in Macie's address. Then I won't have to think. Then my phone will direct me to her house, and hopefully, by morning, I'll have some clarity.

———

I'M awake when Macie's footsteps enter the bedroom. "Hey," I say quietly.

"Oh, you're up."

"Yeah." I did doze, but I'm not sure I ever truly slept. I sit up and swing my legs over the side of the bed. On the other side of it, Archie sigh-purrs as if I've disturbed him mightily.

Macie settles onto the bed beside me. "I got some coffee going. Stop by the shop too, on your way in. I'll pull a chocolate croissant for you."

I give her a small smile. "I look that bad?"

"You don't look rested," she says. Her green eyes hold concern, and she reaches up and pushes my hair back out of my face. The gesture feels loving and motherly, and I lean against her shoulder.

"I...thank you, Mace. Really."

"You're welcome here anytime," she says. "For as long as you need."

She speaks from her heart, but I don't want to be that person who's always living with her because they can't take care of themselves. I should've known better than to use the microwave.

"I heard you won your grand jury yesterday," she says.

"Yes," I say, still confused about how I can be so good in court and so terrible at life.

"I'm surprised Jason didn't come into the shop to brag about it after work." Her eyebrows go up, but I'm not playing into her hand.

"He has a client in from out of town," I say, my voice almost a monotone. "What about you? You had a meeting yesterday. How did it go?"

Her eyes ice over, and then melt again, all in a couple of blinks. "Good, I think," she says. "I think Coy and I are going to *finally* come to an agreement. Oh, and guess what?"

"What?" I ask, still stuck on Coy finally coming around to letting Macie buy half of Legacy Brew. He's been struggling financially, and Macie's been running that shop for a long time as their morning manager. She offered to buy him out, and he refused. But she hasn't given up, and they keep talking and keep talking…

"Andy asked me out." She squeals and jumps to her feet. "We're going to dinner this weekend. His friend is in the band *Outrageous*, and they're playing at Roam Wild. We have dinner reservations." She practically dances to the doorway, then turns back. Her face glows with light I've only seen a woman wear when a really handsome man is in her thoughts.

I grin at Macie and stand too. "That's great, Mace. Two finallys."

"Right?" She trills out a laugh and enters the hall. "I've been so professional with Coy and so flirty with Andy. All of my hard work is *finally* paying off."

"I'm just gonna get dressed," I call after her, and I dig through my bag to find something to wear to the office that day. I have no idea what's on my calendar, but my phone would have a reminder if I had something this morning that required me to be present and ready. It doesn't, which means I can show up to the office a bit comatose and figure things out from there.

It's very early still, or Macie wouldn't be home, and I

dress quickly and head into the kitchen. I want to tell her thanks before she has to go. She looks up from her phone, wonder in her eyes.

"What?" I ask.

"Guess who's asking about you?"

I give her device a look, then pull open the cupboard to find a mug. I keep my back to her as I fill it with coffee and reach for the sugar. "Who?"

"Jason," she says.

I've spilled hot liquid all over myself before when Jason's name was mentioned. This morning, I'm controlled and calm as I stir, then turn to face her. I lift the cup to my lips and sip. "Really? Why?"

"I've told you why, and you don't like the answer."

"He doesn't like me," I say, my lips tingling a little too strongly. The urge to tell Macie about the kiss in the sterile hallway of the courthouse surges, the words very nearly flying out of my mouth. I barely catch them and swallow them down.

Macie grins as she looks at her vibrating phone again. "You're such a liar."

I lean forward to try to read her screen, but she plucks it up and pockets it. "I'm going to be so late."

"Wait. What did he say?"

Macie's eyes dance with delight. "I thought you didn't care?"

"I don't," I say stubbornly. "But you said I was a liar.

Don't you think I should know what I lied about?" I cross my arms, which with Macie is a mistake.

She eyes the sweater I have on. "*Why* are you wearing that?" she asks. "You need to sit down with Jess, and not just so she can find you a house. She could go through your closet and help you match some awesome pieces. No jackets. No cardigans."

"This is a *tunic sweater*," I say, tugging on the open sides to close it across me.

"It's a long cardigan." Macie rolls her eyes. "And the outfit doesn't need it. It's so bulky."

"I..."

"Let me see it without it."

"You're late."

"You're hiding something."

"Yes, I am," I say, surprised the words have come out. More follow, and I can't stop myself. "I'm hiding my uneven chest. I don't need anyone staring at it, and the cardigans and sweatshirts and jackets do a good job."

Macie's eyes widen, and pure humiliation burns through my face and down my throat. "Bri," she says gently.

I pull the tunic closed. "Thank you for letting me stay here. I'll find out if I can get back into my apartment this afternoon."

Macie doesn't just go the way I hope she will. She steps into me and hugs me. "You are beautiful just the way you are. You don't need the cardigan." She pulls away, her eyes burning with fire. "All right?"

I nod, and she nods, and then she says, "All right, Lizzie. Let's get to the shop." Her cat goes with her, and I'm left standing in her kitchen with half a cup of coffee and her words bouncing through my mind.

———

THAT AFTERNOON FINDS me in my office when my phone chimes. "Miss Shadows," Cheryl says. "Mister Buhler would like to see you in his office."

I pause and look up from the file in front of me. "Mister Buhler?" Of the Vincent Buhler, the overlord partner on the top floor? The one whose name sits in the middle of the law firm name of Farmer, Buhler, and Cason?

"Yes, ma'am," Cheryl says. "His secretary just called me. I have the code for the elevator that goes directly to his office."

I jump to my feet. "I'm on my way." I head out of my office and down the hall. Cheryl's standing beside her desk, a resigned look on her face. "Uh oh." I take the slip of paper with the six-digit code on it. I didn't even know Mr. Buhler had a private elevator. I don't even know where it is.

I look at my secretary. "This is bad, right? I'm going to get fired." For what, I don't know. I just had a spectacular win with the grand jury yesterday. Even Jason was impressed.

"Of course not," Cheryl says. "Mister Buhler is just a little...particular, that's all."

"What does that mean?" I glance to the other secretary out in this small lobby. He looks back at me and shrugs. "When you send people up there, do they come back? We're not talking a Sweeney Todd situation, are we?" I swallow, though I know Vincent Buhler isn't killing people in his office on the top floor.

Orion smiles, as does Cheryl. "No Sweeney Todd," she says. "Franny just said he'd like to see you as soon as possible in his office."

"That's all?" I turn the paper over.

"The elevator is the middle one," Orion says. "You put in the code when you get in, then press the button for twenty-five. The code tells the car where you really want to go."

"Fascinating," I murmur to myself, wondering what it would feel like to have an office no one but me knows how to get into. I square my shoulders and tug on my tunic as I stride away from the secretary's desks. I've met with big partners before. I had to for my interview process for junior partner, and perhaps Mr. Buhler wants to promote me to regular partner because of the grand jury.

I punch in the code and hit the button as Orion said, and the elevator takes me up, up, up. I step out into a vestibule with gold and white tiles on the floor. A shiny, silver pitcher of water sits on a desk, and a man in a black suit rounds the corner.

"Ah, Miss Shadows," he says, his smile glorious and filling the small space with more light. "This way, please."

"You're not Franny," I say.

The man give a light laugh. "No," he says. "I'm Ethan, Mister Buhler's butler."

"Of course," I say, though I honestly don't know what a butler does in a law office. Perhaps Mr. Buhler brings his private butler from home to...buttle around the office.

A woman stands from the desk outside an impressive pair of dark, wooden doors, her smile just as jovial as Ethan's. "Sabrina," she says warmly. "You made it."

"Yes, ma'am," I say, deciding I need all the Southern charm I can get. "What does Mister Buhler want?"

Franny's smile dims. "I'll let him know you're here." She turns and opens one of the doors. "Mr. Buhler," she says. "Miss Shadows has arrived." A beat passes, and then Franny steps back, indicates I should enter, and hitches her smile back into place.

There is something seriously wrong here. I can feel it vibrating way down in my toes. I look at Ethan—all smiles. I look at Franny—grins for miles. Are they robots? Clones? Hoping to make it through the day without getting fired themselves?

"Thank you?" I guess, and I face the gaping door. I can't see beyond it. No sound comes out. My only choice is to go in.

I do, and after a couple of steps, the office opens up, windows stretching left and right as far as the eye can see. This office is enormous, and a desk sits at one end of it. Mr. Buhler stands, his own version of a smile on his face.

From one of the plush armchairs in front of his desk, another man gets to his feet too. He brushes his hands down the front of his suit coat and then buttons it. My feet keep taking me closer—until Jason looks up and meets my eyes.

I freeze then, the edge in his eyes screaming something at me. Something I can't decipher immediately but know I'll need to before Mr. Buhler starts asking questions.

CHAPTER SIX

JASON

I CAN'T BELIEVE WHERE I'M STANDING. WHO'S coming toward me. How I've dragged Bri into this mess. She doesn't deserve it.

Neither do you, I tell myself, and she was the only one I could name to help me out of this situation.

"Miss Shadows," Vincent says pleasantly. The man could be an award-winning actor for how well he masks his moods, let me tell you. I thought I'd been called up here to talk about a couple of my recent cases that have brought in a metric ton of money for this firm. Instead, I'm one conversation away from losing my job.

I stare at Bri, praying she can understand my silent pleading. She has to agree with everything I've said, or I'm done here. *She will,* I tell myself. Bri has no reason to lie.

"Hello," Bri says, shaking Vincent's hand, her eyes still

on mine. She switches them to him for a moment, pumps his hand again, then steps back. "Shall I sit?"

"Yes, please," Vincent says, striding around his desk again. He retakes his seat, steeples his fingers, and studies me, then Bri. The tension in the room suffocates me, and there isn't a spare inch for anything else. For such a big, ornate room, that's saying something.

"Sabrina—can I call you Sabrina?"

"Yes, sir," she says confidently. I see her swallow though, and guaranteed Mr. Buhler does. The man has the eyes of a bird of prey. He can see everything, and he's one of the best lawyer in the South because of it.

"Sabrina," he says, leaning back in his chair and crossing his legs. The man spends at least an hour in the gym every morning. I know, as I've seen him in the faculty-provided facility here in the building. Several times.

"Yes, sir," she says again.

"Mister Finch here says you two had some trouble with a client last evening."

To her credit, she doesn't even look at me. "Not much," she says airily. I so wish I'd texted her this morning and told her everything. An email. Something. As my junior, she'd get alerted by her system when I text or email, so even if she's reading a brief or with a client, she'd see it.

"Tell me what happened," he says.

"Sir," I say, but Mr. Buhler silences me with one of his falcon-looks.

"Mister Finch showed up with a client," Bri says. "To a hatchet-throwing facility. I stayed with them, but..." She swallows again, and the nervous eye-flick moves to me.

I reach over and seal my fate by taking her hand in mine. Shock courses through her expression, and I squeeze her hand, desperately hoping she can read minds.

I'm so losing my job.

My mother will be mortified. Tara will question me endlessly.

"Bri—Sabrina—left well before Mister Arnold got going," I say. "I left him at Hotel Ella, then got called back later. I was on the phone with Miss Shadows when the police called."

Bri's eyebrows shoot up, but I don't look at her. I'm holding her hand; she hasn't pulled away yet. I have to say one more thing. "I got the paperwork for my relationship with Bri this morning as well," I say. She sucks in a tight breath low enough to barely reach my ears. All I can do is pray Mr. Buhler didn't hear it.

He leans forward and picks up his phone. All the sunshine in the world comes pouring through those windows, and it feels dark as night in here. "Yes, hello, Franny," he drawls. "I need Malcolm in Human Resources, please." He speaks in a pleasant voice—after all, he's not the one about to take the fall for something he didn't do. He looks at me, then Bri, and both of us barely move to breathe. Bri's hand is tight in mine still, and she's seriously one of the smartest women I've ever known. She knows silence is golden right now. Why say anything she doesn't have to?

She's observant and loyal, and though she doesn't like me much, I can't imagine she'll want me to lose my job over something I didn't do.

"Yes, howdy, Malcolm." Vincent twists in his chair, a light chuckle coming from his mouth. The moment he's facing away from us, I lean closer to Bri.

"Ben got in trouble last night. I should've called you this morning. I didn't. Thought I could handle it. Now he's claiming I did something I didn't, and I needed a corroborating witness."

She nods once and looks at our joined hands. I do too, my chest growing tighter by the moment.

"Thank you, Malcolm." Vincent faces us and hangs up again. I wish I'd paid attention to what he said to the HR manager. "You did pick up the paperwork to disclose a personal relationship with a co-worker," he says.

I swallow. "I'm not sure if I need it," I say. "But Bri and I...just started seeing one another yesterday."

Vincent's eyebrows go up, and his gaze lands on Bri. "Sabrina?"

Her fingers release mine, and she slides her hand back into her own lap. Her back is the straightest I've ever seen it. I draw in a slow breath and hold it.

"I believe we have seventy-two hours to fill out the paperwork from the start of a personal relationship, sir," she says. "By my count." She lifts her wrist and looks at the watch all junior partners get upon their promotion.

I hide my smile, because I doubt Bri knows that Vincent picks out each and every watch. Hers has a red band and goes well with her charcoal sweater and dark hair. "We're just over twenty-four hours."

"So you are seeing him." He doesn't ask. Oh no. He's on high lawyer alert, looking for the truth.

Bri slides me a look. "We're...seeing how things go," she says.

"When's your next date?" he challenges.

"This weekend," Bri says breezily. "We're doubling with our friend at the coffee shop. Redhead? Green eyes. The morning manager at Legacy Brew?" She nods to the to-go cup—clearly marked—on Vincent's desk. "Her name's Macie. We're both friends with her. Anyway, she's been waiting forever for this guy Andy to ask her out. He finally did, and *he* has a friend in a band playing at Roam Wild this weekend. We're going to see them, get some great food, maybe go to that art viewing of the Dead Sea Scrolls." She looks at me, her eyebrows raised. "Right?"

"That's what Macie said," I say, because I know Bri stayed with Macie last night. They obviously had a little girl-talk, and I've never been more grateful.

"Tell me about hatchet-throwing with Ben," Vincent says.

Bri takes another deep breath and blows it out. "Mister Buhler," she says, leaning forward. "The guy's...I don't know what happened last night. I haven't spoken to Jason about it this morning. Last night, I faked having low blood sugar to get away from Mister Arnold. He was clearly interested in me, though I happen to know he's married with a baby on the way. He said he likes having girlfriends in lots of cities."

She puts her elbow on his desk and crosses her legs, and I can't tear my eyes from her. Whatever she says next, I'll believe. "Jason helped me get out of there, and then I had a fire in my apartment, so I called—"

"Wait," I interrupt. "The fire was *in* your apartment?"

"That sounds serious," Vincent says. "Are you okay?"

She waves her hand like these sorts of incidents happen daily. "A mere microwave mishap," she says. I look at Vincent, and he looks at me. Bri continues with, "I called Jason to let him know the case files were inside, and I might not be able to retrieve them—" She looks at me. "I got them, by the way."

I nod like this is very important, and she keeps going. "And he had to end the call because Ben was phoning him."

"Was he home when you called him?"

"Yes," Bri says. "I believe I heard Timber barking in the background." She sits back in her chair and folds her arms, but it's not the tight cinch I've seen before. She's relaxed, almost carefree.

Vincent looks at her, then me. "The police were already there by the time you arrived."

"Yes, sir."

He looks down at the papers on his desk, his sigh mighty and filling the ginormous room. "In for a penny," he says.

"In for a pound," I finish.

Bri takes a breath I can hear, and she says, "You like clichés too."

Vincent looks up, his blue eyes sparkling now. "I trained Jason in the art of clichés," he says with a hearty laugh. "You don't like them?"

She surveys him and then me. "Sometimes, I suppose." She shakes her head at me, but her smile is surprisingly soft. "I didn't like it when he called me a diamond in the rough."

"Jace," Vincent says, another chuckle coming from him. "You don't say them out loud all the time."

"Well," I say, getting to my feet. "If someone wasn't as *old as the hills*, perhaps I would've gotten that memo."

"Or the email reminder," Bri says, clearly joking.

Vincent stands too, and he comes around the desk to shake my hand. "I apologize, Jason. You should've *seen* Ben this morning."

"I did see Ben this morning." I yawn. "Who do you think tried to get him out of jail for hours?"

Vincent shakes his head. "I'm surprised you didn't call me."

"He's my client," I say. Calling Vincent Buhler in the middle of the night had not even crossed my mind.

"I'm going to take his case," Vincent says. "Especially since he threw you under the bus, tossed the driver in the back, and stomped on the accelerator. He doesn't deserve you." He turns his attention to Bri. "And you...are you sure this man deserves you?"

"Hey," I say. "I'm a good catch."

"You're not a fish," Bri and Vincent say together, and they burst out laughing too. I can't tell if Bri's is false or not, but Vincent's isn't. Bri looks at me, sees I'm not laughing, and quiets. "Ooh, someone woke up on the wrong side of the bed."

She shakes Vincent's hand, winks at him, and then precedes me toward the exit. "Clichés are useful," I call after her. I shake my head and nod to Vincent.

"Get that paperwork in," he says.

"Yes, sir." I leave, glad to be out of there. Bri waits at the elevator, and I want to hold her hand again so badly it's like a need inside myself I can't control.

I manage it, though, because Franny is sitting right there. She's over sixty, and she has no problem staring and staring. The car finally comes, and Bri steps into it first. I follow her to find her hitting every button between the private floor we're on and ours—the sixth.

"Wow," I say, my heartbeat doing a dance beneath my breastbone. "You want to get stuck in the elevator with me?"

The doors slide closed, and Bri faces me. It's not happy-smiling Bri, but a slitted-eyed Bri with danger parading across her expression. "You got paperwork to declare our relationship?"

"Yes," I say, my mouth suddenly dry.

"Why?"

"It turned out to be useful," I point out. "Maybe I had a feeling."

She crosses her arms, and now it's the angry kind. "Jason."

I sigh and look up as the car comes to a stop on floor twenty-four. This is going to take forever, which is the point. "I liked kissing you," I mumble.

"I thought you just lost your head."

"I did." I study the floor now, watching the bottom of the doors as they slide closed. I reach over and take her hand in mine again. I don't know what else to say.

"What happened with Ben?"

"We don't have enough time for me to explain that." An insane idea enters my mind. "Maybe over dinner." I look up at her, hopeful.

"You just told our boss that we're dating."

"And you said we were feeling it out. Why can't we do that?"

She holds up one finger on her free hand. "There will be no kissing if I agree to dinner tonight."

"Oh, how can you know that?" I give her a sunny smile. "Maybe it'll be really fun, and you'll want to kiss me."

She pulls her hand away, the fire in her eyes only growing. "Stop it."

The elevator stops again. No one gets on. The doors slide closed. "What do you want?" I ask.

"What do you mean?"

I slowly take her hand in mine again. "In a boyfriend. A man. What do you want?"

She looks at our joined hands as the car comes to another maddening stop.

"For this to maybe be real," I say, laying a lot on the line between us. "What would it take?"

She meets my eye, and wow, she makes me shiver and shake. I love it. I want to see if I can do the same to her. Somehow. "Honesty," she says, her voice calm and even. "The truth. I want a man to be real with me."

She turns toward me fully and takes my other hand in hers. "I want him to be himself." She slides her hand up my chest, and I subconsciously lean down like I'll taste those delicious lips again right here, right now.

Don't do it, I tell myself. It's more of a shouted warning, actually.

"I want to be myself. I want it to be authentic." The elevator opens, and Bri steps back. "I don't know if you're capable of authentic, Mister Finch."

"I am," I say.

"You literally just made up a relationship to get out of a situation," she said. "This *isn't* real. I know it isn't." She looks up at the dial above the doors too. We're only on floor fourteen, and it feels like we'll never get to six.

"What if I want it to be?" I ask.

"Then you have a lot of work to do," she says, putting more distance between us. "I don't want jokes about kissing at the end of a date. That's fake. I don't want you to hold my hand unless you mean it. I don't want you to 'lose your head' and kiss me in the courthouse." She flicks me a glance filled with emotion I can't read. "Kissing means something to me, Mister Finch." Her voice sounds slightly wounded, like a bird with a hurt wing. I want to curl her into my chest and tell her I'll protect her from that hurt until she's ready to fly again.

I clear my throat instead, about to commit more relationship drama for myself. "Dinner tonight," I say as the elevator starts to slow for the umpteenth time.

She holds my gaze as the doors slide open.

"Me and you," I say. "I'll take you out, or we can eat at my place. You tell me what you want. Where to pick you up. What time."

The car moves again, and I wonder if she can feel the authenticity in me now. I've basically opened my heart and shouted that I'm attracted to her. I've laid everything on the line. She won't even let me know if I have a shot. If she even remotely likes me.

At the same time, I can't wait to get back to my office and call Tara. I'll finally be able to tell her I got over my fear, that I'm not a chicken anymore, and that yeah, I may have messed up with that kiss in the courthouse yesterday, but it was also the catalyst to get me out of the stalled space I've been in with Bri for months.

"I suppose this is the calm before the storm," she says with a wry smile, and then she steps off the car.

"Bri," I call after her, annoyed at her use of the cliché. "This isn't our floor."

"I'll text you if I get lost," she calls back. The doors start to slide closed, and I curse under my breath. Then I get to ride down to the sixth floor, stopping every twenty freaking seconds for ghosts to get on the elevator with me.

CHAPTER SEVEN

BRI

Pick me up at Legacy Brew at six-thirty. Bring the HR paperwork, and we'll go over it over dinner.

I stare at the words, trying to muster up the courage to send them. Jason sure has said a lot today. A *lot*. So much, I'm still spinning in my office, all of my briefs and files forgotten. I'd taken the stairs back, told Cheryl to hold all of my calls except for anything from the private floors at the top of the building, and I've been pacing in my office since.

I'm operating on two packages of Starburst—pinks only, thank you very much—and two cans of Diet Coke. And not the caffeine-free kind.

I've texted Macie and asked about the concert-slash-dinner this weekend, because what if Vincent Buhler shows up and Jason and I aren't there with Macie and

Andy? I don't want to crash her first date with him, but desperate times...

I don't finish the stupid cliché. I can't believe *I'm* thinking in them now. I can't believe some of the things I said to Jason—or to Vincent Buhler for that matter. I almost feel like I had an out-of-body experience, and someone else was controlling my mind and mouth.

I look at my fingers, seeing how well Jason's fit in the spaces between them. I feel his skin, the warmth, the smoothness, the rough edges.

I'd told the truth with him. I just want him to be real. I don't want the player. I don't want games. I don't want secrets.

He said a lot too—he's definitely interested in me.

Suddenly too hot, I shrug out of the heavy tunic cardigan. "How can he be interested in you?" I reach up and pull the pencil from my bun, then immediately start winding it up once my hair hits my shoulders. I do it almost as a nervous habit, a trigger for me to get to work. Think. Find the right angle.

I twist my hair, re-secure it with the pencil, and turn again. Cheryl stands in my office doorway. "Are you okay?" she asks.

Numb, but my heart racing, I shake my head no. She slips inside and closes the door. "I have Mister Finch at my desk, insisting he see you before he leaves for the day."

"Leaves for the day?" I glance at my watch again. "Wow, it's after five."

Cheryl watches me. "What happened upstairs?"

I can't tell her. Not yet. I pick up my phone, send the text, and then look at her with determination. "Tell him I'm busy, please. And let me know when he leaves the building."

Cheryl wears doubt on her face, but she nods and turns to go. Before my office door closes all the way, I have a text back from Jason.

Yes, ma'am. See you soon.

I can't tell if he's flirting, upset, excited, hopeful, dreading dinner, or something else entirely. I flop into my desk chair, cringing as it rolls backward and hits the wall behind me. I'm all of the above—upset, excited, hopeful, dreading dinner, ready to flirt, maybe hold his hand, and-slash-or something else entirely.

I'm not even sure why. I've dated before. Handsome men too. Several of them. Why is he so...nervous-inducing? It's like I lose track of who I am when I'm around him. I'm not being real either, and I *hate* that.

My desk phone rings, and I lunge for it. "Yes?"

"He's in his car," Cheryl says.

"Thank you," I say. "I'm headed home too."

"As am I," she says. "Lunch tomorrow, so I can hear the story? Or is it still too soon?"

I smile at the ceiling, and I defy even myself when I say, "Yes, let's go to lunch tomorrow. I'll get you caught up then."

"Thank goodness," she drawls. "If I have to be the final line of defense, I need to know what game we're playing."

"No games," I say, and she laughs. I hang up and add, "I hope," before I get my purse, check for my keys, and exit my office. I'm walking up the front porch steps at Macie's house when I realize—I left my tunic cardigan draped over the chair in my office.

———

SIX-THIRTY COMES, and I'm sitting on the long, orange couch at Legacy Brew. My right foot goes *tap, tap, tap*, and while I'm not wearing heels and my sandal makes no noise against the rug, I feel like I've swallowed jumping beans.

I'm properly clothed for this date, all of my armor in place. Long, black slacks that hide how short my legs are. An oversized sweatshirt that's cropped higher in the front than the back and delicately draws attention away from my mismatched chest by making it appear as though I'm a box, not a woman. It's the color of overnight oats, and I've wrapped a brightly colored scarf around my neck to further hide the abnormality in my chest.

Macie isn't here, as she gets to work at five-thirty in the morning. However, I should've chosen a different meeting place as the door opens and in walks Callie and Dawson Houser. Of course. I'm not entitled to more than one miracle in the same day.

"Hey, Bri," Callie says brightly. "The usual, baby."

Dawson goes to get their coffee, and Callie sighs as she sinks into the sofa. She puts a huge green bag at her feet. "Today has been terrible."

"Oh, no," I say genuinely. "Why?" I switch out of my anxiety and focus on her.

"We lost one of our bigger clients, because a delivery was late. Not our fault."

"Lost-lost?" I ask. "Or lost-like you'll call them tomorrow and get them back when they're thinking more clearly?"

Callie gives me a tired smile. "That last one. I'll try, at least."

"Dawson Dials In is the best marketing firm in Charleston," I tell her. "You'll get them back."

Callie glances over her shoulder, but Dawson is still at the counter. "He handled it far better than I thought he would."

I reach over and pat her hand. "He's changed."

She nods and then looks up. "Hey, Jason." She slides over on the couch, leaving him a spot between us. "Did you want to sit? Or are you getting coffee?"

My heartbeat jackhammers against my breast bone. Then the back of my throat. Then inside my skull. Jason says something that I can barely hear through all the thumping, his smile full of beauty and straight, white teeth.

"Ready?" he asks me, his hand extended toward me. I

hear what he said to Callie as an echo in my ears. *Bri and I are going to dinner to discuss something.*

True. Not false. Not the whole truth and nothing but the truth. Won't hold up in court. I remind myself he's not on the stand, and there are no Bibles anywhere in sight.

I put my hand in his and allow him to pull me to my feet. We turn toward the exit just as Tara comes in. She sees us just as I pull my hand out of Jason's. I don't need to hold it right now, and I tell myself there are many more hours to come that evening.

He's made our dinner sound like business for Callie, but the look on his cousin's face tells a different story. "Have fun, you two," she says, and she's not teasing. I squint at her, and I think she genuinely means it.

Jason's still moving, and I rush to catch him. "You told her," I hiss into his ear right before he opens the door.

Outside, he says, "Yes, I told her."

"Do you tell her everything?"

He takes my hand and slows his step. Suddenly, he's not my partner and the man who makes my blood boil. I'm not his junior partner and the woman who challenges him on everything. We're just a man and a woman walking down the street in downtown Charleston.

"I like your shirt," he says, his voice almost getting swallowed by the sound of traffic.

"Thank you," I say.

"And you should wear more scarves. You look fantastic."

I smile and tilt my head up toward the sinking sun. "Have you even gone home?" I look at his gray slacks. They look like what he had on in the office, though the shirt is different. It's bright blue and a polo—something I've never seen him wear at Farmer, Buhler, and Cason.

He chuckles and says, "I am known for being able to live out of my car." He reaches into his pocket and clicks the button on his key fob. The luxury SUV a few down the curb beeps. "But I did go home. I had to feed Timber and clean up a little."

"Clean up a little?" I look at him as he opens my door and steps back so I can get in. So chivalrous. I remind myself that Jason Finch is no stranger to dating, and of course he's going to treat me like a princess. I can't fall for his Charming act in one night.

"I feel bad leaving Timber home alone again. He's just barely back at the house." He shrugs. "I ordered salads from Veggie World, main dishes from Cooper's, and desserts from Mimi's. If I drive like a bat out of...well, if I scare you to death, we might make it before the first course."

I blink at him, appreciating that he pulled back on the cliché, and I'm impressed he's put some thought into the meal. I step into his SUV and let him close the door.

He seems to strut around the vehicle, gets behind the wheel, and starts the engine. "I won't drive like a crazy person."

"I'll be the judge of that," I tease him, and I hardly recognize myself. Jason laughs and eases onto the street.

"You can change the climate over there," he says. "If you're hot, cold..." He glances at me, his eyes sliding down my body to my lap. "Whatever."

"I never say no to a seat-heater," I say, looking at the controls.

"Even in the summer?"

"Even in the summer."

"Why is that?" he asks, his voice genuinely interested.

"I grew up on a small farm," I say. "Not that far from here, actually. I rode horses a lot." I swallow, realizing how personal this conversation has turned. So soon. I forge onward, telling myself it's time to stop building walls and start opening doors. "I lived in Montana for a while too. Lots of horses there."

"All right," he says, clearly expecting more.

"I fell from one when I was nine. Maybe ten. When I was younger. I didn't break anything, but I swear I can still feel a stitch in my back." I shift in the seat, find the button, and push it to get the seat heating. "Heat always makes it feel better." I give him a smile. "I have one of those electric blankets in my bed. I like to—" I cut off, not ready to tell him about the nightly romance novel reading just yet.

"Is that how the fire started in your apartment?" he asks. "Wait, you said that was a microwave mishap."

"Yes," I say, swallowing. "I should probably get this out

of the way up front." I shift again, ready for him to tease me. "I can't cook."

"Oh, lots of people can't cook," he says like this is something everyone is cursed with. Not at my level. I'm the Jedi Master of bad cooks.

"No," I say. "I mean...I started a fire in my microwave last night, because I used it to store dishes in, then wanted to heat up my muffin, and figured it wouldn't matter if there was a stack of dishes in it."

"Sounds innocent enough." He glances at me and makes a turn that will take us out of the city. I've been to his farmhouse when he briefly listed it for sale, months ago. "I once exploded a grape in our microwave after a boy at school told me that's what would happen." He chuckles. "My mama was not happy."

I shake my head, because he's not getting it. "I put a pot of water to boil on the stove so I could make egg salad. Then I remembered I wanted to go to the bookstore, so I ran out to do that. When I got home, it took me several long seconds to figure out what was wrong with my apartment."

Jason comes to a stop at a light and meets my eyes fully. "And?"

"And the eggs had exploded everywhere. All of the water boiled out. So then it's just a dry pot with eggs in it. I lost the security deposit on that apartment."

"Wait, this just happened?"

"Like a couple months ago," I mumble, turning away

from him and looking out my window. "Remember how I just moved *again*?"

"Yeah," he says slowly. "That was because of this...egg mishap?"

"Yes," I say.

"Wow," he says.

"I almost lost the apartment I'm in now over a crock pot of beef stew," I say. "My neighbors thought I was boiling bodies, and trust me, from the smell, the FBI would've believed them."

He bursts out laughing, and the sound is so happy and light, I want to as well. I hold back, because those two stories are only the tip of the iceberg when it comes to my cooking issues.

"My sister is a foodie and married to a chef," I say. "She'll be thrilled I'm getting the proper nutrients tonight."

"Do you talk to her a lot?"

"Yes," I say. "She lives in California, and it's just the two of us. We text almost every day."

"That's great," he says sincerely. "It's just me and Connor too, so I get the closeness of a pair of siblings."

"Did he give you that scar?" I ask, and I cross my legs —the flirtiest move I know. It's pathetic, I know, but I've not been out with someone new in a long, long time. I dated Max for so long, and I swore off men after that. It's been three-plus years since I left Montana, and I'm lucky I have the crossing-legs move in my arsenal at all.

I lean into the console and nod to the mark above his right eye, almost obscured by his sexy eyebrow. He reaches up and touches it, a slight laugh coming from his throat. "I make up a new story every time someone asks me about this scar," he says, giving me a flirty smile. "But I seem to remember you saying you wanted a man who was real."

"A story that makes you a hero, no doubt."

"No doubt," he says.

"So you can get a woman to give you her number."

"Lucky for me, I already have your number, and when I text, you get an email, and a phone and computer notification, and probably a fax." He laughs again, and I join in this time.

"Nah," I say. "Cheryl calls when you message me, night or day." I grin at him, noting that we've left the city behind.

"I hope not," he says. "I don't want to bother her at home."

"So it's just me you want to bother after hours."

He looks at me, and in the last rays of sunshine before dusk falls, I see the desire shining in his gaze. "Yeah," he says simply. "Just you."

A few minutes later, he slows and turns onto a dirt drive I've been down before. "I got this scar when I was nine years old, funnily enough." He comes to a stop in front of the charming white farmhouse that still looks like it needs a lot of tender loving care. "Same as when you fell from the horse."

Our eyes meet, and I smile at him to get him to go on. "Connor and I helped on a farm for our neighbor, and they'd just had these calves born. Cutest things ever."

"A farm?" Wow, I hadn't expected that from the polished, professional Jason Finch.

"Yeah, and we fought over who got to feed the babies their bottles, and he pushed me into the fencing." He touches his eyebrow, and I suddenly want to do the same. "Bam. Scar."

"So no capes. No leaping a tall building to save the city. No damsels in distress." I grin as his hand falls and mine moves toward his face. "That's all the clichés I've got."

He doesn't chuckle. Doesn't move a muscle as I trace a single fingertip along the once-cut, then gingerly move all of them through his hair. In fact, he leans into the touch.

A car pulls up beside us, or I'm sure I'd have done something crazy—like kiss him right there in his car, less than twenty minutes into our first date.

"That'll be the first course, m'lady," he whispers, and I bring my hand back into my own personal space. "I'll come get your door."

"Thank you," I murmur, my thoughts spinning like lettuce in one of those fancy driers. Chelsea's shown them to me before, and her husband has a fleet of them in the restaurant where he works.

I watch Jason round the car, his step sure and slow. He greets the driver, takes a big white bag from her, and waits until she backs up and heads down the drive. That extra time has given me my wits back, and I remind myself that Jason and I are not really dating at all.

I told him he owed me dinner so we could set rules for our half-fake relationship. Not so I could touch his hair, cross my legs, and almost kiss him all in under a half-hour.

Get a grip, I tell myself as he opens the door.

"Salads," he announces, holding up the bag. As tires crunch down the dirt road, he turns his attention in that direction. "And there's our main course. Hope you're ready to eat."

"So ready," I say, taking his free hand and letting him help me out of the SUV.

He stills the moment and moves his fingers through my hair too. "It's down tonight," he murmurs.

I say nothing, because it's obvious I've tried to spruce myself up for this dinner. For him. My hair isn't bad when down; it's just not my battle mode, and that's what I need in the office.

"Is this real?" I ask, suddenly needing to know. Jason's expression turns confused, and my pulse flies through my body like a hummingbird flitting from flower to flower. "Because I thought we'd establish some dating rules tonight, get the paperwork filled out, and devise a plan to make Vincent *think* we were dating, but..."

The delivery car comes to a stop, but Jason doesn't turn toward it. "But what?" he asks.

I shake my head, embarrassment heating me from sole to scalp. "Nothing."

"Delivery for Jason?" The man slams the car door, and that breaks everything between us. Jason backs up, his eyes falling closed as he breathes in through his nose.

"Yes," he says, turning around.

I edge away from the car, thinking the rest of what I didn't say. *But...this feels real.*

CHAPTER EIGHT

JASON

I know Bri doesn't say anything unless it's something, but I haven't been able to circle back to our conversation in front of the farmhouse yet. She's all smiles and easy conversation, and I can't say I'm upset about that. I'm not.

The salad course and main course have been fantastic, even for having to wait an extra twenty minutes after they were ready. "All right," I say in a lull in the conversation. She's been telling me about Archie, the stray who adopted her when she moved into the apartment she has now. "Dessert."

I get to my feet and leave her at the table. I had come home and changed my clothes, started the dishwasher, sprayed some air freshener, and put a cloth and some candles on the table. I've been out with a lot of women, and while Bri isn't remotely like anyone I've ever picked up in a bar or met on the sidewalk out in front of a club, she is still a woman.

She does like candlelight and things that smell pretty —and hopefully chocolate.

"Have you been to Mimi's?" I ask as I open the white pastry box.

"I've lived here for three years," she says. "Yes, I've been to Mimi's."

"Such sass," I tease her, glancing over to find her smiling. It has been a great night, and no paperwork has made an appearance yet. That still has to happen, and she mentioned something about rules out in the driveway. I've never had dating rules before, but then again, I've never dated anyone at my law firm before either.

"They have a mousse tasting pretty regularly," I say. "Turns out, you can call them and ask for a sampler. So let's see what we've got."

Bri's chair scrapes as she gets up to join me. She scents the air with her floral perfume, and her hair drifts down as she leans over the counter to peer into the box. "Smells good," she says. "Do you know all of these?" She looks up at me, her expression open, trusting, and oh-so-beautiful.

The room spins, and I blink to try to right it. I just need some sugar. This woman hasn't rocked my world or anything. "Uh," I say, trying to focus. "I'm pretty sure that one's chocolate." I point to the deep, dark brown one in the corner. "This lighter one will be caramel. This pink one is raspberry."

My brain kicks in then, because I have gone to Mimi's loads of times and gotten their mousses. "Oh, lemon," I say. "That one is fantastic."

Bri plucks the yellow custard from the box and picks up a tasting spoon. "We can share, right?" She doesn't wait for me to confirm before she dunks her spoon into the side of the mousse and lifts the bite to her lips. I stand there and watch, mesmerized by her movement.

"Mm," she says. "This one is great." She hands it to me, and stupidly, I fumble it. My fingers feel numb, and the plastic cup falls toward the countertop.

She yelps, and I cry out, and together, we manage to catch the cup before it goes splat. "Sorry," I say, my chest heaving for a reason I can't name.

"You were like a ninja," she says. "I mean, after you dropped it." She licks her lips, and Southern fried chicken. She has *got* to stop doing that.

I force my attention to the lemon mousse. It didn't spill, but it's been disturbed. "I think they sent whipped cream," I say, and I step away from Bri. My head clears with the distance, and I take a deep breath as I pass the sink. The air is clear. Okay. I'm okay.

In the fridge, there is a container of whipped cream, and I dollop some onto each of the nine mousse cups. Bri picks up the box and turns to go back to the table, leaving me to follow. I do, of course, and I snag the paperwork from Malcolm in HR as I pass my built-in desk.

I put it on the table between us, and Bri's eyes fall to it.

A sigh comes out of her mouth just before a spoonful of a dark red mousse goes in. "Ooh," she says around the tiny plastic spoon. She swallows and adds, "That one's raspberry, and it's good."

"The other one must be strawberry," I say. "The fruity ones aren't my favorite."

"No?" She gives me a teasing look. "More of a chocolate guy?"

"Yeah," I say, lifting that one from the corner of the box. "The white chocolate is good too." I nod to the white cream on white mousse in the box.

"The lemon was really good too." She doesn't go in for another bite though. Instead she sets her spoon down and pulls the paperwork in front of her. "Let's see..."

"I can do that," I say. "You just sounded like you might have something to add."

Her eyes flit left and right as she reads, and when she raises her head, she doesn't do it to meet my eyes. "I did?"

"Yeah," I say, taking another bite of the chocolate mousse. It's rich and creamy and absolutely sinful. I push it toward her. "Outside. Earlier."

"This says the relationship can't impact our work," she says.

I know what it says. I read it immediately after leaving Vincent's office that afternoon. While I waited with bated breath for Bri to text me and let me know if this dinner was happening or not. It was torture—and not just the reading. As a lawyer, I'm used to reading huge amounts of text and knowing what it all means.

"It won't," I say. "You've got your cases. We're counseling on a couple, but you've got them well in hand."

She glances up from the pages again. "Well in hand," she says, and it sure sounds like she's teasing me.

"That's not a cliché," I say.

"What is it then?" she challenges, and this time, her eyes do lock onto mine. She hasn't had a problem doing so during dinner either, and I can't help but wonder what changed the moment the paperwork came out.

"A compliment." I fold my arms, because heaven knows she's done it a thousand times since we met. Probably just this week.

She does a half-roll of her eyes and goes back to the papers. "They want to know when it started, who initiated it, all kinds of things."

I gently extract the papers from their spot in front of her. "I told you I'd handle it."

"I need to know what you're going to put," she says.

I smile at her. "I'll show them to you before I turn them in." I fold them in half and tuck the papers under my thigh. "Talk to me about the rules you want."

She shutters right off, and I've hit some unknown bullseye. She says nothing, and while I'm no orator when it comes to feelings, I might be better than Bri. "I've never dated anyone at work before," I say. "It's probably really smart to have some rules."

"Have you ever had rules in a relationship before?" she asks, her focus solely on the lemon mousse. I'm not going to get any of that, I can tell.

"No," I say. "You?"

"No," she says.

"Then maybe we don't need rules at all."

"Yes." She looks up with panic in her gaze. "We do. For this, we do."

I gaze at her until she shifts, then I drop my attention to the dessert box and take out the white chocolate mousse. "Why?"

"Because," she says. "The situation is...delicate. We need to be sure to treat it with...delicateness."

I laugh and point my tasting spoon at her. "Delicateness is not a word."

"Yes, it is."

"Sure," I say, grinning at her. All I can think about is kissing her—kissing that mouth that's fighting against a smile. If she's not thinking about kissing me, may the Good Lord Himself smite me and make my lips into frogs.

Since I don't get smitten, I'm pretty sure Bri is thinking about kissing me too. I remind myself of my pledge, and I will not be doing any moves on her tonight. None. Not even holding her hand—though I kind of broke that one at the coffee shop.

I give myself a mental shake. "Okay, so what rules?"

"I think we should stick to the no-kissing one," she says.

Alarm pulls through me. "At work," I say slowly. "Right?" Her body language suggests otherwise, if the cinching across her chest is any indication.

Her eyes narrow, and I don't like that either. "Why would we need to kiss at all?"

"Come on," I say with a scoff, but she's serious. Dead serious. "Do you not...kiss your boyfriends?"

"You're not my boyfriend," she fires at me.

"Yet," I shoot back.

She leans forward, those eyes still lasered in on me. I have the inexplicable urge to move closer to her too. I do, thinking I'm going to get my eye poked out or something equally as horrifying. "This isn't a real relationship," she says in the same slow, unsure voice I just used to say *At work*. "Right?"

Squinting, I study her. "What do you mean?"

"I mean," she says, and then she clears her throat. For a moment—the briefest speck of time—I see Bri without any of her safeguards in place. And she is terrified. A blip, then the strong, sure-of-everything woman slides back into place. "You told Vincent we were dating as a reason I could be your alibi with Ben. This dinner is to go over paperwork and rules; it's not a real date." She takes a breath and starts talking again, something about how I didn't even pick her up at her apartment, but my chest has gone hollow.

Every word she says continues to make her voice reverberate around inside my head, and I get to my feet and pace away. I'm not sure if she's stopped talking or not, and I exhale and run my hands through my hair.

How have I not been clear enough? Are the wires between me and Bri always going to be so crazy-crossed? I tilt my head back and think, *Help me communicate clearly with this woman.*

I have to speak from the heart, which almost ensures I'm going to mess it up, but I turn toward her. She sits at the table, but Bri rises to her feet as I fully face her. She looks somewhat upset, and I wish I could erase that.

"I don't know the last part of what you said," I admit. "I sort of tuned you out as I tried to think of what to say to be super-duper clear with you."

"I'd love for you to be *super-duper* clear with me." More arm-folding. My *word*. I want to pull those arms apart and fasten them to her sides. Irritation shoots through me, and I'll admit, it's hard to tell the difference between it and attraction to Bri.

I gesture to her and then me, my arm flapping like a flag. "This is a real date."

She's already shaking her head before I'm even done speaking.

"Yes," I say before she can interject. "I ordered dinner with you in mind. I lit candles. I changed my clothes. It's not business. It's for pleasure. You and me. I picked you up where you told me to, but I'd have gladly come to Macie's or your apartment or the blasted moon." My voice nearly shouts, and I take a deep breath.

At least Bri doesn't look like she'll argue with me.

I throw my hands into the air and push all of the air out of my lungs. My mindfulness coach taught me to focus on my breath to find my center. Let everything relax as the air goes out. I try, but I can't really achieve it in this situation.

"I like you," I blurt out. "I want to get to know you better—and not as my junior partner. I want to see you outside of work, and find out if your hair shines a little red in the sunshine or not, and maybe go on a weekend trip to Kimli Island. You know, as a couple. That's what couples do. People who like each other and are learning about each other. For real."

Bri's eyes get wider and wider with every word I say. I feel like I've been blubbering for an hour, and I press my lips together. That's all she's getting. If she doesn't say she wants this huge, hulking, sparking thing between us to be real, I should probably march into Vincent's office in the morning and quit.

Seeing her will be too painful. I've never been rejected like that before, and I can't even imagine how I'll feel.

"I—" she starts, then promptly closes her mouth.

"For real," I say again, taking a step toward her. "This is *not* fake for me. Not even close. I *feel* something for you, and I don't know what it is, but I want to find out. So I got the form from HR. I'm going to fill it out and turn it in... unless you tell me right now—*right now*, Miss Shadows— that you feel nothing for me."

I swallow, my heartbeat drumming through my veins. The one in my neck pulses, and I wish I could slap my hand over it so Bri won't know how nervous I am. I didn't crash and burn on the delivery, though, so I'm still standing here.

"Jason," she says just as Timber fills the house with his big, booming barks.

"Hey." I shout at him and whip my attention to where he's been hogging the entire couch in the living room. "No barking!"

He jumps down from the couch, all one hundred and forty pounds of his black and white flesh and trots toward the front door, his voice still echoing off the walls and ceiling.

"He's so loud," Bri yells, and I find her with both hands clapped over her ears.

Timber comes scampering back into the kitchen, and even from fifteen feet away, I know I'm getting knocked to the floor. "Hey," I say in a stern voice, stepping in front of Bri. "Stop, Timber. Slow down!"

He doesn't, and he jumps—all four paws off the freaking floor—toward me as if I can catch him and cradle him against my chest until the fright has been soothed out of him.

I can't, of course, and we both go tumbling to the ground. Me, on the bottom—not a great position to be in when there's a lot of dog coming down on top of you, trust me.

Timber yelps and wails like a little child, and I groan. The terrible sound of bones and bodies and dining room chairs clatters about, and Bri cries out, "Are you okay?"

I'd like to think she's asking me, but she could be directing the question at Timber.

The doorbell rings.

"Oh, boy," I say just before Timber stomps one big, bony foot into my stomach, pushes off, and streaks toward the door, barking, barking, barking.

CHAPTER NINE

BRI

Jason lays on the floor, half under the table, in the fetal position. I'm not sure if I should go after the dog, answer the door, or get him some ice.

For real, echoes in my head.

This is not fake for me.

Tell me you feel nothing for me.

I can't tell him that. I haven't told him anything yet.

I drop to my knees and put one hand on his forehead. "Hey," I say, turning my back to his huge Great Dane. I might regret that later, but right now, my body-blocking creates a pocket for the two of us. "Look at me, Jason."

His eyes come open, and he blinks once and twice and then sees me. "My dog is a menace," he says.

I give him a smile even as the doorbell rings again. "Are you expecting someone? Should I get that?"

"It's probably second dessert," he says, starting to sit up.

"Watch your—" I say just before his very hard skull hits the lip on the bottom of the table. I cringe, and Jason falls back to the floor. "Head," drips from my lips. "I'll get the door." After scooting back, I get to my feet, tug down my sweatshirt, and march toward where Timber has his front paws up on the door. There's a rectangular window in the top one-sixth of the door, and the silly dog is looking through it.

"Timber," I bark at him. "Get down. Now." To my surprise, the Great Dane obeys me. "In the office," I command next, adding a stern point of my hand to go with the words. "Just a second," I call to whoever is on the other side of the door. I look at Timber; he looks at me.

I cock an eyebrow, and the beast trots toward Jason's office. I got a decent tour of the first floor when we arrived, and then he whisked me away for salad and barbecue meatloaf.

With the door closed to the office, I run my hands over my hair and determine I'm presentable, then I open the door.

There's no one there, but there is a huge carton of ice cream on the porch and a pair of taillights heading down the drive. "They had to ring the doorbell twice to drop off ice cream?" I bend to get it, but it's not just a carton. It's like a barrel.

I can't lift it, and I turn back to the house for help. "Jason," I call.

"Coming." A few seconds later, he appears at the end of the hall, one hand against the wall. "Sorry. I forgot it's huge."

"How many dates are we going to have to eat this on?" I tease as he approaches.

He stalls, those dark eyes full of quizzes again.

"Listen," I say, my throat narrowing by the moment. "I'd like to..."

He slides his hand into mine. "Kiss me?"

"No," I say quickly, though my eyes do drop to that gorgeous mouth. I can't even remember what it feels like to be kissed by a man. Not right now, anyway. "Not tonight."

"Not tonight or not ever?" he asks.

"Not tonight," I say.

He nods, releases me, and retrieves the ginormous bucket of ice cream from the porch. "It's chocolate chocolate chip," he says. "You can take it home with you."

I giggle and follow him back into the kitchen. "I don't think so," I say. "How will I get it home? Where will I put it?"

"I'll give you a small container," he says. "And bring you some at work."

"Is that allowed?" I ask, clearly flirting with him.

Everything in his house suddenly warms as he smiles at me. He lifts the giant barrel to his head and rests it against his hairline. A sigh slips from between his lips.

I laugh, the sound coming straight from my gut. I can't remember the last time I felt this happy and let it come out of my soul. "I'll get you some ice." I move toward his fridge. The ice cream thunks onto the counter, and he walks away from me.

"I need to lie down." His voice is pathetic, and I watch him as I fill a zipper bag with ice and head toward where he lays on the couch. I'm not sure if he's really injured or just hamming it up, and right now I don't care.

I kneel in his personal space, once again creating an intimate pocket I want to exist inside for a while. I gently lower the ice to his forehead and cover it with my hand. His goes on top of mine, and our eyes meet. There are no more questions swimming in his eyes, but I say, "For real," anyway.

Down the hall and in the office, Timber barks.

Jason jumps and asks, "Where'd you put him?" with plenty of worry in his expression now.

"Your office," I say just as a colossal crash fills the house. The windows legit shake and everything. My shoulders hunch, almost like they're trying to hide my head. "Uh oh."

Jason sags back into the couch. "Leave him," he says. "What's done is done."

Our eyes meet, and we laugh together—him chuckling and me giggling. It feels really, really...nice.

Real.

Like maybe the past decade hasn't been one hard

lesson after another about how I can't trust men, but an exercise in patience until I find the right one.

I dismiss the thought quickly and get up to dish up our second dessert. This is our first date, after all, and I can't get too far ahead of myself.

———

"THERE IT IS," Jessie Dunaway says, pointing though I've got the address pulled up on my phone's map app too. I peer at the house through my window, noticing how nicely the gray exterior blends into the sky today.

For the beginning of May, it sure has been cloudy lately, and I expect rain any moment. Sure enough, the first drops of it pelt the windshield as Jessie turns into the driveway of the house she's brought me to see today.

I'm back in my apartment, but I don't want to stay there. My landlord is fining me a full month's rent to replace the microwave and surrounding plaster. I talked to Jillian Redstone, who owns the building where Callie and Dawson work, and she said that's fair. Her father owns a lot of rentals around the city and the surrounding suburbs, and when she's not running her spa, her artist yoga classes, or doing photo shoots for her husband's rowhouse renovations, she manages those properties for her daddy.

"I'm tired of renting," I say to Jessie out of nowhere. I'd told her the same thing almost a week ago when I'd slumped into the orange couch at Legacy Brew and told everyone about the fine. I'd conveniently left out the part about the stench of smoke still hanging in the apartment, but Mr. Winslow will charge me for that once I move out, I'm sure.

"I know you are, sweetie," Jessie says. "This is the place, I know it."

"You've been here before?" I ask.

"Yes," she says somewhat evasively.

"So another client didn't want it." I'm not asking. If she's been here before, she's shown this property, and it didn't get bought. Plain and simple.

She parks her car and we both look at the house. It's nothing too spectacular. I still lift my phone and take a quick pic, because Chelsea will want to see it. She's the one who called and in no uncertain terms told me to "One, Bri, find a house you can buy and fix up, and two, send me more pictures of this hot new lawyer boyfriend of yours."

I'd done the latter, but I'm still working on the house thing.

Jason and I have made it through a full work week in our new relationship, and to be honest, the whole thing was kind of...boring. He's got a case going to court next week, and I'll be at his side, observing. He has the court-room experience I don't, and I'm really excited about it.

"Looks like it needs new shutters," I say.

"Project number one," Jessie trills out just before she opens her door. "Come on, Bri. We're going to have to run." She squeals as she enters the rain, and she dashes in such a feminine way toward the front porch, which offers some safety from the downpour.

I grew up in the South—so did Jessie—so I sit in my seat and wait another sixty seconds. Then seventy. The thrumming of the droplets begins to fade, and then I open my door and get out. It's still raining, but not cats and dogs —ha! Jason would love that—and I do a quick mall-walk-jog through the weather to the porch.

It creaks, something I note mentally. A creaky porch? Can't have that, and the Ms. Fix-It inside me actually brightens.

Jessie has gone inside, and I nudge open the door to follow her. I take a deep breath, because the scent of a place can tell you a lot about it. This air smells like lilacs and dryer sheets, which is so fake, I cough.

So something to cover up, I think as if this house has bodies buried somewhere.

The living room opens up before me, and while it's not as big as Jason's farmhouse, the wall to my left is made of old brick that screams charm. The floor is original—I can tell just by looking—and a staircase rises ten feet in front of me, creating a little foyer in this little country house.

I love it.

I keep my smile to myself as I move into the living room. There's a cupboard under the stairs for Archie and maybe more feline friends, and the back corner of the house behind the living room holds the kitchen. Jessie waits there, and she spreads her arms wide. "Huh? What do you think? First impressions."

"I love the brick wall." I indicate it. It runs unstopped from corner to corner, through the living room and kitchen. It bears a fireplace too, and that's a huge plus. "The floor is in good shape for being a hundred years old."

"Mm hm," she says, her bright blue eyes dazzling like sapphires. "Yes, good. Yeah."

I reach back and gather my hair, already twisting it into battle mode. I don't have a pencil or a hair tie, so I just let it fall back across my shoulders after a moment of holding the bun in place. "It needs new appliances and countertops."

"Yes," Jessie says, a hint of dreariness now coating her voice. "These are terrible." She gives me the brightest smile ever. "Projects two and three."

I can't stop myself from smiling back. "Master bedroom?"

"Nope," she says cheerfully. "That will require you to knock down some walls. Allow me." She leads me into the bedroom, which is only accessed from a doorway beside the fridge. That's pretty tacky, but I go with it for now. The bedroom is a box, and not the good kind that bears assorted chocolates or nine varieties of mousses from a premier downtown restaurant.

There's no attached bath, but a narrow hallway runs along the wall, jogs around the staircase, and ends in a laundry room. The bathroom sits between that and the bedroom, and I can suddenly see this whole half of the house as my personal sanctuary.

Yes, some walls will have to come down. New beams put up. All the carpet torn out, and the laundry room relocated.

But I can do it.

As I go back around through the kitchen and living room and up the stairs, I *want* to do it. I say nothing as Jessie shows me the three bedrooms and single bath upstairs—again, nothing to get too excited about. Things here are functional at best—but the excitement builds in my chest.

The back yard sprawls out from behind the deck, with huge, mature sycamores and live oaks, and I can see myself out there, a romance novel in one hand and a tall glass of sweet tea in the other. Jason waltzes into my fantasy life, and I don't immediately push him back out.

He fits here too.

The thought terrifies me, so I turn back to Jessie, realizing I've gone down the steps of the deck and taken a few steps toward one of the trees. "This is in my budget?"

"Below budget," she says. "Do you love it or do you love it?"

I walk up to her, glancing left and right. Our eyes meet, and I say, "You know what? I love it."

Jessie squeals and grabs onto me, and while normally I'm not the huggy, jumpy type of woman, I allow myself to get caught up in this moment. I laugh with Jess, and she starts talking in acronyms at the speed of sound. All I get out of it is that I should go in with an offer a few thousand below asking, because this property has been on the market for thirty-two days.

Apparently, thirty is good, but thirty-one is a death knell. And thirty-two?

"Let's definitely go in eight thousand below asking," Jessie says as she drives us back to her office. "Then the games can begin."

"I don't like games," I tell her, smiling all the while.

She glances at me. "Surprising, given you and Jason." Her voice holds coolness, and I'm not sure what to make of it.

I watch her drive, but she doesn't say anything else. She does crumple after only a few seconds, saying, "Sorry, that was mean."

I tilt my head and continue to study her. "Was it?"

"He's changed a lot in the past several months." She kneads the steering wheel. "I shouldn't have said anything. Lord knows I'm not the same woman I was last year."

I look away from her, and the tension in the car recedes. "Yeah," I say. "I get that." The silence envelops us, and I start to smile. "He's *really* good-looking, though, right?"

Jessie bursts out laughing. "Oh, girl, he's more than good-looking."

I'm not one to kiss and tell, and I haven't had female friends for a while. But Jessie feels safe, as do Tara, Callie, and Macie. We see each other almost every day at the coffee shop, and I giggle and realize how very content I am in this moment.

My life is humming along with a couple of exciting cases that are going well at work, a possible new house on the horizon, true friends I can call when I start a fire in my apartment, and the best-looking boyfriend on the planet— for real.

"So he's being good to you?" Jessie asks, shooting me a look with wide eyes.

"Yes," I say easily. "He's practically a prince." With an exaggerated sigh floating on the air, Jessie giggles again, and I feel like sunshine is beaming from my face. That's not a cliché, but Jason's not here to tease about it. If he was, I'd probably say I'm as fit as a fiddle—mentally, spiritually, emotionally, and physically.

That's cringe-worthy, but right now, it only makes me smile even harder.

CHAPTER TEN

JASON

"Objection," I say from the table, almost in a bored voice. I look up to Judge Crouch, and he looks back at me. "Leading."

"Sustained."

That's right, I think as I look at the prosecutor. *Can't lead the witness like that.* Jarrod Donovan will do whatever he can get away with—most lawyers will—which is why my client has a lawyer too. I don't look over to Sarah Daniels. We've met at least a zillion times (and I *never* exaggerate), and I know her case inside and out. I know the defense I've come up with, and Bri and I went over it and over it last night, the night before that, and the night before that too.

It's not my job to decide if Sarah's guilty or not. It's my job to make sure she gets treated fairly and has someone

who understands the law so she can be properly repre-
sented in court. So I don't know if she should be convicted
of neglect or not. I know she had a lot of people in her face,
giving her substances and advice, and if I've learned
anything over the past almost fifteen years of my career in
law school and practicing family law, it's that no situation
is exactly how we think it is.

Everyone has layers and facets. Every story has dozens
of sides, not just two. Some have called me callous or hard-
hearted. They don't see the running on the treadmill to get
children out of my head. They don't see the vats of ice
cream I consume. They don't see the countless hours spent
in prep to make sure I'm not the reason someone doesn't
get what they deserve.

The prosecutor tries once again to lead the witness to
an answer—and one that's hearsay anyway. This time, I
get to my feet. I take a moment to button my expensive
designer jacket. "Your Honor," I say, gesturing to the
witness and making sure my voice is heavy with weariness.
"Is he going to testify for her?"

"Mister Donovan," Judge Crouch warns. "Do you
have a *question* for this witness?"

The woman in the hot seat squirms, and I move to the
end of the table. I'm aware of the eyes on me, but none
more than Bri's. It's like she's scribbling mental notes
about where I'm standing, when I chose to get to my feet,
and who I look at. I haven't thought so hard about my presence in the courtroom in a long, long time.

I pick up my glass of water and take a sip while Donovan returns to his table and takes a piece of paper from someone on his legal team. He slides his reading glasses onto his face, and I see myself in him in ten years. Gray around the temples, glasses, a bit of a gut. He's a family man, married, with three children between the ages of seven and twelve.

My future unfolds in front of me, and for the first time, I want to reach out and grab it. Bri and I have been seeing each other for about two and a half weeks now officially. There have been no instances of PDA at work. Half the people on our floor don't even know we're a couple. I can and will be professional with her when necessary, and I'm still playing my cards right to get that kiss.

A real one, not one stolen in the hallway here in the county courthouse.

"Mrs. Kelley," Donovan says. "How many pills did Sarah Daniels take on the night of July the twenty-third?" He speaks like a Southern gentleman, and that'll endear him to the jury. I can do the same; I usually don't in court.

The woman leans forward and swallows. "I don't know."

I stand up straight and practically drop my glass. I manage to use my ninja skills to save it, but it still thumps loudly on the table. I don't care. My eyes are locked on the witness.

"Wasn't it four?" Donovan asks.

"Objection," I bark.

"Sustained," Judge Crouch said.

"Didn't you see her take the pills?" Donovan asks.

The witness swallows, her big eyes darting to mine. I cock my head ever so slightly, praying she'll just tell the truth. The whole truth. Nothing but the truth.

"No," she says.

A murmur runs through the congregation in the room, and it echoes the excitement now pouring through my veins.

"But your statement to the police says you did," Donovan says, clearly confused. He moves between me and his witness, which is a really smart move. I never said he was dumb, that's for sure. "Four pills, because you counted the ones left in the bottle and had been keeping a tally of it for days."

He looks up from his paper, his unspoken question hanging in the air. She doesn't answer it, and I want to rejoice. I hold my tongue when I want to jump in. Mama would be proud of my restraint, as she's always said I'm too impulsive.

"On the night of July twenty-third," Donovan starts again. "How many pills did Sarah Daniels swallow before she passed out, leaving her three-year-old son alone?"

"Asked and answered," I call to the judge.

"Sustained," he said. "Mister Donovan, do you—?"

"Recess, Your Honor," he says, swinging toward the judge. "I need a recess to confer with my witness."

"No," I say, striding forward. "We just got back from lunch thirty minutes ago. She's been on the stand for less than ten minutes. Are we to waste this court's time? All these jurors? He's been preparing this case for seven and a half months. Why isn't he ready?" I shoot Jarrod Donovan a glare. Afterward, we'll probably get drinks down the street, but his look suggests he might follow me home, stalker-style instead.

"If he has no questions for his witness," I say. "I'm ready for my cross-examine."

"Ten minutes," Donovan says. "She's testifying against the police report."

"Perhaps she's finally telling the truth," I say.

"My chambers." The judge gets to his feet, and my shoulders sink. That's never good. I'm going to get a tongue-lashing, and Donovan is getting his recess—just in a different way. "Now."

He walks off the stand, and Jarrod and I go through another door, down a short hallway, and into the judge's office. Two cops stand inside, with two more behind us that stand guard outside the door once it closes.

I'm still deciding if I should be the first to talk or not when Donovan says, "She's throwing me out there, Judge Crouch. I need to know why."

"She can't even answer the questions," I say. "Are you sure she was even there?"

Jarrod glares at me, and it's not easy to withstand. "She

was found in the home when the police brought the little boy home."

"Maybe *she* took the pills," I say with a shrug as I sit in one of Judge Crouch's oversized wingbacks. This thing is *nice*, and I relax back into it. "Maybe *she* was supposed to be watching the boy the night he wandered into the storm."

It's like Bri reached into my brain and planted a lightbulb. I jump to my feet. "What if *she* was supposed to be babysitting the child?"

"No," Jarrod says, shaking his head mightily. "No way."

I turn to Judge Crouch, who's sitting at his desk with a jar of onion dip and a bag of ridged potato chips. My mouth waters, but now is no time to be thinking about junk food. "Judge, let me ask her."

"She won't say." Jarrod takes a seat. "She likes talking to women more than men." He sighs. "With a recess, Judge, I can have Linda Ellison from my team resume the questioning. Perhaps Jenny-Anne will respond to her better."

"If he gets a woman, so do I." I lift my chin and stare down Judge Crouch.

"I wasn't aware you had any females on your legal team on this case," he says.

"I have a junior partner I can call up," I say. "We've gone over the case extensively. She's in the audience.

Sabrina Shadows, junior partner at Farmer, Buhler, and Cason."

"Add her name to your filing during the recess," the judge says dryly. "You both have ten minutes."

"Thank you," Donovan says. I say nothing, because I'm already striding toward the exit. I have less than ten minutes to find Bri, get all the ideas out of my head, and put her on the list of defense attorneys in this case so she can cross-examine Jenny-Anne Kelley once the recess ends.

———

"OKAY?" I ask nine minutes and fifty-two seconds later. I'm sweating through my undershirt, but I've got a white shirt on over that, and then my suit coat. No one will know. I glance over to Bri, and I swear she's turned a shade of green no human being should ever be.

"Hey." I step in front of her. "This is just the grand jury again."

"No, it's not," she hisses at me. "This is a real case, in front of a real judge, with a real jury, and real people's lives on the line."

I smile at her. "And we have real ice cream back at the farmhouse. You've got this."

"I don't even know—"

"All rise," the bailiff yells, cutting her off. Judge Crouch returns, and Bri presses her palms to the table in front of her the whole time he comes in and sits behind his bench.

"Mister Donovan," he says, and all eyes move to the prosecutor.

"Miss Ellison is going to resume questioning," he says, not bothering to stand from the end seat at the table. A short, smartly-dressed woman rises to her feet. She's wearing heels and a pencil skirt, and if I saw her in the grocery store, I'd know she lawyered for a living. Everything about her screams buttoned up and polished, and one look to Jenny-Anne shows that she knows who she's talking to.

Jarrod Donovan in female clothes.

I lean over and hiss, "Let your hair down."

"What?" Bri whispers back.

I nod to the witness, and Bri follows my gaze. Five seconds later, she reaches up casually and removes the clip in her hair keeping her bun in place. Her hair falls softly over her shoulders and tumbles down her back. It's seriously one of the sexiest things I've ever seen, and not only because she's beautiful. But because she's smart enough to see what I see.

The witness bumbles through the questions again, still clearly nervous and out of her element.

"Your witness," Miss Ellison says, and I write something on a paper.

"Miss Shadows is going to conduct our cross-examination." My voice almost sounds bored. I don't look at the witness. Or Bri as she gets to her feet. I stare openly when she shrugs out of her jacket and drapes it over the back of her chair.

I've never seen her without a jacket, a cardigan, a sweater, a bulky sweatshirt, or something very similar to keep herself covered and shapeless. Watching her swing her hips past me and around the table, I wonder why in the world she'd keep all of that covered up.

She reaches up and runs her hand through her hair. "Mrs. Kelley, how many children do you have?"

She seems surprised by the question. "Uh, three."

Bri nods. "Girls or boys?"

"Two girls and a boy," she says. We know the witness's history. We know everything about them. We've read the police reports too.

"What do you do for a living?" Bri pauses near the podium and casually puts one elbow up on it as if she's at a bar waiting for a drink.

"I stay home with the kids," she says. "My oldest is eleven."

"What about your husband?" Bri asks. This isn't a line of questioning I'd have gone down. I'd probably pound questions at the poor woman to try to break her into saying she wasn't at Sarah's house that night, or that she took the drugs too, or something. I'm honestly not sure, because I'm not the one doing it.

My mind zips through the hoops Bri is laying out for Jenny-Anne, but I can't see where she's going yet.

"He works in construction," Jenny-Anne says, finally leaning away from the microphone.

"My father did that," Bri says. "For a while. The work is on and off, isn't it? Sometimes you have a job. Sometimes you don't."

"Is there a question in there?" Miss Ellison asks.

"Did your husband have steady employment, Mrs. Kelley?" Bri asks.

The woman shakes her head and gives a light laugh. "He's been on and off, like your daddy, for a while. He hurt his back and can't do as much."

"Doesn't he get some aid for his injury?" Bri asks, cocking her head. I can't see her face from this angle, but I can imagine the slightly confused look that goes with her question.

"A little," Jenny-Anne says.

"Did you try to pick up any odd jobs to make ends meet?"

"Here and there."

"What kind of things?"

"I picked up a sewing job," she says. "I did some shopping for people, because I can take the kids with me to do that."

"Mm." Bri doesn't ask another question. The silence stretches, but it doesn't make me uncomfortable.

"I started doing some babysitting," Jenny-Anne says.

"Is that how you met Miss Daniels?" Bri finally pushes away from the podium, and now she retreats to our table, leans back against it, just perching on the very front of it. She puts her hands down to balance herself, and I find myself once again in awe of her.

She's a natural in the courtroom, though she acts like she's terrified to be here. She doesn't have much experience, but every time she steps up to the plate, she knocks it out of the park.

"Yes," Jenny-Anne says. "She was working at the grocery store, long hours. I took Marty for her sometimes if Dale was working."

"Because you live close to her, don't you?"

"A few streets over," Jenny-Anne says.

"Mm." Bri glances down at the table, where a paper sits. I never saw her put it there, but there it is. She takes a deep breath. "Last July, Jenny-Anne." She looks up. "It's the twenty-third. Hot here in Charleston." She half-laughs as she blows out her breath. "Do you remember that day?"

"Yes." Jenny-Anne swallows, leaning into the microphone again. I want to tell Bri to proceed with caution, but the woman has eyes.

"Was your husband working that day?"

"Yes."

"Did you take Marty for Sarah?"

"Yes."

Bri pushes to a stand. "When? That morning? Afternoon? Evening?"

Tears flow down Jenny-Anne's face. "That afternoon," she sobs into the microphone. "I couldn't keep him when

Dale got home, and I called her and called her. When she finally picked up, I said she had to come get him. So she did."

Bri walks closer, slowly. She goes all the way to the witness stand and puts her hand over Jenny-Anne's. "What state was she in when she picked up her son?"

I can't see her face, nor Jenny-Anne's as Bri blocks her. All the jurors are locked on the witness, and all I have is my ears to guide me. "Not good," Jenny-Anne whispers.

"You could tell?" Bri asks.

"Yes."

"Do you think she was high?"

"Yes."

"Did you call the police?"

"No."

"Did you ask her about it?" There's a pause, and then Bri says, "I'm so sorry, Jenny-Anne, but we need you to answer out loud for the court."

"She said her boyfriend gave them to her at work," she whispers. "Forced her to take them. Her boss found them and fired her, and she went home and crashed. Then I called."

"Who was the boyfriend?" Bri asks, and I hear the sharp edge in her voice. "Do you know his name?"

"Landon Bills," Jenny-Anne says.

My eyelids sink closed. *Yes*, I think. There's our defense right there, and Bri led Jenny-Anne right to it.

"He got the pills. They were in his name. He made her take them. She loved her son."

"Objection," Donovan calls, but Judge Crouch holds up his hand.

"Overruled. Let the witness speak."

And speak she does. Bri stays right at her side as she does, prompting her with questions when she falters, and before I know it, the judge raps his gavel and says, "Reconvene at nine a.m. tomorrow morning."

Activity flurries around me, and I get to my feet, expecting Bri to skip back to me like a dutiful protégé, ready for her praise. She deserves it. Instead, she stands near the podium and watches Jenny-Anne Kelley leave the courtroom with a police officer. Only then does she turn toward me, and her face isn't beaming with rainbows and sunshine. She almost looks like she might cry.

I want to take her into my arms and comfort her, but that would be against our act-professional-while-at-work agreement. I nod to her, my eyes searching hers, as she approaches the table. "Excellent work, Bri," I murmur.

"Thank you," Sarah Daniels says, throwing herself at Bri. They both grunt as they collide, and then Sarah has to go with her police escort too. I tell her we'll be in touch before tomorrow to go over some things now that the case has taken a turn, and then I put my hand on the small of Bri's back and guide her out of the courtroom.

We drove over together earlier that day, and she falls into zombie-mode as we walk toward my SUV. Only when we make it inside do I say, "Bri." That thaws her, and she looks over to me. "You can't get wrapped up in the emotions of the case."

"I'm not," she says. "I'm wrapped in the emotions of a human being." She looks away and her hands grab at a phantom jacket that's usually there. She startles and says, "My jacket."

"I got it," I say, reaching into the backseat to retrieve it. I hand it to her, and she slides her arms through it backward as if cold. It rained on and off last week, but this week it's been nothing but humidity and heat. She can't possibly be cold.

"Why do you always wear a jacket?" I ask. "You have to be sweltering sometimes."

She looks at me, her gaze perfectly even now. "You also always wear a jacket."

"It goes with my suit," I say. "That's a denim jacket you don't need with what else you have on."

"I..." She focuses out her window. "I feel safer inside jackets and cardigans."

"Mm." I wonder if I leave it at that and let the silence ask my questions if she'll answer the way Jenny-Anne did. "I sense a story there."

"There's one," she says.

"Do I get to hear it?"

"Maybe not tonight," she says. She leans her head back and lets it roll toward me. "Can I take a pass tonight?"

"Sure." I reach over and take one of her hands, bringing it all the way to my lips for a kiss. "What are you feeling like? Ritzy? Low-key? Quiet? Loud?"

"Pizza," she says, and I grin.

"I know the best place."

"I'm sure you do." She squeezes my hand and closes her eyes. I bask in her company, because it's nice to have her with me. In court. At the office. In my car. In the evenings. She has me thinking things about myself and my future I haven't before, and I like that I'm not alone and so keenly aware of it.

She teases me about my clichés, but she loves that I know all the best restaurants and hole-in-the-wall places in the city. I love food, and I love getting to know people off the beaten path, and both of those make me the best man to go to when a meal is needed in Charleston.

"Here we are," I say a few minutes later. She opens her eyes and squints up at the half-burnt out sign.

"Porky's?" she asks. "This place looks like I might be on the pizza tomorrow night if I'm not careful."

I burst out laughing and set the SUV in park. "Come on," I say. "You're going to love the artichoke dip pie here. It has your name written all over it."

She smiles softly at me, and neither of us move to get out of the car. "How'd I do in court?" she asks. "Honestly."

"You were brilliant," I whisper. "As always."

"You don't have a wife and family somewhere else, do you?" Her eyes shoot open wider as she sucks in a breath.

"Bri," I say slowly. "What?"

"Nothing," she says, tugging her hand free and reaching for the door handle.

I meet her at the front bumper and hold up one hand. Anyone with only one good eye can see Bri doesn't want to be touched right now. "No," I say, standing my ground. "It's not nothing. It's something, and I want to know what."

CHAPTER ELEVEN

BRI

I CANNOT BELIEVE WHAT'S COME OUT OF MY MOUTH. I just want a lot of carbs, a huge barrel of ice cream, and a big Great Dane to start barking. Then everything will get jumbled, and I won't have to delve into this part of my past.

Standing here, though, there is no ice cream, no dogs, and no distractions. In fact, if we're not careful, someone will come upon us unaware, and then I won't have to tell the story.

"Can we go in?" I ask. "This alley is creepy."

"It's not an alley," Jason says, a hefty roll of his eyes. He turns and leads me inside. Plenty of people pack the interior of the building, which I wouldn't have guessed from the outside.

"Jason," someone booms, and I let him get swept away into a group of men and women who clearly know him.

Nothing about that surprises me. He's lived in the city for a long time, and he's accustomed to the nightlife. He told me once that he used to go out with a different woman four or five times per week, but that he stopped several months ago when he realized it wasn't making him happy.

I asked him what he needed to be happy, and he shrugged. *I'm still figuring that part out*, he said.

Welcome to the club.

"Guys, guys," he says with a laugh. "This is Bri. Bri, come on over." He gestures to me, and I hitch a smile to my face. I should've told him I wanted quiet, a farmhouse, and a big black and white dog. Then he'd have taken me to his place and fed me something from his freezer. "She had an amazing day in court today."

The crowd swells in noise and smiles, and I let myself get swept up in it. Jason finally rescues us by claiming he's about to starve to death, and a tall, portly man leads us to a table in the corner.

I slide onto the high barstool and nod to the water being poured. "Sweet tea and Diet Coke," I say. "Both with lemon if you've got it."

The waitress looks at Jason. "Whiskey sour?"

"I'm driving," he says casually. "I'll take a ginger ale and a tonic water with a whole lime, please." He gives her his movie-star smile, the one the Player-Jason wears. I don't hate it as much as I used to, but it's nothing compared to the softer smiles of Jason, or the ones he gives when he's truly being himself.

The façade he's put on for his friends here falls, and he meets my eyes. "Did your last boyfriend have a wife and family you didn't know about?" He takes his silverware out of the napkin they're rolled in and lays it across his lap like this is polite dinner conversation.

My chest storms something fierce. "Yes," I say.

"In Montana."

"Yes."

"That's why you left."

"Objection," I sneer at him. "Leading the witness."

He doesn't smile. He tilts his head and studies me. "You're not my witness."

"Then stop throwing questions at me."

"I wasn't, as your objection proves. There wasn't a question in there at all, besides the first one." He carries bite in his tone, and for some reason I like it as much as it tires me. He flashes a tight grin at the woman who brings our drinks, and he squeezes all of his lime into his sparkling water before he speaks again.

"I'm really sorry, Bri."

"Some people suck," I say. "As you well know." I lift my Diet Coke to my lips, then squeeze in my lemon wedge. The cola is so much better with the citrus, and I gulp a couple of mouthfuls. "That was exhausting." I roll my neck forward and press on the back of it with my fingertips. "I need a massage."

"I've got a great woman," he says.

"I bet you do." I look at him, and the tension between

us fades. "I'm sorry." I reach across the table and cover his hands with mine. "I'm tired. I'm hungry. I'm emotionally spent. I didn't mean to add to things tonight with my complaining about my ex-boyfriend."

He twines his fingers through mine. "I'm kinda mad at you that you didn't bring him up when I spilled my guts about my party days." He keeps his eyes on our hands, and I actually believe he's "kinda mad" at me.

"It's embarrassing," I say to the tabletop. "I mean, how do you date someone for five years and not know they're married? That they've had two kids with another woman while you've been together?" I shake my head. I really don't want to talk about this tonight. The questions and emotions from the courtroom stir through me, and I should've asked him to take me back to the firm so I could get my car and go home.

He looks up, so much energy in his eyes. "I may be a lot of things, but I would never do that to someone."

I swallow, because there's truth in his words. "What kind of things might you be?" I somehow add the right amount of lilt to my voice to make it flirty, and he rewards me with the Fun-Jason smile.

"Oh, you know," he says airily. "I think you've called me a player before. Arrogant." He holds up one finger. "Yep, definitely been called that. Cheater. Loser. Uncommitted. Lazy. Too handsome for his own good."

I start to laugh. "Who's called you that?"

"Tara," he says with a grin.

He makes my life brighter, and I sure do appreciate that. I wonder what would happen if I told him that. My eyes drop to his mouth, and I want to kiss him. Tonight. Right now. I glance away, and while we're seated out of the way, plenty of people are still looking at him.

Maybe not here, but definitely tonight.

"I don't believe anyone could call you lazy," I say.

"My mama would disagree," he says coolly.

"You don't get along with her."

"No."

"She makes you see red."

"Yes." He points at me. "Leading the witness—and a cliché."

I hold up my free hand in concession, smiling as I do. "But I actually think 'seeing red' is an idiom."

"They're the same thing," he says.

"If you say so." I snuggle down into my denim jacket as the waitress returns and we order our food. I can't believe he's noticed my cardigans and jackets. Or rather, that he's noticed I wear them as a shield. Anyone can see I wear them all the time.

My phone chimes, and I reach for it. "It's my sister," I say.

"Is she wondering what you're eating tonight?"

I smile at him and return to Chelsea's text. "No," I say slowly. "She has news."

"What kind of news?"

"She hasn't given it yet." I turn my phone over, my

heart suddenly pounding. "Do you ever think you might not be happy for someone when they tell you good news?"

He doesn't answer right away, which I appreciate. "You mean like when Tara told me she and Alec were serious and were probably going to get married."

He's really close with his cousin Tara, I know that. I didn't know him—or her—that well at the time, but I can imagine what that might've looked like and felt like for him. "Yeah," I say through a narrowing throat. "Like that."

"I am happy for her now," he says. "I just think I had to...mourn something. That we weren't going to be the same, if that makes sense."

"You're still close with her."

"Yes," he says. "But it's still not the same."

I nod. "I think Chelsea is going to tell me she's pregnant."

Jason nods. "And you...well, what does that do to you?"

I appreciate that he's asked, but I'm not sure how to answer. The day feels heavy enough. "It's nothing."

"You know what?" He leans forward. "You don't get to use that word anymore."

"What word?"

"Oh, come on." He grins and shakes his head.

"No, you come on."

"Nothing," he says. "You can't use that to get out of a conversation you don't want to have."

"Objection."

He laughs, which makes me smile, and some of the heavy chains I've been wearing since talking to Jenny-Anne disappear.

"You want kids," he says.

"Do you?"

"Yes."

The moment sobers between us again, and sometimes I feel like I'm being whipped back and forth. Happy, laughing, teasing in one moment. Then quiet, contemplative, and real in the next.

"I do too," I say, my phone chiming and buzzing against the table.

"I'll look at it." Jason picks up my phone and reads the text. He smiles that wonderful, gorgeous smile as his thumb and first finger fly across my screen.

"She's going to know it's not me texting back," I say.

"That's okay," he says. "We can take a selfie together, so you can show her your—and I quote—'drop-dead gorgeous boyfriend' who you're out to dinner with."

My chest caves in on itself. "I'm sure I didn't use those words."

"Nope." He hands me my phone. "She is pregnant. Due in January."

I take the device and shove it under my thigh.

"Those are the words I used for myself." He gives me a devilish look that says he knows I'd describe him the same way, and then our pizzas arrive. "So we better take that photo so I'm not a liar."

"Yes, sir," I say, my mouth watering. "After we eat, though."

He chuckles, but there's nothing to laugh about with the food in front of us. He's done it again—delivered the perfect dining experience, with the perfect amount of humor and heart.

Yep, I'm definitely kissing him tonight, so he knows how very important he is to me. It's time he knew, and I take a deep breath and tell myself it's time to truly move past Max. He's in the past, and I've told Jason about him now. I'm even wearing a thick jacket.

There's nothing holding me back. I take a big bite of my artichoke dip pizza, getting a blast of garlic on every taste bud.

Well, maybe this pizza will be my downfall after all. The moan coming from my mouth suggests otherwise, and Jason chuckles as he lifts his three cheese and honey slice to his mouth and bites off an equally huge mouthful of it.

I like how comfortable he makes me, and I like how much of myself I get to be when I'm with him. I like that he's real with me, and I hope he gets to be perfectly himself when we're together.

Because I want him to know I don't want this time with him to end too fast, I lean toward him and ask, "Where's second dessert tonight? Want to stop by somewhere and take some cake to my apartment?"

His eyes shine like stars as he swallows and says, "Definitely."

CHAPTER TWELVE

JASON

I DASH UP THE STEPS, FEELING TORN IN TWO. BRI waits in my SUV, but Timber is howling behind the door. He likely heard me crunch up over the gravel, and he's not happy I wasn't home an hour ago.

I'm not even sure I can get the dog in the back of my SUV. Bri insisted it was fine, that Timber could come to her apartment, but I don't think she understands how destructive he can be. I'm not even sure I know that.

I ram the door with my shoulder, because the lock doesn't disengage as quickly as I think it should. I grunt, and Timber howls. Literally howls, like I'm going to enter and dice him into tiny pieces.

"It's just me," I say as I finally get the knob to twist. "My word, Timber. Calm down." He's on me before I've taken another step, and I get knocked backward. "No, no."

I throw my hands up to ward him off, but he weighs almost as much as I do.

"You have to be on your best behavior tonight." I glance over my shoulder as if Bri will be there to witness yet another embarrassment at the paws of my dog. She's met him before, and he actually minded her better than he does me. Maybe tonight won't be a complete loss.

Dinner was fantastic, so it's already not a loss. I just... Bri is acting different tonight, and the fact that she invited me to her apartment to prolong our time together is huge for her. It's different. It's something new for us, and I don't want to cut the night short because of a Great Dane.

"You're coming," I tell him. "Let's get your leash." It's hanging just inside the garage door, and there's no way I can muscle the beast the several feet to that door, then hold him while I open the door and get the leash.

I shove him off me and say, "Go to the car." He won't, but I figure he can't do too much damage here on my own property. I hurry to retrieve the leash while Timber barks and scratches his way out onto the porch. His voice is so loud, and my hand gets caught on the leash as I try to get it.

After managing it, I follow him outside. He's down the steps and barreling toward Bri, and my heart sinks to my designer soles. She yells something not in English and holds up her hand. Timber comes to a complete stop in front of her. The stern look on her face makes me hold up too.

She's seriously the sexiest woman I've dated in a long time. Maybe ever. The thought gets me moving again, and I fly down the steps, saying, "Come on, bud. In the back."

With Bri's help, I get Timber in the very back of the SUV, and while he looks hunched and uncomfortable, he's in. I get behind the wheel and exhale as Bri clicks her seatbelt into place.

"Maybe you should take Timber," I say, and I'm only half-kidding. Maybe a third kidding. Maybe not kidding at all.

She gives me a look that I'm well-versed in. She's not amused, and she's not taking Timber. The end.

I chuckle, the sound silencing as Bri reaches over and takes my hand in hers. I don't know why it surprises me, only that it does. I look at her, and she offers me a small smile. I give one back to her, wondering where my quick comment is.

In the past, with a different woman in my passenger seat, I wouldn't be driving this boring SUV, and I'd say something fake about her hair or eyes or necklace. Then she'd look at me like I'm a Rockstar—and with the flashy, red convertible and the summer evening sunshine, I'd feel like a Rockstar—and I'd kiss her later.

With Bri, I have no idea what might happen next, and I am *here* for it.

She settles out hands on her lap and says, "You'll whip the cream, right?"

I focus on the road again, because I don't want to drive

us into a ditch before we get to her place. No time is a good time for driving into a ditch, and I think of my mama's advice every time I left the house after I'd gotten my driver's license.

"Today's not a good day to die, Jace!" she'd call after me as I ran from the house. The memory makes me smile, and I glance over to Bri.

"Yes, ma'am," I drawl. "I can whip cream."

Her smile widens, and she reaches up with her free hand and trails her fingers through her hair. I'm instantly jealous of her hand, which is so ridiculous I give a little scoff. To cover it, I say, "Tell me more about your parents."

"What do you want to know?"

"What they do for a living," I say. "Where they live. Anything."

"They're in Savannah now," she says. "I grew up in a little tiny town called Peach Grove." Her voice takes on a wistful quality, and I like listening to her. "Mama had friends from college—that's how I know Macie. Her mom and mine are old friends—that she spent time with. A couple of them got together and started a party-planning business. She still does that from time to time. My daddy was a truck driver for a lot of years."

"Really?" I ask. "Cross-country?"

"Nope," she says. "Just around town, filling up soda pop machines. He used to come home and say people had cheered for him that day, that he was a real celebrity." She giggles, and I laugh with her.

"I'll bet," I say. "I don't even want to know what would happen if we ran out of Diet Coke on the sixth floor."

"Rioting," she says. "Meltdowns. Nuclear war." We laugh together again for a moment, though there's nothing really funny about war. War over Diet Coke, though...sort of funny. Or maybe I'm just floating from such a great day with Bri.

We arrive at her apartment, and she says, "I'll get the desserts. You wrangle that dog." She gives Timber another stern look, and I squeeze her hand as she starts to pull it away.

"He likes you better," I say. "How about I get the desserts, and you leash him and make him walk calmly into your place?"

"He likes me better?" she repeats, her eyes narrowing. "Is this like when my sister would tell me I made chocolate milk better than her? *It tastes better when you make it.* So then I'd make it, thinking I was going to be some master chef."

I grin at her. "I bet she's eating her request now. You can't even boil eggs."

"Exactly." She stabs one finger at me.

"Did you really make chocolate milk?"

"It was putting in powder and stirring," she says. "Yes, I did it."

"No National Guard were called in?"

"Very funny." She tugs her hand free and gets out of the SUV.

"Hey, you're the one who said you can't even boil water."

"Wrong," she says. "I *can* boil water...until it's all gone. That's the real problem." She opens the back door and retrieves the leash I tossed on the back seat. Relief fills me, because we might have a shot of getting inside her apartment if she's in charge of Timber.

I collect the chocolate cake we'd stopped by Babycakes to get, along with a container of cream we have to whip ourselves. I've been to her place before, but I let her lead the way.

Timber walks like a leashed lion at her side, the king of Charleston itself. I shake my head at him and wonder where I went wrong. Probably when I gave him to Connor to dogsit and then never went to pick him up. He legit probably feels abandoned, and he sticks to Bri like glue despite the slack in the leash.

Inside her apartment, I take a moment to inhale, searching for the scent of fire. If it's there, I can't detect it. Timber immediately puts his nose to the floor and starts exploring, and Bri releases the leash so it can trail along behind him.

I go into the kitchen and set down the desserts. "Mixer?" I ask.

"Oh, I'm not to be trusted with small appliances," she says.

My eyebrows go toward the ceiling. "You don't have a mixer?"

"No," she says. "No blender either. Once, I thought it would be a good idea to make smoothies for breakfast. You know, when you're busy in law school and studying for the bar and all of that? Brain food. Something."

I open a drawer as she talks, but there's nothing in it. Literally, nothing. Shock starts to move through me in waves. Sure, she's said she's not a great cook, and I'd laughed at the stories she's told about dead-body-beef-stew and Boiled Eggsplosion Salad.

But I really didn't think she wouldn't have any utensils at all.

"So I stuff my blender full of spinach, strawberries, chia seeds, the whole nine yards. It's pushing a button, right?" She's smiling, everything about her relaxed and calm, and I'm glad for that. I think I used to make her nervous—or irate—so relaxed is a huge improvement. "Well, you would be wrong. I pushed the button, and the lid goes flying toward the ceiling. There were bits of spinach in this gross, pink muck. I just stood there like I'd walked in on a crime scene." She laughs, and I once again join her.

"So your mama didn't cook," I say.

"Oh, heavens no," she says. "Mama is the type to go to lunch every single day and not be hungry for dinner." She cradles her face in her hands and gazes at me. A moment later, she startles. "You need a whisk."

"That would be ideal," I say. A hand mixer would be ideal, but I keep that to myself. She opens a drawer next to the fridge and pulls out a whisk with a red handle. It looks brand new, but again, I don't comment on that.

"Bowl," I say, reaching to open a cupboard.

"Not in there," she says, her voice a bit on the panicked side, and I yank my hand back.

"What's in there?" I ask.

She wears a look of guilt, her cheeks pinking up. Then she opens the cupboard. Archie looks at us like we've committed a horrible, heinous crime by letting in any light at all. "He likes to sleep in here."

I blink. "You have a cat sleeping in your kitchen cupboard." I've never quite strung together such ridiculous words.

She closes the cupboard door and nods to the one on the other side of the sink. "Bowls are over there."

I move in that direction and open the cupboard. A few bowls—cereal bowls—sit stacked inside. "I need a big bowl," I say, turning back to her. "You know, like you'd make egg salad in."

"Why are you talking so slow?" she asks.

"You literally just pointed me to a bowl that won't hold all of this." I lift the carton of cream, my smile growing by the millisecond. "As if I could whip it *by hand*, mind you, in one of them."

She raises her chin in a very dignified manner and turns to open the cake box. "Maybe we don't need cream."

"Maybe you have no way of whipping it."

"Maybe you should find a couple of forks before I eat

this with my fists." She gives me a half-dangerous, half-flir-
tatious look, and I start yanking at drawer pulls. Thankfully, the second one I open holds utensils, and I grab a
couple of forks. I hold them up triumphantly, and she
rewards me with a smile.

She takes one and lifts the cake out of the box. I want
to take a moment to open all of her cupboards and drawers
and see what I'm working with here. I can't wait to see
what's in her fridge, and I pick up the carton of cream and
move to put it inside.

With the fridge open, I can only stare. There is literally three things inside. A gallon of milk. A bottle of
mustard—the fancy kind my brother and I used to laugh
about when the commercials of stuffy, rich men came on
asking for the Grey Poupon—and a box of baking soda.

Pardon me, sir, I think.

This can't be real. No one has this little in their fridge.

Behind me, Bri moans, and I spin back to her. She's
pulling her fork from her mouth real slow, and every
hormone in my body is screaming now. "You cheated," I
say, my voice hoarse.

Her eyes open, and they carry an edge of delight that
almost looks sharp enough to cut. "Cheating?" she says
around the mouthful of chocolate cake.

"You can't just go in," I say, abandoning the fridge to
return to her side. "It's second dessert. We're supposed to
share it."

"You were staring into my fridge," she says.

"There's nothing in that thing." I point over my shoulder with my fork. "It's like...surreal."

She giggles and shakes her head. "I told you, I'm a disaster in the kitchen."

"A beautiful disaster," I say, poking my fork into the cake. It's rich and moist, and I'm moaning and it's not even in my mouth yet. I take the bite, and *ohhh, yeaaaahhh*, there's nothing better than chocolate cake from Babycakes.

Absolutely nothing.

My eyes roll back in my head as they close, but I'm still aware of how close Bri moves to me. Her hand slides along my shoulder, and I open my eyes to look at her. I lick my fork, the silence and tension between us off the charts.

The chemistry sizzles in the air, and she doesn't remove her eyes from mine as she reaches up and takes my fork from me, as if I'm done eating my second dessert. I'm not.

I take her into my arms and lean down, getting halfway to her and leaving only a few inches between us. "Is this third dessert?" I whisper.

"Mm."

Just like she did in the courtroom when she wanted the witness to keep going. Keep talking. Now, I take her "Mm" as a *yes, go on, Jason, kiss me*, so I close that distance between us and do exactly that.

My heartbeat flutters through my veins like baby bird wings, and there's always been popping and fizzing and bubbling between us.

Everything boils now, the heat in my body raging into a huge inferno as it devours dry grass. I've never tasted a mouth like hers. I've never had a woman send such strong shivers down my spine, *alllll* the way to my feet, just by slipping her fingers through my hair. I've never felt my pulse prance around like this during a kiss.

All of it adds up to how very wrong I was a moment ago. Dead wrong. There is something better than the delectable double-chocolate cake from Babycakes.

And that's kissing Sabrina Shadows.

CHAPTER THIRTEEN

BRI

WHO KNEW THE BEST KISS OF MY LIFE WOULD HAPPEN while I stood in my kitchen? This room has always been a site of misery and humiliation.

Not anymore.

Oh, no.

I will never move again. I want to be buried right here, under this old tile, in this apartment dozens of people have probably lived in.

Because it's now holy ground.

Kissing Jason is ten times better than I imagined it would be, and given the man's dating history and that he's super-nova hot, I'd been expecting great.

This is better than great. This is life-changing, knee-weakening, bone-melting amazing. He moves slow and fast at the same time, bringing me flush against him in a swift movement, but keeping his lips soft as he kisses me almost leisurely.

There's no doubt he knows what he's doing, though. Every stroke is calculated, drawn out, filled with passion. Every time I try to go a little faster, he holds me back. It's almost irritating, and if I had any brain capacity outside of, *Holy smokes, I never want to stop doing this*, I might pull away and tell him to stop being so bossy with the kissing.

I don't pull away, because I don't want to stop kissing him.

He deepens the kiss, finally increasing the pace, and his hand slips under the hem of my jacket. I'm still wearing my dress, and he hasn't entered any danger zones yet. We breathe in tandem, and then he gently breaks the kiss.

I suddenly can't breathe, though now my nose and mouth are available to get the job done. He doesn't release me but keeps me within the immediate circle of his arms, one hand pushing my hair back and the other sliding up my back.

I open my eyes while the darkness created by closed eyelids is still spinning. He comes into focus, and he's not smiling, laughing, or joking. He wears one of the more serious looks I've seen on his face, and I realize I'm looking at a brand-new version of Jason Finch.

Boyfriend-Jason.

Real-Boyfriend-Jason.

And he is sexy, and strong, and utterly dedicated to

making sure I'm okay. To ensuring I'm happy—and not just me. But that I'm happy with us. That I'm happy with him.

"Good?" he asks, his voice the perfect level of husky and hoarse and oh-so-sexy. He must practice that after work, recording himself so he can get the pitch and the sandy quality of it just-so.

"Yeah," I sigh, leaning my head against his chest. My heartbeat sprints through my body, rushing into my head and making it throb a couple of times. I focus on my breath, taking in a long, deep lungful of air and imagining my ribs spreading to make room for it.

My chest rises, pressing against his ribcage, and then I exhale, letting all the tension and tightness go.

"Do you do meditation?" he whispers.

"A little," I say. "My roommate in Butte taught yoga, and her studio had some meditation classes. She started teaching those, so she'd practice on me."

"I've been trying to be more mindful," he says. "Slow down. Be in the moment."

"Sounds nice," I say, wanting to live inside this one for a good, long while. A Southern summer day's worth of moments.

"Yeah." He shifts, and I step back a teensy bit. Our eyes meet, and it's like we act at the exact same time, both of us moving toward the other. I'm not sure if he kisses me or I kiss him, but it hardly matters. I'm a different woman than the one he kissed a minute ago.

That kiss... That kiss changed me, and I have to find out if this second one will too.

———

"WHAT DO YOU MEAN?" I ask, getting to my feet. Confusion races through my mind, and I look first to Jason and then to Vincent Buhler. Getting called up to his office again? Not fun. Seeing Jason at the man's desk for the second time in a month? Never want to do that again.

But this phone call?

By far the worst one I've ever experienced—even worse than calling Max and asking him if he was married.

"I mean, Miss Shadows," the District Attorney says on the other end of the line. "You're off the case. You're not allowed to be in the courtroom at all."

"This is insane," Jason says, leaning forward to shout into the speaker on the desk phone. "She's my junior partner. She's on my legal team."

"She touched a witness on the stand," the DA says. "She's off the case. It's inappropriate, and jurors could see it as a personal relationship she's exploiting to twist testimony."

I pace away from Vincent's desk. "I don't know Jenny-Anne Kelley," I say.

"You're doing this because she beat you in court," Jason says.

"I'm not trying this case, Mister Finch," the DA says

crisply, though he totally represents the city of Charleston, and that's who brought the case against our client. "It doesn't matter to me if they're friends or not. It only matters what could be seen by others. Do you want the case thrown out because Miss Shadows acted inappropriately with a witness?"

I throw my hands into the air. "Inappropriately? I was *comforting* her." I shouldn't have touched Jenny-Anne. I know that—I knew it a couple of days ago when I did it. I've been at the table with Jason since, though I haven't done anything else in court. He hasn't needed me, and Jenny-Anne hasn't re-taken the stand.

We've been planning to call her up again, though, before closing arguments.

Now, we won't.

I untwist my bun and let my hair fall down while Jason continues to argue with the DA. It doesn't matter. He's not going to win. Still, I like listening to him fight for me. It's sweet and sexy at the same time.

Frustrated with the whole situation—and because I can't kiss Jason in front of Vincent—I take off my glasses and clean them on the hem of my cardigan. That job done, I gather my hair again, pile it up, twist it, and secure it into its battle position.

I meet Jason's eye and shake my head. Vincent watches the exchange, then says, "Thank you, Gilroy. Good to hear from you."

"I'm sorry, Vince."

"We understand," he says. "Come down to the yacht club this weekend. Byron's got a new toy." They laugh, and I find it somewhat strange how we can be at each other's throats in one moment and laughing about wealth and boats in the next.

The call ends, and it takes some of the tension with it. I survey the two men still in the vicinity of Vincent's desk. I shake my head. "I'm sorry."

"You did a great job with Jenny-Anne," Jason says earnestly. "He's just worried they're going to lose."

"No," I say, accepting my consequence. "It's my fault. I shouldn't have touched her. What's that? Law 101?" Disgusted, I turn away. I press my eyes closed, because I suddenly want to cry, and I can't do it here, not in front of these two. "I have to go."

My voice breaks on the last word, but I've got my eyes open and I'm already striding for the door. I pray they'll just let me leave, but Jason calls, "Bri," from behind me.

I don't run, because I don't have the body for that, but Franny must hear my slapping steps, because she appears at the end of the hall. Concern writes itself across her face, and she steps back as the outer edges of my storm reaches her.

"Miss Shadows," she says, and unfortunately, the first of my tears have appeared. They slide down my face, and I swipe them angrily away. Determination strengthens her face, and she indicates a doorway to her right. "In here."

I detour, because I can't go stomping and sobbing back to my office. There are way too many eyes along the way.

"Bri," Jason says, and he's so close to me.

Franny's gaze slips to him, and I have the very real feeling she's going to seal me in the room with him. I'm not sure if I'm upset by that or not. I go inside and continue around the massive conference room table to the window. I want to open it and let in some fresh air. Take it deep into my lungs and let it air-dry my tears.

I wipe my eyes again as the door closes. Jason doesn't jog to my side, but his breathing does hitch in his chest. It quiets quickly, because he's admitted to running a few miles every morning. His resting heart rate must be one step above death, honestly, and his recovery time vastly outstrips mine.

My chest still heaves from the striding, and I take a deep breath to calm it. My face feels wet and cracked, and I duck my head away from him and wipe it again.

"It's okay," he says.

I simply shake my head, because of course it's okay. I haven't compromised his case. I've only been in court the one time, and I did a good job. "I feel stupid," I say, my voice too tinny despite the fact that my tears have dried up.

Jason slips his hand into mine. "I'm sure you do."

"I hate feeling like this."

"Everyone feels like this sometimes." He lowers his head, his voice barely loud enough for me to hear even though he's standing so close. "I kinda like that this happened."

I jerk away from him and give him my mightiest glare. "Are you joking?"

He grins and shakes his head. The smile fades away, and he says, "You're so...perfect, Bri. I like that you make mistakes too. It makes you...real. Human."

My muscles unwind, and I soften toward him. "Of course I'm human."

"You're a very good lawyer," he whispers. "I feel like I have a lot to live up to when it comes to you."

I lean into him, and he releases my hand and puts his arm around me. "I think I'll just say thank you."

He squeezes my shoulder, and we look out the window and over the city together. The silence is kind, and needed, and I'm so glad I'm not standing here alone, reliving my failure in the courtroom the other day.

"What do you need?" he asks.

I think for a moment, my fantasy of the perfect man coming to the front of my mind. "Cookies," I say. "Home-made cookies. Chocolate chip cookies."

He chuckles, the sound soft and lovely, and he morphs once more into a different man, one I hope I get to see and know a lot more. "I will make you some homemade choco-late chip cookies, okay?"

"Really?"

He nods soberly and lowers his head to kiss me. My eyes drift closed, and my pulse skips in anticipation. His lips don't touch mine until he says, "Really, Bri. Whenever you want." He kisses me before I can tell him I want cookies every day after work, but only if we get to go home together so he can make them.

The thought is scary and too big for me to handle right now, so I simply let Jason erase a small portion of my humiliation with his slow, sensual kiss.

CHAPTER FOURTEEN

CALLIE

My hands shake as I reach for a yellow-red combination of Skittles. My emotions have existed on the edge of a knife for days now, and I glance toward my boss's office. The man at his desk is also my husband, and I adore working with him, living with him, commuting with him, and learning from him.

We've been married for a little over nine months now, and every day still feels like a new adventure with Dawson. Life around the office is about the same, except I don't have to have any come-to-Jesus talks with him, and he picks up his own pens on Saturdays now. I'm still over-watering the plants before we stop by the spa next door and do a couples' yoga class, and he's still running and running and running in the mornings while I sleep in as long as possible.

Claude Monet curls into his chest most evenings, and

I snuggle into his side while he works on his phone, his sexy reading glasses perched on the end of his nose.

We've talked about having kids but having them isn't our top priority.

"It might be," I murmur to myself, the sugar and sweetness in the candy not doing its usual trick. The fruit-flavored goodness gets me through difficult afternoons, but today, all it does is make my pulse race.

The phone rings, and I startle. I reach for the headset and slip it over my ear, and then punch the button. Unfortunately, I'm too aggressive today, and I rock the receiver from the cradle. The shrieking noise stops; I've hung up on the caller.

A sigh sinks through my whole body, finally rebounding to my mouth. "They'll call back," I say.

I can't focus right now, and I know I won't be able to until I get this test over with. I glance to my purse, which sits on the floor at my feet, the top zipped tight. I'm not sure why I want this to be a secret. I just don't want to add any more stress to Dawson's shoulders.

He's been working sixteen hours a day since we lost the Warner Copier portfolio. I couldn't call and get them back, though I tried. He's been trying to replace their huge account for a couple of weeks now, even though we don't need the clients.

The man has a *ton* of money, and his mother pulls his attention more and more from Dawson Dials In. I'm not sure why he feels such a drive to keep and maintain his level of business here, and I can't get him to tell me.

He claims it's because he wants to prove to his mother —to everyone—that he isn't just going to take Mommy's money and sail into the sunset. I've argued with him several times over the job his mother has for him. There's no sailing, let me tell you.

Lila Fowler runs a huge organization called Fowler International, and she named Dawson the heir of it last year. He's been attending meetings, answering texts, and organizing the major gala for months now. He claims to like the work—and it's work—but he doesn't want to give up his marketing firm to do only that.

I think he should, but we've agreed to disagree.

"Cal," he says, and I blink out of my scattered thoughts. "Hmm?"

"Tara's on line two," he says, frowning as he comes out of his office. "You didn't pick up the phone." He perches on the edge of my desk, his eyes sweeping the empty candy wrapper there. They come back to mine, and I don't know what to tell him.

I might be pregnant, sounds too loud inside my head.

"Oh," I say. "I'm just waiting for my sugar high to kick in." I bend to open my purse and retrieve my cellphone. "I put this on silent when I met with Jillian."

She wants to do more to get people into her artist yoga classes on the third weekend of every month, and we went over a simple marketing plan that could help her. She and her spa—Withdraw Spa—won't be huge clients, but they should make Dawson happy.

I've missed three calls from Tara, my very best friend in the whole world, and I wonder what has her all worked up. Maybe she's pregnant too.

You don't even know if you are, I tell myself as I look back at my husband. He hasn't moved, and his eyebrows draw down into a sexy frown as he watches me. "You okay?"

"Yes," I say. "Just fine." I tack a smile onto the words and stand up. I'm wearing the cutest shoes today, and they add a good three inches to my height. My skirt is long and flowing, so I don't have to mince around in a pencil skirt. "I'm chilly," I say. "I'm going to go call her outside in the sunshine."

"All right," he says, still not moving as I start to walk away. His eyes follow me, and I won't be able to hide much from him for long. Of course I won't. I don't even want to.

I tap to call Tara before I leave the office, and my skin warms the moment I step outside. May in Carolina is one of my favorite months, and I take a deep breath and focus on the air in my lungs as it leaves. A new kind of calm enters me, and I'm able to say, "Hey, girl," when Tara answers.

"There you are," she says.

"Sorry, I put my phone on silent earlier." I cross my

free arm across my middle, wishing I could detect a pregnancy by feel. I haven't been sick in the mornings, but I am terribly tired. And I'm late. Really late.

"I was wondering what you and Dawson are doing tonight," Tara says. "I'm having a little party at Mister Reynolds' about six-thirty to sample the Dutch oven offerings Alec and I have put together for the Cattleman's Bureau."

"You don't have to say anything else," I say, glad there's still part of me that's the same. I'm not the one who forgets to turn my phone back on after a meeting. I never miss calls like this. My brain feels one step above completely fried, and I could really use some good, down-home cooking tonight.

"Perfect," Tara says. "You can meet the new chicks too."

I giggle and say, "I don't think we need to go that far."

"Oh, we do," she says. "Come early if you want to grill Jason about Bri. Apparently, she's going to be a little late, and we'll have a tiny window to get the goods out of him."

"That sounds fun." I'm actually surprised Jason managed to get Bri to go out with him at all, but she seems completely enamored with him. Tara says he can be one of the sweetest men on the planet, and I have no reason to have a poor opinion of her cousin. He's always been kind to me, and I've never been on the receiving end of his dating-multiple-women techniques.

He's given all of that up anyway.

"I can't believe I'm saying this," Tara says. "But I think she might be the one to tame him."

"He's not a lion."

"No, but he's...loud," Tara says.

I watch a couple of women leave the spa next door. "What does that mean?"

"I mean, he has a big personality," she says. "He's hard to contain. He lives life at level ten all the time. He's loud."

"Bri doesn't seem to mind."

"She quiets him," Tara says. "It's actually really cute to watch."

"Kind of like you and Alec," I say, smiling. "Remember how grumpy he was in the kitchen what? A year ago?"

"Like you have room to talk," she says.

"Oh, come on," I say. "I'm the cute one, but don't you dare let Dawson hear you call him that." We laugh together, and I tell Tara we'll be at her Dutch oven dinner party in a few hours. After the call ends, I turn back to the office and go inside.

Dawson's not perched on my desk anymore, and I drop my phone in my bag and swipe the pregnancy test out in the same fluid motion. It's time to know for sure.

Several minutes later, my hands shake as I walk toward the entrance to the marketing office. I twist the lock on the glass door as if we're now closed, sniffle, and turn to go back to Dawson's office. I pause just out of his line of sight and tell myself that I've had really hard conversations with him in the past.

He kissed me for the first time in that office. I tried to quit by putting my keys on his desk in that office. I've asked for raises in there, and we've had countless meetings with high tension and plenty of glaring.

I can do this too.

I'm not sure why I'm so nervous, only that adding a baby to everything else we have going on feels like a burden not a blessing.

I step into the doorway, which draws my husband's attention. He's on his feet instantly, his dark eyes firing compassion in my direction. "Hey, honey." He comes around the desk. "What's wrong? What's going on? Is Tara okay?"

He arrives in front of me and takes me by the shoulders. I shake my head, which is probably the wrong thing to do. "It's not Tara."

"Okay," he says. "Talk to me, Cal."

I hold up the pregnancy test. His eyes move to it. "I'm going to have a baby," I say, watching him closely for his reaction. "*We're* going to have a baby."

Dawson transforms in front of me in the blink of an eye. A smile flashes across his face, and then widens. "We are?" His gaze comes back to mine, and pure joy lives there. "That's spectacular."

He folds me into a hug so warm and so right, more tears leak from my eyes. "Is it?"

"Absolutely," he whispers into my neck. "This is so great."

His reaction gives me courage, and the fact that he hasn't brought up how a baby will impact his work with Fowler International or what we do here at the firm calms me.

He pulls back, his face alight with happiness. "I can't wait to be a dad."

"Yeah?" I'm not sure why I need so many reassurances. "Your mother might be upset."

"Why would she be?" His furrowed brow only stays for a moment. "She'll be thrilled. She's wanted a grandchild for ages." He laughs, tipping his head back and letting the sound fly toward the ceiling. "And your mama." He shakes his head. "Let's go tell her right now."

He actually starts to lead me out of his office. My heart lifts, some of his elation entering me. "Dawson," I say, resisting him. "We can't go tell her now."

"Why not?"

"Because," I say. "I'm like one month along. People don't usually make announcements like this until the second trimester."

He pauses, clearly thinking. "All right," he says slowly. "So it'll be our little secret for a while."

I put both hands on his chest and lean into his strength. "You can't tell Lance."

"That might be hard," he muses.

"Tara invited us to a Dutch oven tasting at her place tonight."

"You didn't tell her."

"I didn't know at the time, but no, I'm not going to tell her."

He gives me a small smile, and I return it. "Such restraint," he murmurs. He kisses me, and it's not the explosive, heat-filled kind we shared the first time we kissed. This union is tender and sweet, and everything about it reminds me of why I fell for him in the first place.

"Are you not happy about the baby?" He slides his mouth away from mine and along my jaw.

"I am." I hold onto his shoulders and lean into his touch. "I was worried it might cause more stress, and that's the last thing you need."

He lifts his head and looks right into my eyes. "Callie."

I shrug one shoulder. "I worry about you, Dawson."

"You don't need to."

"That doesn't make it go away," I say.

He exhales and looks over my shoulder. "Things need to change."

I don't know what to say, so I let him disappear inside his mind. He's brilliant, and I know he'll do the right thing for him, for me, and for our baby. For all of us.

He looks at me again. "Maybe it's time to start talking about pulling back on this place."

I fiddle with his tie, not wanting to blurt out that I've been saying that for a couple of months now. Dawson usually needs time to come to things in his own way. "Maybe you're right."

Another sigh, and he takes me into his arms. "I don't want to," he whispers. "I love it here, and I don't want to give all of this up."

"You like the work at Fowler too," I say. "You won't be able to do both for much longer, and when the baby comes..."

"I will not work sixteen hours a day and miss my baby's life," he says, and I know he means it. "I've made hard changes before. I can do it again."

I look up and stroke my hand down the side of his face. "I will help you any way I can."

"I know you will." His eyes crinkle as he smiles. "Just like you always do, and it's why I love you so much."

I laugh as he twirls me back into his office. "No, you love me so much because I let you eat dessert before your dinner."

He chuckles too, but the moment is still heavy between us. "That too," he says.

"Or because I have such cute clothes."

"Definitely that."

"It's because I make sure our house is safe from serial killers, isn't it?"

His eyes glitter like dark diamonds as he laughs again. "You're going to make me double- and triple-check everything before the baby comes, aren't you?"

"Oh, we're going to have to move," I say, grinning at

him and gripping his shoulders so there's no space between us. "Our house is nowhere near safe enough for a baby."

"A baby," he repeats, wonder in the words. "I can't believe we're going to have a baby."

I can hardly believe it myself, and as he kisses me again, I count myself one of the luckiest women in the world.

"I love you, Dawson," I say.

"I love you too, Callie."

His phone rings, and it's the special ringtone he's given to Lance. "You really can't tell him," I warn as his attention moves to his desk.

"I'm not going to tell him," he says, releasing me to answer his phone. "Lance, what's up?" He sits on the front of his desk, his smile seemingly stuck in place. "You'll never guess what Callie just told me..."

"Dawson," I hiss.

"Tara's feeding us dinner at Mister Reynolds' tonight. Dutch oven specialties. You and Jess will be there, right?" He grins at me, and I roll my eyes and head back to my desk. I have to tell Tara to expect two more for dinner tonight, after all.

CHAPTER FIFTEEN

MACIE

I FIT MY KEY INTO THE LOCK ON THE BACK DOOR AT Legacy Brew, surprised when the knob turns before I unlock it. Someone's already here.

My heart sinks to the soles of my cute, wide-width runners. I know who's here, and it's no one I want to see. With any luck, I can simply hang up my purse and windbreaker, get out into the front of the shop, and start getting set up. We open in an hour, and there's about two hours worth of work to be done.

Coy Cochran will hopefully stay in his office, where he belongs. I know how to make coffee better than most people, and I know how to deal with frustrated, rushed customers that allows them to leave with a smile on their face.

I keep Legacy Brew staffed, and I make sure everyone knows their job. There's no downtime in the coffee shop, as there's always something that needs to be baked, and something that needs to be cleaned.

The scent of coffee fills my nose, and I sigh. That's not good, though I do adore all things coffee, especially the smell of it. A mess waits in the kitchen, and Coy's been making muffins. Why, I have no idea, but I'm sure I'll find out. The man never holds back with me, and I hang my purse and jacket just as a timer goes off on the counter.

I pick it up and silence it, then grab the nearby oven mitts and open the industrial oven. A huge, twenty-four well muffin tin sits there, and a blast of blueberry-scented heat hits me in the face.

The muffin tin goes into the cooling rack, where three others already wait. Coy's been here a long time, and I wonder what had him up in the middle of the night. Nothing good for me, that's for sure. We've had some of our worst fights when he hasn't slept.

He bumps into the kitchen from the front of the shop, and our eyes meet. "The timer went off," I say, wishing I don't feel like smoothing my hands over my hair to make sure it hasn't been wind-blown on the walk from my parking spot out back. There's something deep and mysterious about Coy that makes me want to look my best for him, though I barely tolerate his presence in my life.

"Thanks," he says, and while I've quelled my urge to smooth my hair, that goes out the window with his somewhat abnormal congeniality. "I started the regular and the decaf."

Irritation fires inside me, but I can mirror his behavior. "Thanks." I nod toward the nearly one hundred muffins cooling in the rack. "What time did you get here?"

He looks at the muffins too. "Early." His tone carries darkness, and I take a breath. Do I want to do this right now?

There's never a good time to talk to Coy, but there's no one around right now, so perhaps this is it. "If you'd let me come on as a partner, maybe you'd be able to sleep past three a.m."

"Macie," he says, his voice filled with exhaustion.

"I'm just saying," I say. "You don't have to do this alone. I've worked here for years. I've talked to the credit union. I can have the money today, Coy. Fifty-fifty. It's fair. You keep doing what you're doing, and I'll keep doing what I'm doing. No changes. No one would even have to know I came on as a partner here."

"Everyone will know," he says. "You're a commanding presence here, and you don't even own the place."

I cock my hip and fold my arms. "I'm not going to strut around on a power trip." He's said those words in the past, and let me tell you, his face almost had a collision with a leftover piece of pumpkin pound cake. He can duck like lightning, let me tell you.

"Maybe not," he concedes. "But it won't be a secret."

"Then it's not a secret," I say.

He shakes his head, rubs his hand across his full beard, and heads for his office. I watch him go, and not just because he's as handsome as the day is long. I can admit that to myself, but I'll never, ever tell anyone else.

I don't have feelings for him, but I can admire the midnight quality of his hair and the way he can grow a beard in only a handful of hours without those. My mind flies to Andy, and a pinch of guilt hits my stomach.

I twist away from Coy's office and bump the black plastic door with my hip to get it swinging. Out in the front of the shop, I survey the long counter. I met Andy at this counter for the first time, and I had to work dang hard to get him to ask me out.

We've been out several times now, and I enjoy spending time with him. He gets me out of this shop, and that's been an interesting development I actually like. I like hanging out on the couches up front with my friends who work day jobs too, and my shift ends at two, so I actually come back to do that.

I know I spend too much time here at Legacy Brew. I love this place, and my heart squeezes with the want to buy out half of it. Yes, I'd co-own it with Coy, and that would be hard from time to time. But we've been working together for a decade, and after every argument, we manage to come back together for the good of the shop.

"Not this time," I mutter as I start to set out our daily offerings. I leave a space for the blueberry muffins Coy baked that morning, but yesterday's lemon poppyseed muffins get retrieved from the fridge, and I lay out the bunches of bananas, the peanut butter granola bars, and our pre-baked and wrapped biscotti.

Janice will be here soon, and she'll start on assembling the fruit pizzas that usually sell out in under an hour. Kathleen arrives at open, and she makes our coffee cakes daily. I'm not sure what's on the menu today, but we don't normally put them out until mid-morning, as they sell better during the lunch rush.

I bring out the creams, syrups, and refill the straws, sticks, and spoons behind the counter. The shop where customers sit and sip should've been cleaned, swept, mopped, and stocked last night, but I take a trip around the room to make sure.

"Mace," Kathleen says. "Muffins here?"

I turn toward her, and she's the cutest little thing in her gray leggings with wide pockets on the front as if they're jeans. "Yes," I say. "Did you taste one?"

She slides a huge round platter of muffins into the empty spot. "No." She looks up at me. "Do I need to?"

"Coy made them," I say, all the explanation she needs. He's not bad in the kitchen, but he once mixed up the sugar canister with the salt one. They're vastly different sizes, and honestly, they smell so different, I don't understand how that mistake can be made.

Kathleen picks up a muffin and pinches off a piece of the best part—the top. She pops it into her mouth, no fear on her face. I watch as she chews, and she nods and offers me the muffin. I'm probably twice as big as her, but she teaches yoga for a second job, and I'm not shy about the chunk of muffin I take.

Blueberries are one of my favorite fruits in the whole world, and if she didn't spit out the muffin, I'm sure I'll love it. It melts in my mouth, and I can admit—silently—that Coy has done an amazing job on these. "They're good," I say, a hint of mild surprise in my tone.

Someone knocks on the door behind me, and instant irritation spikes in me. "My word," I say. "Just because we're in here doesn't mean we're open." I twist toward the door, but I don't see anyone there.

I shake my head and go behind the cash register to get it open and ready for business. I have a key that activates it, and I insert that and twist it. Coy will have the till in his office, but I don't have time to turn to go get it before Kathleen says, "Macie, it's Andy."

My chest expands and my heartbeat jumps into the back of my throat. "Really?" She's looking toward the front door, and I follow her gaze. More knocking, and Andy waves to me from the other side of the glass.

I hurry toward him, only a tiny bit annoyed now. I press the bar to open the door and get greeted with his laughter. I giggle too as he scoops me into his arms. "Good morning, beautiful," he says, no Southern drawl in his voice at all. He's from Maryland, and he came to Carolina to work in the tech industry. He's told me what he does, but I don't really understand cloud storage on a basic level, and I've zoned out a couple of times during our conversations about his job.

"What are you doin' here?" I ask, plenty of the South in my accent.

"Just wanted to say good morning." He smiles down at me and lowers his head to kiss me. I feel fifteen again, kissing the most popular boy in school, and I don't mind that anyone and everyone can see. I *want* them to see.

He pulls away as a car honks at us. Instant heat fills my face, so maybe I don't want to put my feelings for this man on public display. "I won't see you until Monday," he says, not bothered by the car-honking at all.

I pout and say, "I hope your trip to Charlotte is really terrible."

He laughs, and I do too.

"Macie," Coy barks, and I jump out of Andy's arms like we've been caught by my father. Coy wears a dark look and a frown and adds, "We're not open." It's what he doesn't say that rubs me the wrong way the most. *Say goodbye and close the door, for the love of hot coffee.*

Even worse is when I do that, waving to Andy as he jogs to catch the bus that just pulled up to the curb a bit down the block, like Coy must be obeyed. I pull the door closed and watch Andy board the bus, then sigh as I turn around. Coy is gone, thankfully, but Kathleen and Janice both pretend not to watch me as I walk toward the counter. They move around packets of organic sugar and little cups of fake cream.

"What?" I ask, because there's something.

"Nothing," Kathleen says as Janice goes, "Coy sure didn't like you kissin' him, did he?" She wears a knowing look on her face that catches me completely by surprise.

"I..." ...don't know what to say. I snap my mouth closed and switch my glare to the black door behind them. "It's really none of his business."

Janice grins at me, but Kathleen wears worry in her eyes. "He said to ask you to please come to his office once you got back to work," she says.

More surprise fills me. "He said please?"

"Mm hm." She nods and moves a muffin a half a millimeter. "And ask, and then he was all salty with the part about you getting back to work."

I look at the black door again, wondering what waits to devour me back there. "All right." I can handle Coy Cochran. I don't care what he thinks about me and Andy, but my confusion over his half-polite, half-condescending request to find him in his office matches Kathleen's. "If I'm not back in ten minutes to open the doors, someone come find my body."

We all laugh, but I'm only half-kidding. Fine, like eighty percent. There is something dark and dangerous and...delicious about Coy, but we have way too much history for us to ever be anything like me and Andy.

I pause in his open doorway. "You wanted to see me?" I ask.

He doesn't even look away from his computer. He says nothing.

"Sir?" I add.

"Yes," he says, and I roll my eyes. "Come in, Macie." He looks up then, and he doesn't sound mad. He didn't clip out my name in irritation, as he's done before. "Come in and close the door behind you."

Oh, this freaky calm version of Coy is definitely scarier than the man who just griped at me to close the door and stop kissing my boyfriend. And yet, I step into his office and close the door behind me.

CHAPTER SIXTEEN

COY

I DO MY BEST NOT TO WATCH, STARE AT, OR EVEN LOOK in the direction of the gorgeous, curvaceous Macie Wilheim as she does what I've asked her—nicely too, I might add—to do. She didn't take long to come back here either, which means she did stop kissing that fool of a boyfriend of hers, close the front door, and get back to work pretty quickly.

I didn't mean to snipe at her, but the very thought of her kissing someone else has my vision going red around the edges.

I've imagined kissing her plenty of times. I'm not going to say it's a daily daydream, but then I'd be lying. And if I'm anything bad, a liar isn't one of them.

I fail in my quest to keep my eyes solidly on the computer screen in front of me. I catch the end of Macie's slide into the only chair in front of my desk, and she sighs, wipes her hair out of her face, and looks at me.

I'm caught, and heat fills me from toes to trachea.

"We open in a few minutes," she says. And she's the one to open the door and welcome everyone to Legacy Brew. I'm not an idiot, and I know Macie's the reason a lot of our customers come back morning after morning. Lunchtime after lunchtime. Afternoon after afternoon.

I also can't believe I just thought the word "our."

I own Legacy Brew. Just me.

"Yes," I say crisply. She's been asking me to let her buy half of this place to alleviate the debt I've fallen into. Everyone complains about the price of a cup of coffee, and I even saw someone compare it to a gallon of gasoline a week or two ago. They don't understand that it takes a ton of time and energy to get coffee beans to grow. Then they have to be harvested, shipped, ground, and brewed into that liquid caffeine people can't get enough of.

It's expensive, and not just because I can't grow it in my backyard. In fact, out of the very limited places coffee is grown in the United States, they're all super far west of here. California or Hawaii, and shipping across an ocean?

Not cheap, people.

I also find the coffee that comes from the US commercial farms to be light on flavor and color, and our richer, darker blends from places like Zimbabwe and Columbia do far better in this shop. I glance at my computer screen, which bears the burden of my issues.

"Coy," Macie says, and I look back to her. "What do you need?" She sounds tired already, but I think she's probably just tired of me.

I open my mouth to say I need *her*. I've been stewing over letting her become my partner for months now, and we've had fight after fight about it. Another quick look at the numbers tells me Legacy Brew only has twenty-four days left to live, and then I'll be forced to shut her down.

I can't let that happen.

I think of my father, and all he poured into this business—and that's no pun. His entire soul resides here, and I can't lose this place because of a bad economy and a couple of poor decisions on my part.

Letting Macie buy half of Legacy might just *save* her legacy. Macie is smart; she's inventive; she thinks of things I never do. I'd just decided to find her and talk more about her offer when I found her in Andy's arms.

I scoff then, unable to stop myself. I really don't see the two of them together, but that's because when I picture who Macie should be with…it's me.

I've never told her. I've never told *anyone* how I feel about her. Most of the time, I brush aside my feelings as an innocent schoolboy crush on the super-sexy celebrity—the way I felt about Madonna as a pre-teen in the eighties.

"I have to get to work," she says, standing.

I jump to my feet too, not about to let my pride—or my jealousy—get in the way. Not anymore. Well, at least the pride. The green-eyed monster inside me is still roaring and kicking at the image of her kissing her boyfriend.

"Wait," I say. "Macie, I—" I don't know how else to say it. "I need you."

Her eyes widen, and I'm not surprised. I've fought her for so long. Nerves jangle through me, because I can barely handle working with her as closely as I do now, and that's hardly close at all. She's my morning manager, and she often stays hours past her shift end-time to make sure the afternoon rush goes well.

I spend most of my time in the office, and she's the public face of Legacy. I make the schedule, pay the bills, and take care of the behind-the-scenes administrative work, like ordering more cups and making sure our ovens work. She handles all staffing issues, and all customer service, and everyone within a two hundred mile radius of the shop adores her.

Myself included.

I hope I've never been transparent enough for her to know. Humiliation creeps up my throat even now, especially considering what I just said.

I need you.

Better clarify that one, Coy, I tell myself.

"I need you to help me save Legacy," I say, clearing my throat. "Are you really still interested in buying half of the company?"

"Yes," she says before I'm even finished with the

sentence. Her eyes burn with bright green fire, reminding me of how amazing she is. "Is this a joke?"

"No," I say, sighing as I retake my seat. "It's me being desperate." On more than one front, but I vow she'll never know that. I should find a therapist who can help me past her, so I can find a woman who's in my league and who I might have a shot with.

She sits down too. "Is it that bad?"

"Yes," I say honestly. I don't have time to turn the computer screen and show her, but yes. "Do you want to maybe sit down with me this afternoon, and we'll go over everything? You might not be as interested when you see real numbers."

Misery coats my insides, but when she says, "Sure, absolutely," without a glimmer of waning enthusiasm, my heart takes courage.

"Okay," I say, giving her a smile which she returns. I think this is our most civil conversation in the past six months, and I want a whole lot more of them. "You're done at two, but you never stop at two. Four o'clock? The afternoon rush is usually done by then." We close at seven, and Macie is often here then too, sitting on the front couches with her friends.

"Four o'clock," she says, grinning from ear to ear now. "Thanks, Coy."

We stand, and she looks like she's not sure if she should lunge across the desk and hug me, shake my hand, or just walk out. I extend my hand toward her, and she pumps it nice and hard a couple of times. She leaves giggling to herself, and I stand there, my eyes drifting closed.

I love that laugh.

My skin tingles where she touched it.

"Pull yourself together," I mutter-lecture myself, and then I do exactly that. I'm going to need to spend the next several hours preparing a presentation for her—and rebuilding all of the walls I've put between us. I don't want her to know of my stupid crush on her. I'm thirty-one, not fourteen, and it's embarrassing how long I've been fixated on her.

Too long, I think. *Get help. Move on.*

If only life is as easily lived as two-word sentences are thought.

———

"I ASKED MACIE," I say to my sister over lunch. She's chosen to go vegetarian lately, and she's on day eleven. Her fad diets usually run out within a month, but she's dragged me to this vegan, vegetarian, gluten-free joint on the fringes of downtown Charleston. I look at my vegetarian chili, the spice wafting from it bound to give me a grumbling stomach by four o'clock. I mean, chefs have to do something with vegetarian "meat" to make it taste good, right?

I dig my spoon in and glance over to Anna-Lee. Her

fork is suspended halfway between her mouth—which gapes open—and her salad bowl. A leaf of lettuce falls from it. "I think she'll come on board."

I do my best not to roll my eyes, and I succeed. "You don't have to look so shocked."

Anna-Lee shoves her forkful of salad into her mouth. "I'm not shocked," she says around the veggies. She chews and swallows. "I'm surprised. There's a difference."

"Why are you surprised?" I take my first bite of the vegetarian chili. It burns my tongue on contact, the heat moving through my entire mouth and down my throat before I even swallow.

"Because you've told her no like, five hundred times."

"Five hundred times?" I do roll my eyes then. Anna-Lee has a penchant for exaggeration and hyperbole. "She's only offered four hundred and ninety-nine times."

Anna-Lee grins, and where I'm serious, she's not. Where I'm dark, she's lighter. Where I'm stoic, she's a free spirit. She's five years younger than me, and I remember being twenty-six and full of hopes and dreams. The world is open then, and she hasn't had any doors slammed in her face yet.

She hasn't had her heart ripped out by a gorgeous woman, stomped on, and then sewn back together backward before being shoved into the wrong place inside her chest. I don't wish that on her—on anyone—but she simply doesn't understand me sometimes.

I don't expect her to, and she is always supportive and the absolute safest place for me.

"And I said yes to this one," I say. "So definitely not five hundred times."

Anna-Lee mixes up her salad and stabs another bite. She wears her hair short, like Macie, but Macie's got bangs while Anna-Lee's hair falls in stick-straight lines down the sides of her face, somewhat like Morticia from *The Addams Family*. I've never told her that, though, because I value having sight in both of my eyes.

"What made you say yes this time?" she asks. She has no interest in coffee, and I haven't bored her with too many of the sordid details of the past year.

"It's time," I say. "I don't want to lose Legacy, and by my calculations, if I can get some funding from someone like her, then I have more time to correct the things that went wrong." We'll be six months from closing instead of a few weeks.

Everything inside me relaxes at the thought of that. I need to keep Legacy Brew open, as it's important to me, and I know Daddy would want me to fight for this.

"That's great," she says. "Maybe Daegan would want to contribute."

I shake my head, because one, I'm not taking money from her boyfriend-of-the-month. Two, it's not a GoFundMe. Third, Daegan told me last week that he prefers black tea to coffee, and there's no way I'm ever letting someone like that near Legacy Brew.

"It's not like a political campaign," I say. "Macie is going to come on as a partner. An investor in the business. She'll own part of it, Anna-Lee. You get that, right?"

"Sure," she says, but I'm not sure she does. She's a smart woman, and I love her dearly. But finances and math and other "boring things" are not her strong suit. She can dress a room and stage a house like nobody's business. She's sought after by lots of realtors and housewives looking to make their friends jealous with their stylish interior decorating. But she doesn't concern herself with my failing coffee shop.

It's not failing, I think. *It fell on hard times.*

The economy has been down for a while, and I had to raise wages to get and keep good people. Then there was this whole shipping fiasco out of South America, and the cost of coffee rose through the roof. I didn't want to raise prices—mistake numero uno—and we started making less than we needed to pay bills.

I let it go on too long—mistake numero dos—and I'm still paying the price for those negative months. Four of them in a row, and though I've now had four positive months in a row, they haven't made up for the negative ones yet.

Yet being the operative word.

I'm confident I can keep growing and improving, and soon enough, I'll be out of the woods. But bringing on Macie will make turning a bigger profit ten times easier, and she's worked for Legacy for as long as I can remember. I think Daddy even hired her a year or two before his death. She's the only constant at Legacy besides the shop itself, and maybe that's why I'm so infatuated with her.

She remembers my father, and that makes her more important to me?

I'm honestly grasping at straws, and yes, I know how pathetic that makes me.

"So she'll be a partner," Anna-Lee says, her dark eyes framed by big, thick, false eyelashes. She smiles. "Just in business?"

I suck in a breath and nervously stroke my beard. "Of course," I say. "What else would she be?"

"Oh, come on," she teases. "You clearly like her."

"I do?" How clearly? Is it that obvious? I feel like I've worked mega-hard to make sure no one knows I even like Macie as a person. Probably too hard.

"Yeah." Anna-Lee goes back to her salad, picking out a grape tomato and popping it into her mouth. "She'd be the first woman you'll date after Lena."

"First, I'm not going to date her," I say. "She has a boyfriend. Secondly, she's just my barista. A coffee-maker —and a really good one. Plus, she has the money I need to take Legacy to the next level."

Anna-Lee watches me during my soliloquy. "Third?" she prompts when I fall silent.

"Third, I don't like her," I say, and it sounds pretty convincing to me. I hope it is to my sister—and anyone else

I need to say it to. "I don't need or want to date after Lena. I'm not interested in women."

"So you're interested in men," she says, pretending terribly to be serious.

I toss my napkin over the too-spicy bowl of non-meat chili and growl. That's Coy-speak for *no, I'm not interested in men. Stop being cute.*

"Listen, honey," she says. "I'm just saying you can't go home to a couple of bearded dragons every night and think you're not lonely."

"I'm *not* lonely," I say. I can't sleep at night, but that's because I can't shut off my mind, not because I'm talking to myself or my reptiles... Oh, wow. I might be lonely.

I choose not to tell her about the full-blown, one-sided "discussion" I had with Elmer and Orion last night about three a.m. Just like my feelings for Macie, no one needs to know about that.

"All right," Anna-Lee says in a false voice. "Well, let me know how the meeting goes this afternoon."

"I will," I say. "Are you goin' to Mama's this weekend?"

She sighs, and I get why. Mama is...a unique person, and that's being kind. "Yeah," she says. "I'm going to take Daegan. She hasn't met him yet, and we started talking about marriage."

My jaw drops. "Are you joking?"

Anna-Lee spears me with a sharp look. "No," she whips at me. "I'm not joking."

I don't particularly like Daegan, and I don't see her with him for much longer. I say nothing, and nod instead.

"Are you coming?"

"No," I say. "I think I'm going to be really busy this weekend with a split and then a merger." I give her a smile. "But give Mama a hug for me."

"You're going next time," she says, pointing her fork at me. "I'm going to be so busy, I won't be able to visit her for six months."

I laugh, because if Anna-Lee really does get engaged, she'll be out at Mama's every day to get the wedding planned. The Cochrans don't know how to do anything small, and Mama is the worst of us all.

Lunch ends, and I head home for a couple of minutes. I present my facts and portfolio to the dragons, who blink lazily at me. I count that as applause, gather my things, and head back to Legacy Brew.

It's almost four o'clock, and I pray I can get through this without embarrassing myself any more than necessary. Just presenting the true numbers will do that, and I cement my vow to be nothing but a pure professional with Macie.

I can do it, because I've been practicing for years. One more hour is nothing.

CHAPTER SEVENTEEN

JASON

I pull open the door at Legacy Brew, the laughter inside too jovial for this early in the morning on a Saturday. I brighten, though, because Tara's there, her head thrown back in laughter. Her husband sits at her side, and Alec is chuckling too.

Callie, Dawson, Lance, and Jessie loiter in the couch area, and I'm not the only one who got the memo to convene for early-morning weekend coffees. I don't see Bri yet, but we texted last night until almost midnight, and she said she'd be here. I head for the couches and recliners where my friends are, but I don't feel like I belong quite the same way.

"There you are," Tara says, jumping up when she catches sight of me hanging out on the fringes of the group. Her smile tells the world how happy she is, and I haven't seen her quite like this in a while. Maybe since she opened Saucebilities to some of the best reviews a catering company had ever gotten in the city.

She hugs me, and I wrap my arms around her. I sink into the embrace, because she's my favorite cousin and we've been through a lot together. She was at my side when I made partner at Farmer, Buhler, and Cason, and she was there for the five years previous to that.

She's kept me fed all these years, and she's listened to me complain about the transmission in my car, the farmhouse I can't seem to sell, and my family.

"You okay?" she asks, keeping her mouth right at my ear.

"Yeah." I smile as I step back. "You?"

"Peachy," she says.

"Surviving with that bird in your house?" I grin at her and then Alec, who came to his marriage with Tara with a green and white parrot who took a while to warm up to her. She has a zillion chickens pecking around in a coop and neighboring field, but she and Peaches...let's just say it wasn't love at first sight.

"Yeah, she's okay," Tara says. "Except when she tries to shower with me."

I laugh, trying to get that picture out of my head. "Does she shower with Alec?"

"Oh, yes," Tara says. "They chit and chat and prattle and sing in there. It's quite the show." She smiles at me and gestures for me to follow her.

"I'm gonna wait for Bri," I say. "And there's not room

for her on the couch." I glance toward the door, but she doesn't walk through it.

Tara turns back to me. "How's Timber?"

"Uh, good," I say, running my hand up the back of my neck. That's a huge tell for me, and Tara narrows her eyes at me.

"What does that mean?"

A booming *woof!* answers for me, and I know that bark. I turn toward the entrance to the coffee shop just as the door opens. Timber leads the way inside, giving one more deafening bark. My heart lodges somewhere in the back of my throat.

"What in the world?" I ask as my feet take me toward my dog.

Bri enters behind the canine, and he's leashed and waiting expectantly for her. I can't believe my eyes as she looks at him and holds up her fist. Timber sits right down, his huge tongue lolling out of the side of his mouth.

"My word," I say, arriving in front of both of them. "You brought him today?"

"I didn't want to leave him in the apartment," she says, her eyes mirroring his—big, puppy-dog eyes that beg me not to be upset.

"I thought we were going boating after this," I say. I've got my bag packed and in the back of the SUV. A client of mine—Nessa Winters—has a yacht that she just docked after being out at sea for a couple of weeks, and she said we could use it for the afternoon.

I may have dated her at one point, and I've spent plenty of time on boats. I've been looking forward to a summer day with Bri for a long time, and nowhere was Timber in the picture.

"We are," she says.

"You'll never get Timber on a boat." I automatically reach to pat him, and love for him fills me unexpectedly. He is a good dog. He's just huge and untrained, and I suppose one of those is my fault.

"He'll be fine," Bri says. "Look how good he's sitting." She beams down at him, offers him something from her hand, and he gobbles it right up. "You don't have coffee. Should we get some?" She surveys the shop. "No one's seen Macie?"

"Not yet," I say. "But I just got here."

"Bri," Tara says, drawing her away from me. I don't like the look in her eye, and I really don't like how she leads my girlfriend toward Callie. The two of them hounded me to death—to *death*—last week about Bri before she arrived at Mr. Reynolds' for a Dutch oven dinner. I'm a lawyer, and I was shocked at how many questions they can fire off in four minutes.

Timber goes with Bri until she turns back and tosses me the leash. "I want a vanilla cappuccino with cinnamon," she says.

I catch the leash and look at it. Am I supposed to walk him through the line and get two coffees? This has disaster written all over it. Timber looks up at me, and I look down at him. "All right," I say, resigning myself to my fate. "Come on, bud."

We make it to the cash register without incident, and I say, "Vanilla cappuccino with cinnamon and a dark roast, twelve-ounce, with hazelnut whip."

I pay, and Timber is calm and quiet at my side, like a gentle giant. I don't see Macie, and I'm honestly a little surprised. Of course, I'm not usually in Legacy Brew this early on the weekend. They serve coffee all day long, so it's not like the early bird gets the worm or anything.

"Down here, man," someone says, and I tuck my wallet into my back pocket and get out of the way. I feel like I've never ordered coffee before, because I've certainly never done it with over a hundred pounds of dog flesh at my side.

I collect my cups of coffee from the end of the counter and face the seating area. No one's looking my way, and it feels like a piece of glass separates me from my friends. I'm not even sure why. I've always been the guy who fits in. The one with story after story—most stranger than fiction. The one making the jokes and getting everyone to laugh.

Today, Lance and Jessie are tag-teaming their way through a tale about a couple buying their first house, and since I've missed most of it, I don't get why everyone suddenly erupts into more laughter.

"Bri," I say, and she turns toward me. The sight of her makes my heartbeat hop, and it apparently does the same to Timber. He tugs against the leash, anxious to get to Bri.

"No," I say. "Wait." Timber does not wait. He never listens to me, and I get jerked forward. Frustration fills me, and I drop the leash. *No*, my mind screams, because Timber can't be loose in Legacy Brew.

I stomp on the leash, and that causes Timber to come to a stop once the slack gets pulled tight.

"Stop it," Bri says in a voice I haven't heard her use in a while. She used to throw words my way in that hard, commanding, disapproving tone. They apparently work on Timber, because he stops. She bends and picks up his leash, and I turn to collect her cappuccino.

She takes it from me just as Macie yells, "Can I have everyone's attention?"

I turn and she's standing on the counter only a few feet from me. That means several pairs of eyes are on me instead of her, and I edge out of the way. I step on Timber's paw, and he yelps and bucks.

Everything slows down, and I swear I watch my coffee cup fall toward the floor for a good twenty seconds.

Macie says something else that enters my ears distorted, and Bri gets jerked forward in slow motion, the whiplash of her neck making my eyes widen.

Her cappuccino goes flying too, the china shattering against the counter at Macie's feet as time rushes forward again.

The crowd is silent now, and not because of Macie's request.

"It's okay," Bri yells into the silence. She hands me

Timber's leash, seeing as how I'm frozen. "Nothing to worry about. We don't cry over spilled milk." She throws me a sly look as she accepts a towel from another barista. Everyone in the shop laughs and twitters, even me.

"Sorry, Mace, go ahead." Bri starts to mop up my coffee on the floor while the other woman takes care of the shards and liquid on the counter.

"You have an announcement too," she says.

I'm still reeling over Bri's use of a cliché when I whip my head in her direction. "You have an announcement?"

"You go first," Bri says.

"If I do, you won't be able to make yours."

"Someone say something," Callie calls. "I've been here for an hour, and I've drunk half my body weight in coffee, and I seriously can't make my foot hold still."

More laughter fills the shop, and I marvel at how joyful these people are. Did I mention it's barely eight o'clock in the *morning*?

Bri straightens and glances at me first. I catalog the quick swallow, and then she faces the shop and our friends. "I finally closed on my house," she says. "I'm moving in at the end of June."

Jessie squeals, and Lance lifts his fingers to his mouth and whistles. Tara rushes at Bri and hugs her, and there's some female jumping up and down I don't understand. Bri retreats to my side as the applause dies down, her face bright red.

"You didn't tell me," I murmur.

"Surprise," she says. "That's where I was on Thursday night so late."

"I suppose you're going to use me for my muscles when you move." I grin at her, ready and willing to be used by her.

"I suppose," she says coolly.

"All right," Macie yells. "I know I asked a lot of you to be here for this, so thank you for coming." Pure sunshine beams from her face. "I'm thrilled to announce that I, Macie Wilheim, am now the co-owner of Legacy Brew."

Silence fills the shop as Macie throws both arms into the air. "I own half of this shop, guys, so this morning, your coffee is on me." She lifts one foot, which is clad in a cute, pink sneaker. "Literally, in some cases."

The shop erupts into congratulations and clapping, and I join in. Timber doesn't like all the noise, and he chooses to let everyone know by adding his voice to the fray.

Woof, woof! Woof, woof!

He is so blasted loud, and I try to shush him. He pays me no mind at all. Bri looks at him, strokes one hand over his face and ears, and says, "Shush."

The traitorous dog goes silent. I stare at him and pull his leash tight when Bri walks away to talk to Macie. A group has gathered around her, everyone offering personal congratulations and hugs and handshakes.

"So you like her better than me, huh?" I ask Timber. He looks up at me, his doggy eyes somewhat forlorn. I run my hand along his face and ears, exactly the same way Bri just did. Timber opens his mouth and barks in my face.

I jump back, but one cannot escape dog slobber from a Great Dane. It's scientifically impossible.

He pulls away from me as I'm wiping my face and trying not to gag. "Timber," I say, but he trots around the potted plants to the couch area, and I yell, "Watch out!" just before he jumps up onto the couch where Tara and Alec sit.

He clearly doesn't fit, but he simply tromps across both of their laps and lays down while they protest. Then Tara laughs and hugs Timber's huge head. No wonder he thinks he's a lap dog and that he can sit wherever he wants.

He can.

Macie jumps to the ground, and I step forward to say, "Congrats, Macie. This is great news for you."

"And the shop," she says.

"Yeah," I say, though I don't know much about the shop. Bri mentioned once that Macie wanted to buy into it, and I'm glad she finally had the opportunity. I move over to the couches, coffeeless and dogless, and Dawson smiles at me. I return the smile and ask, "How's the firm?"

"Good," he says. "I think I'm going to be moving over to Fowler International soon. Can I have you look at a contract for me?"

"Yeah, of course," I say. "Any time. I just finished a case, so my schedule is a bit more open now."

"Yes, Bri said you were brilliant," Callie says.

"She did, huh?" I ask, some of my former ego shoving its way forward.

"Don't get a big head," Bri says as she arrives at my side. "You can't even get your dog to sit."

"Hey," I say. "We all can't be good at everything."

"I'm not good at everything," Bri says with a scoff.

"Yeah," Macie says, joining us. "That jacket is a testament of that." She eyes it like the black sweater will come alive and strangle us all.

"I like this jacket," Bri says, pulling it tighter across her chest. "I don't insult your clothes."

"That's because Macie dresses like a million bucks," Callie says.

"Did she tell you I'm designing a dress for her to wear to the official ribbon-cutting?" Jess asks, and she seems animated and happy too. A slip of embarrassment moves through me at how shamelessly I flirted with her last year.

She and Lance are like cotton-candy-sickeningly-sweet together, and I'm glad they found one another.

"Are you going to wear the sweater on the yacht?" I ask.

"You're going on a yacht?" Macie swings her attention back to me. "When?"

"Today," I say, sliding my eyes down Bri's clothes. She's wearing a pair of white skinny jeans with her oversized black sweater, and I can't tell if she's got a shirt on underneath that. She must be sweltering and sweaty, and I cock one eyebrow at her.

"You can leave it in my office," Macie says, pure determination on her face.

"I'm not leaving it in your office," Bri shoots back.

"You're not wearing a black sweater out on a yacht at the end of May," Macie says, her eyebrows pulling down.

I almost want to edge away, but watching the two of them square off is kind of exciting too.

"Macie," Bri warns.

"Bri," she says back.

"Hey!" a man yells. "What is going on here? No one's paying for their coffee?"

"Lions and tigers and bears," Macie says under her breath. She steps away from us and calls, "It's fine, Coy. It's all on me."

"On you?" The dark-haired man looks at her like she's lost her mind. He cocks his head and narrows his eyes at her. "Can I see you in my office for a sec?"

"No, you may not," Macie fires back at him. "But I'd love to see you in mine for just a moment." They take their storm through the black plastic door and into the back of the shop, and Bri exchanges a glance with Tara.

"What's that about?" I ask.

"That's her co-owner," Bri says. She moves toward the couch and adds, "Come on, Timber. On the floor. Get down. Go on." He does, and she takes a spot on the end of the couch beside Tara. They bend their heads together and start talking in low voices.

Bri keeps a tight grip on two things: Timber's leash and the tie on her black sweater even as she laughs quietly and glances over to me. And though I return her smile and think she's the most beautiful woman in the world, I have to get to the bottom of all of these sweaters and jackets.

CHAPTER EIGHTEEN

BRI

I STARE AT MYSELF IN THE MIRROR IN THE BEDROOM on the yacht. First, I can't even believe I'm on a yacht. Boats are so not my thing. I can feel every wave and swell, and I hate how unsolid the ground is.

I reach back and gather my hair into a ponytail, revealing my neck and more of my shoulders. I'm not sure if I like it or not. I hardly recognize myself from the woman I was a few years ago. Montana doesn't exactly have crystalline blue water or huge boats that cost more than the house I just bought.

I didn't have many occasions to wear swimming suits, cover-ups, or fluffy white robes. Two of those hang in the closet, along with matching slippers, and I just stared at them before jerking to attention and getting into my suit.

It's black from shoulder strap to the skirt that brushes the tops of my thighs. The tiniest hint of cleavage peeks out from the scooped neck, and I can't tell if I look lopsided or not. I can't get myself to move away from the mirror either.

I slip the hair tie off my wrist and secure my hair into a bun, then push my glasses back into place. I've opted to wear my second pair today, and they're bright red with a white edge around them. They don't go with my suit, but I always feel powerful in them.

I rarely wear bright colors, instead choosing skirts and suits in black, gray, charcoal, mahogany, navy, or eggplant. The brightest items of clothing I own are scarves, and sometimes I wear them as belts and sometimes as wraps around my bun.

My nerves choke me, and I reach up and remove the hair tie holding my bun in place. My locks tumble around my shoulders and down my back, and I release the breath in my lungs. My face relaxes, and then my shoulders. Several things tumble through my mind, one of which is the words Jason said to me earlier this week when he invited me to come out on the yacht with him.

I'd been standing at the window in his office, and he'd come up behind me. His hands spread warmth through my body as he slid them along my hips and up my arms, and I'd leaned back into his chest. "Do you own a swimming suit?"

"Of course," I said, giggling.

"I can't wait to see it." He kissed my neck and added, "You're gorgeous, and it's going to be an amazing day."

You're gorgeous.

Sometimes, I feel like I'm hiding underneath so many layers—physically, emotionally, mentally—that no one really sees who I am.

Jason does, and I repeat what he'd said. "It's going to be an amazing day." I turn away from the mirror, pull my cover-up over my head, and glance at the Great Dane lying on the bed. "Come on. If I have to go up there wearing this, you have to come with me."

Timber puts his head down, and I cock my head at him. "Really?"

He whines, and I step over to the door and open it. "Go on." I wait for the dog to jump down from the bed and trot past me. He looks up at me like I'm making him do something absolutely horrific instead of heading for sunshine and fancy food.

I know several versions of Jason, and one of them adores good food, good service, and expensive things. He's taken me to some of the ritziest places around Charleston, and the hostesses and hosts there know him by name.

He's promised me "the best oysters of my life" at a place without a name where we have a reservation in a few weeks. Apparently, they book out super far in advance, and we've already been waiting for a couple of weeks.

I follow Timber up the stairs and through the galley kitchen. One more short flight of stairs, and I'm squinting into sunshine. I pluck my sunglasses from the buffet beside the door and switch out my regular ones for those.

Jason turns as Timber noses his hand, and he pats his dog then looks for me. My chest vibrates, but I force my feet to move. I'm not wearing the robe or the slippers, but Jason devours me with a simple look from a dozen feet away.

He comes toward me, his sunglasses mirrored and reflecting blue glass at me. His smile is as dazzling as the sparkling ocean, and everything in my world tilts. I know what it is—it's me falling in love with him.

I don't want to do that. I can't see his eyes, but he's kissed me passionately and sweetly and lovingly. Can he be falling in love with me too?

"Wow," he says, pausing in the shade of an umbrella attached to the side of the boat. It extends up and over a seating area, and he waits for me there.

My cover up is sheer, and Jason can see my suit through it. He drinks me up, and I'm pretty busy taking in his ridged muscles on his bare chest and the bright green, yellow, and black pattern on his swim trunks. He's wearing a pair of leather flip flops, and he's absolutely the sexiest man alive. He should be on the cover of a dozen magazines to prove it.

I move almost into his arms, and then I stop and cock my hip. "What do you think?"

"I'm stunned," he says. "I can't even think right now at all." He reaches for my hand, and I link my fingers into his. He tugs me closer, and I sort of stumble into his arms.

He cradles my chin in his hand and leans down to kiss me. This is one of those slow, sensual kisses that tells me he's more than good looks and quick wit. That he appreciates more than physical attractiveness. That he's falling for me too.

After breaking the connection, Jason whispers, "Are you going to wear the coverup all day?"

"If I don't want to get fried to a crisp," I say.

"Will you answer a question for me?" he asks, his voice serious and the moment between us still intimate.

"If I can."

He hesitates for a moment, and the tension between us increases. "Why do you always wear sweaters and jackets?"

I pull in a breath. "I just like—"

"Don't lie to me," he says.

I step out of his arms, and I can't see his eyes behind the lenses. I hate that, but I can read body language really well. Facial tics. Expressions. We learn it all in law school and accompanying trainings once we start at a firm. At least I did.

I draw a deep breath. "Personal reasons."

"I thought it might be a scar or something." He reaches up and touches his eyebrow. "But you seem blemish-free." He offers me a smile. "Perfect, as usual."

Timber barks, and I look over to him. He's got his front

paws up on the railing, and my stomach swoops. "He's going to fall."

"He's fine," Jason says. "You're going to use him to—" He cuts off with a sigh as I walk away from him and toward the dog. I know what he's going to say—I'm using Timber as a distraction, so I won't have to have a hard conversation.

So what? I ask myself. I don't need to get into my body issues with Jason. He thinks I'm perfect, but I'm so not. He's told me he's not good at having hard conversations, especially if feelings are involved, and we haven't had a lot of those.

I'm just as bad at them as he is.

"Timber," I call just as the yacht sways. I stumble, throwing my hand out for something to steady myself. There's nothing there, and for some reason, I close my eyes as I fall to my knees.

"Whoa," Jason says, and a crash sounds in my ears. Timber yelps, and then Jason yells.

I open my eyes—and there's no giant Great Dane at the railing. Jason pauses beside me and extends his hand. "Timber went over," he says, plenty of panic in his voice.

I take his hand and get to my feet. We sprint over to the railing and look overboard. The black and white canine bobs in the water several yards behind the boat. He doesn't seem to be in any distress, and he's paddling after us as if he'll be able to catch us.

"I'll tell the captain to stop the boat," he says, and he

turns and jogs off. I look back at Timber, my pulse pounding in my body. *Only me*, I think. Just when things are starting to get real and get serious, something major happens that allows me to put distance between me and everyone else. I bond better with cats and dogs than humans, and I hate that about myself.

The yacht slows, but I have no idea how we're going to get Timber back on board.

Jason returns with a couple of people, and one of them throws a bright red ring into the water. This can't be happening. How in the world is Timber going to grab onto that? He doesn't have hands, and when Jason leans over the railing and yells, "Swim to the ring, buddy!" I legit start giggling.

He looks at me, shock on his face. "What?" he asks.

"Swim to the ring?" I grin and turn back to the water. The Great Dane is getting closer and closer to the ring, and he looks absolutely delighted to be swimming.

Jason moves over next to me. "They're going to handle it."

"He looks so happy," I say. The lapping of water fills the silence between us, and one of the men yells at the dog that he's almost to the ring. Timber's a great dog, but trust me when I say he doesn't know the word "ring."

"This is not how I pictured this afternoon," he says. The two men lean over the railing and start heaving the rope in. Down below, Timber barks, and I swear he's telling me to come clean with Jason.

I turn into him and place my palms against his chest. "Listen."

"Here we go." He smiles at me, but it doesn't stay long.

I can't look at him. "I like to cover up, because..." I can't tell him. This is stupid. I step back and turn away from him. "I have some body issues with my chest."

"Are you serious?"

I spin back to him, my eyebrows sky-high. "Do I look like I'm not serious?"

"Here you go," a man says, and he groans as he heaves the Great Dane over the railing. Timber's claws slip, and then the canine shakes himself dry.

"Timber," Jason chastises, and I just close my eyes and let the saltwater splash me from head to toe. The dog stops and comes over to nose me.

"Hey, bud," I say, wiping my face with my free hand. "You can't go over the side again, okay?"

Timber barks right in my face, as if I shoved him over the side, and I fall backward.

"Hey," Jason says, and he jumps between me and his dog. He says something else I don't catch, because my ears echo with the volume of the Dane's voice. My hands burn against the deck, the summer sun having heated it past comfortable.

I pull them in and dust them off, then push myself to standing. Jason's taken Timber back inside, and he emerges from the doorway leading into the cabin, his eyes finding mine easily. "You okay?" he asks, coming toward me with the *flip-thwack* of his sandals filling the silence between us. "I put him in time-out."

"He's just going to howl," I say.

"Let him." Jason arrives in front of me, and there's new tension. I can tell, because he doesn't take me immediately into his arms. His eyes scan me down to my feet, then rebound to mine. "I think you're..."

"Please," I say with a smile. "Don't say whatever you're going to say. You're just going to embarrass yourself."

He grins at me too. "Probably." He swings his arm a little and catches my fingers in the tips of his. "I just want to have this amazing afternoon with you. No pressure. No clients. No phones ringing. No dogs abandoning ship."

I inch closer to him, the heat all coming from his body now. He's smoking hot, and he has to know it. No body issues for him. "Well, three out of four isn't bad, right?" I tip my head back and look up at him.

"It's not perfect," he says.

"Oh, practice makes perfect." I love using his clichés against him. "So we'll just have to come out on the yacht again."

"Mm." He bends down and kisses me, and the way he moves in such a slow, caring manner—like I'm precious and he wants to handle me carefully—makes me feel strong and powerful. It makes me feel beautiful.

I step back, and he protests, but I reach down to the hem of my swimming suit cover-up and lift it over my head. Arms all the way up, all the issues I have on display for him now. My heart thrums through my body, but I casually toss the cover-up onto the nearby couch.

Our eyes lock, and I cock my hip. "Will you put sunscreen on my back? I rarely leave the building while the sun is out, so I'm afraid I'm going to fry to a crisp."

"Absolutely," he says, his voice made mostly of air. He reaches for the can of spray on the table in the corner between the two couches under this shade, and looks at me again. "I don't know what body issues you have, but Bri, you are *gorgeous*."

I smile, because what woman doesn't want to hear that? "Thank you," I murmur, letting my eyes drip down his ridged abs too. "You're not bad yourself."

He laughs, the sound flying away into the wide sky. "I think that sums up everything in my life. I'm not bad at it."

"Oh, come on," I say, turning and gathering my hair and twisting it into its trademark bun. "You're a great lawyer."

"No," he says. "I'm not a bad lawyer." The sunscreen can hisses as he sprays it, and I flinch as the cool liquid spritzes my bare back. His hands warm me right up as he rubs it into my skin, and he adds, "Yeah, I want to practice this a lot more."

I giggle and say, "We'll see how many strikes we get before the day ends."

"How many do I get?" he asks, his breath washing over my shoulder.

I shiver and manage to say, "I think the traditional count is three."

"Oh, are we traditional?" He touches his lips to my neck, and I reach back with one hand and thread my fingers through his hair.

"I guess not," I murmur.

"So five or six?"

Or eight or nine, I think, but to answer him, I just turn in his arms and kiss him firmly on the mouth. I hate to admit it, but I'm pretty sure the earth moves with this kiss. Or maybe that's just the yacht on all this undulating water.

CHAPTER NINETEEN

JASON

I pull up to Tara's house, noting the lack of vehicles. A look next door tells me no one is waiting at Mr. Reynolds' either. "This can't be right," I mutter. The verdict for my court case came down today, and thanks to Bri's brilliant performance a few weeks ago, we won. Easily. Big time.

Tara said she'd make a celebratory dinner and to be at Mr. Reynolds' about six. It's six-fifteen, and there's not another soul in sight. I pull into my cousin's driveway and move all the way up to the house. Even Alec's car isn't here. They usually drive to work together, as they both cook at Saucebilities, and it's very suspicious that neither of them are here.

I step out of my SUV, then duck back in to get my phone. I'd told Bri to meet me here, as we'd been having drinks with my team but she'd wanted to run home and check on Timber.

A quick glance down the street shows me empty pavement, and then a round of laughter fills the air. It's coming from the direction of Tara's backyard, and I head that way. She's got one of these cute suburban houses with green grass everywhere. She and Alec both love doing yard work —or at least paying someone to do it—and I seriously need to get someone out to my farmhouse to get things cleaned up.

The moment I reach the back corner of the house, I know something is up. There's no one there. No laughter. No talking. Nothing.

Well, nothing besides a baker's dozen of hens clucking and pecking and bobbing around. "Where are they?" I ask the chickens. None of them answer. "Come on," I say, unlatching the gate and stepping into the backyard. A scent floats on the air, and it smells suspiciously like chocolate mixed with a woman's perfume.

"I know you know, Nuggets," I say, really loudly. Tara hates it when I call her chickens by the wrong name, and I'm not even sure she has one named Nuggets. "What about you, Eggheart? Is she hiding in the henhouse?" I do duck that way, because I don't put anything past Tara.

I whip my attention back to the house and scramble for the deck. I've just heard something that's a dead giveaway, and I yank open the screen door to "Bacon-motorbike!" in Peaches's voice. Then I remember that Alec and Peaches live here now.

"Breaking and entering," Tara says, and I spin around. She's standing on the back deck, both hands cocked on her hips.

"Why are you hiding from me?" I ask, opening the door and going back outside.

"Surprise!" she yells, and several people jump out from the other side of the house. "Congrats on winning your case!" Tara's eyes shine with joy as she hugs me. I smile and laugh, though me winning isn't a surprise.

"They handed down the verdict a few hours ago," I say, holding her tight. "Why is this a surprise party?" It's not my birthday, and I don't really like surprises.

"We just thought it would be more fun." Tara steps back, her smile morphing into a cocked-eyebrow glare. "Eggheart?"

I laugh and shake my head. "I know you have one named Chick Fillet. I couldn't use that."

"At least you got Nuggets right."

I see Bri laughing with Callie, and they're both watching Timber as he bounds through the yard, and I just want to hold her, laugh with her, and kiss her. Our time on the yacht last weekend was fantastic—after the overboard fiasco. I'm still not sure what her body issues are, but I've decided that I'm not going to push her on them. She's never really had a problem telling me what she thinks, but it's usually something I'm doing that annoys her.

"Your girlfriend awaits," Tara teases, and I focus on her again.

"I'm..." I was going to deny staring at Bri, but I can't.

"You're *smitten*," Tara teases just as the doorbell rings. "Oh, that'll be Mister Reynolds. Get him a chair out by the food tables, would you?"

"There aren't any food tables."

Tara dashes by me, and sure enough, out in the back corner of her yard are now a couple of round tables. Dawson and Lance set up chairs around them, and Alec is hot-stepping toward them with two huge trays in his hands. "Oh, there they are," I say.

I go down the steps and approach Callie and Bri. "Heya, Cal," I say.

"There you are." She takes me into a hug and holds on tight. "Congrats on your win."

"Thank you."

She steps back, and I think there are legit tears in her eyes. Confusion runs through me, and I glance over to Bri. She smiles and nods out to Timber. "He needs a yard."

"He had a yard at the farmhouse," I say, taking her hand in mine. "He abused it. Lost his privileges."

She laughs, and I wish we were back at the firm, crammed into some closet somewhere, kissing. We've kept everything at Farmer, Buhler, and Cason on the up-and-up, but man, I want to get a little crazy over there. Soon.

"He's a dog," Callie says.

"He's a manipulator," I fire back. "Just like Claude

Monet. Is he curling into *you* now?" I blink at her, and she stares back. "Last I heard, he preferred that husband of yours."

She swats at my arm, and I flinch away. "You... that...cat..."

I laugh, because Claude Monet *is* manipulating her and Dawson, and they let him. Just like Bri and I allow Timber to do the same to us.

"I'm going to go help with the food," Callie says, her chin and nose high in the air.

"I'm supposed to have a chair for Mister Reynolds," I tell Bri. "Do we need to take anything out?"

Alec is coming back this way, and I repeat my question for him. "Nope," he says with a grin. "Just go sit. We've got it covered."

"Go sit," I say. "Man, I'm tired. I just want to watch a movie and maybe fall asleep on my couch." I reach up and loosen my tie.

"Yeah?" Bri asks. "With one of those romantic comedies on?"

I look at her and let loose a wounded scoff. "You weren't supposed to look in that cupboard." She'd come over earlier this week and found my stash of hidden romcoms.

"Oh, I'm searching that whole house," she teases. "What if you have board games?" She gasps and covers her mouth in mock horror. "In a closet somewhere? I need to know these things."

We start across the lawn just as the chickens go into a clucking uproar. I honestly don't know how Tara deals with all that noise, all the time. I give them a cursory glance and then focus on Bri again. "At least I can boil water," I mock whisper.

"There are cooking classes," she fires back.

"I'm sure there are male romcom support groups." She laughs, and I give myself a single point. "Besides, you said you had a habit you wanted to tell me about."

"Did I?"

"Oh, don't play all innocent." We're getting closer to the tables in the back corner, and I slow. "I've waited all week to hear about your dirty little secret."

She rolls her eyes. "It's not dirty."

"Spill it, then." I smile at her, liking this game between us.

She narrows her eyes at me, really searching my face. "I like—" She cuts off as her phone rings. "That's Nate." She digs her phone out of her skirt pocket and slides on the call. A turn and a step, and I've lost her to another junior partner at the firm.

Jealousy roars up through me, but I tamp it back down. Nathan Hatters is a great lawyer. A nice guy. Good-looking. Loves dogs. Probably has money. Single.

No wonder I don't want Bri talking to him.

But they've been assigned a case together, and she's spent almost all of her time in his office this week, going over things, laying out the evidence they've been given, all of it. Bri is nothing if not dedicated to her job, and she takes cases home and spreads them out in new ways to see details she hasn't before.

All lawyers take cases home, I tell myself as Bri laughs. It sounds like the kind she gives me when we're flirting, and I frown at her back.

"Come on, Jace," Tara says, and I turn, not realizing she and Mr. Reynolds have already made it to the tables. I commit to going the rest of the way alone, and I shake Mr. Reynolds' hand as I arrive.

"Congratulations, young man," he says.

"Thank you."

"All right," Alec says, clapping his hands together. "Tara and I are going to the Miami Food and Wine Festival at the end of the summer, and this year, Saucebilities is taking some food."

"What?" I ask. Every eye flies to Tara, even Alec's. He grins at her with the edge of love only a man in deep can have.

"It's nothing," Tara says, but it's something. "It's a Food Festival."

"The biggest one," Callie says, shock in her voice.

"We're entering the Southern delicacies," Alec says. "So it's something." He lifts the lid on one of the trays. "Which is why we have Southern shrimp and grits tonight."

The scent coming from that makes my mouth water.

Savory and salty and creamy, and I adore shrimp and grits. Especially when Tara's made them.

"Tomato pie," Alec continues, glancing toward the house as his parrot screeches. The chickens squabble back, and everyone twitters with laughter, even me. In that moment, I realize I'm standing there alone, and I glance around for Bri. She's off at the corner of the house, her shoulders square and boxy, still on the phone.

I want to rescue her from Nate, but Alec's lifting another lid.

"Lowcountry red rice," he says. "And fried green tomatoes." Everything looks moist and delicious, with the fried green tomatoes browned and perfectly crisped. "With a jalapeño dipping sauce."

"Two tomato dishes," Lance says.

"Risky," Jessie adds, both of them clearly teasing.

Tara grins back at them. "They passed the Finley and Frank taste-test, so now we've brought in the big guns. Baby, will you do the fried green tomatoes first?"

"Sure thing," Alec says, and I once again turn to find Bri. She's coming toward me, a storm on her face. Her hair isn't down anymore either but twisted back into her battle-mode bun. At least that's what she calls it.

"Hey," I say, taking a couple of quick steps away from the group. "Everything okay?"

"Yeah," she says. "Fine." In the next breath, she smooths away all the emotion on her face, and it's almost freaky how she can do that. "Sorry. What did I miss?"

"Nothing," I say. "What did Nate have to say?"

She frowns and says, "The defense attorneys just dropped off four more boxes of discovery evidence."

And she wants to leave to start going through it. I know, because I would.

"I'll make you a plate," I say. "You can take it with you." I swallow, because I don't want to be here at my celebratory party without her. But we're both lawyers; we're busy people. Sometimes cases come first.

"No," she says, further frowning. "I'm not leaving."

"Don't look so happy about it then," I tease.

Her expression lightens, but she doesn't smile. "Where's Timber?"

We both glance around, and when I don't see him immediately, my heart drops to my shiny shoes. Just then, an enormous racket starts by the chicken coop. "Timber!" I yell, and I take off in a jog. "Tara, my dog is going to eat your chickens!"

I can't let that happen; Tara will fillet me alive, carefully slicing the flesh from my bones. As I get closer, though, I see Timber barking and jumping left and right. The chickens are in a frenzy, feathers flapping and flying here and there. Their voices double and then triple, and I yell at my dog again.

He flattens himself to the ground and barks, barks, barks, but he hasn't taken a single bird into his jowls. He's playing with them.

It's the strangest, weirdest, funniest thing I've ever

seen, and as Dawson and then Lance arrive, we all just stand there and watch as the hens hurry into their house and Timber continues to beg them to stay outside and play with him, his tail whapping the ground with big thuds.

Tara opens the gate and goes inside, her firm don't-mess-with-me voice on as she commands Timber out of the pasture. He slinks to my side, and Tara glares at both of us. "Scared Hennifer half to death," she says. "Come on. The food is getting cold now."

"Wait," Lance says. "You have a chicken named Hennifer?"

I can't help it—I laugh. As they always say, laughter is the best medicine, and I need a pretty strong dose about now.

———

THE END of June finally arrives, and Carolina is in the midst of a heat wave. So moving Bri out of her apartment and into her new house is on the agenda for today. Easy peasy. Sweaty squeezy.

"Where does this go?" I ask her as I carry in one of the biggest lamps I've ever seen.

"My bedroom," she says, and I feel like I've been given keys to the promised land. She heads back out the front door, already calling to Dawson about something, and I turn down the hallway between the living room and the kitchen, her master bedroom at the end of the hall.

It's a short hall, with a jog to the right in it, and I pass Macie coming out. "She wants that by the recliner," she says. "There's a plug there too."

"Okay." My hand starts to slip on the enormous neck of the lamp, and I adjust it. The lamp slips, and I drop it. It's so dang heavy and made of wood or iron or granite, so it thuds against the floor like I've crashed a truck into the side of the house.

I grunt and try to pick up the lamp again. I can't even get my fingers around the girth of this thing, and I wipe the sweat off my forehead. Bri's had the air conditioning pumping for hours, but it's done nothing to stave off the heat of today.

Grumbling, I try again, and with two hands, I get the lamp up off the floor. Into the bedroom I go, and since Bri stayed here last night—yes, we've been moving her for two days in a marathon event instead of a sprint—her bed is there, set up, and made.

I glance at it, because I'm a male, and she's my girl-friend. The comforter is bright blue, with pink and white stripes and patterns, and I barely know what's happening in that moment. Bri never wears anything like that. She's all navies and blacks, olive green and mustard yellow. Her hair is dark, her skin easily tanned, and her eyes like liquid midnight.

This comforter doesn't belong to her. It can't.

"Just another piece of her puzzle," I say to myself as I spot the recliner. That's a normal, dark red leather, and it screams Bri. It sits to the side of the window, with tall, towering, overflowing bookshelves behind it.

I put the lamp down by dropping it again, and I swear a sliver embeds in my palm. I curse and look at it, but the books on the shelf catch my attention. Bri has dozens and dozens of them. I expect them to be law volumes, perhaps her textbooks from school.

That is not what they are. The stinging pain in my hand ebbs away as I reach for the first book. This is not even non-fiction.

It's a romance novel, if the handsome man holding the woman on the front cover is any indication. Bri reads romance novels? When?

"What are you doing?" she demands, and I drop the book like she's caught me going through her personal papers. I turn back to her and catch her throwing something on her bed. She strides toward me and picks up the book, looks at it, and then cradles it to her chest.

"Sorry," I say automatically. Our eyes meet, and the lightning in her gaze fizzles out.

"So...this is like your secret stash of romantic comedy DVDs," she says.

Stunned, I stare at her. Then look at the array of romance novels on her shelves. There's more than dozens. Probably at least a hundred books. Maybe more. A smile forms on my face. "First," I say. "They're Blu-ray discs, not DVDs."

"Okay," she says, rolling her eyes.

"Second, you're *reading* the same stuff I'm watching. How dare you laugh at me?" I pluck the book from her hands and study the cover again. "Love Burns," I read out loud. "What? Is this guy a firefighter?"

"As a matter of fact." She hits the T hard and pulls the book back to her. I don't let go of it, though, and a small tug-of-war starts. I let her have the volume after a couple of rounds. I can't stop smiling at her. "Any lawyers in there?"

"No," she clips out.

"Do people not write about lawyers in romance novels?"

"No," she says again.

"Why not?"

"Because." She steps over to her shelves and studies them for a moment before placing the book precisely where I'd taken it from. She turns back to me, her eyebrows drawn down. "The hero of a book has to be swoon-worthy, Jason."

"Ouch," I say, chuckling. "Are you saying lawyers aren't swoon-worthy? I dress nice. I have money."

"You're sweating like a cow." She folds her arms and cocks her head and her hip simultaneously. She is stunning, and I think I fall all the way in love with her right there in that corner of her bedroom.

"Who's pulling out the clichés now?" I fire back. When she remains silent, I continue with, "I'm employed. I take you out to nice restaurants. I show up on time. I'm here on a weekend helping you move for the second day in a row." I take a tiny step closer to her. "Women don't want that?"

I touch her hip and slide my hand around to her back. She arches into the touch, and yeah, she likes that. All of it. I instantly pull back on the thoughts, because they're the kind the old me would have. The arrogant me. The man who thought he could get whatever and whoever he wanted.

"Maybe," she concedes.

I laugh, because she's so much fun to tease. "Why can't you just say I'd be a good book hero?" I lean down and run the tip of my nose down the side of her face. We breathe in together. "I win a lot of cases too," I whisper. "I can boil eggs and make you egg salad. Or fix up some of that store-bought cookie dough. If that's not swoon-worthy, I don't know what is."

Her arms go around me too, and she says, "The cookies do help."

"Guess what I have in my car?" I ask.

"It better not be the store-bought cookie dough," she says in all seriousness. "Do you know how hot it is outside? We'll be poisoned."

I laugh and step away from her. "You *bake* cookies, Bri."

"Not in your car," she says.

"I'll go get them right now."

I flash her my best smile as I turn, and she says, "Jason, wait."

I turn back to her, and Bri braids her fingers together and then pulls them apart. "Thank you," she says, not truly looking at me. "For helping me move, and being..." She looks at me then, and I swear choirs of angels sing from heaven above. "You."

I've always wanted to be myself with someone and have that be enough, have me as who I am be okay. Bri makes me feel like that, and I rush back to her and take her into my arms and kiss her all in one swift movement as my way of accepting her gratitude and hopefully showing her mine that she's accepted me for who I am.

"Hey," Tara barks. "You can't be in here kissing while the rest of us work."

"Yeah, Bri," I say as I step away again. I give her a secret smile and turn to face my cousin. "She just can't stay away from me," I say to Tara, who scoffs as I go past her and into the hallway.

"Whoa," someone says, but I'm not sure who the voice belongs to. A man, I know that. I see something large coming toward me. Maybe another lamp? I duck; my knees hit the ground; a dog licks my face—and not my dog.

"Jason," Bri says, and then she's on the ground with me while voices clamor around us. "Sorry, sorry," she yells.

I pull her into my side, and we squeeze against the wall while a corgi prances around us.

"Cha-Cha," Lance says—he belongs to the voice—as

he goes by with a nightstand, not a lamp. "Get out of the way, you silly thing." He enters the room, leaving me and Bri in the hallway together.

Bri looks at me, and I look at her, and I say, "You and your dog-netic personality." She giggles, leans her head against my chest, and pats Cha-Cha like they're best of friends, no excuse in sight.

CHAPTER TWENTY

TARA

I'm running so late, but I can't just leave the chickens without anything to eat or drink. Alec's working late tonight on a party, and as I toss another handful of feed for my hens, a stitch of guilt pulls tightly through me.

I remind myself the way Callie did that I used to schedule Alec to work nights without me, no guilt necessary. Saucebilities is busier than ever, and we're interviewing for new chefs next week. We desperately need them, because I'm pulled in ten different directions every minute. My chefs are too, and they deserve to have a life. They chose a catering job over a restaurant job for a reason.

I sigh as the last of the feed hits the ground, and I watch Hennifer peck her way through it. She's the top hen in the flock, and I sometimes want to shake her and tell her to leave Alfredo alone. The poor chicken doesn't have any tail feathers left, and it's not even molting season.

As I go up the steps to the back deck, my phone chimes several times in a row. A couple of them are from Alec, and I pause just inside the back door of the house to read the messages. The cool air conditioning blows on me, and Peaches is blessedly quiet tonight.

Tommy's claws clickety-clack on the hard floor as he walks toward me, but I don't hear Goose.

Alec's said, *Everything going great here. I added garlic powder to your shopping list.* His second message says, *Why are you still at home? Callie's probably thinking you got kidnapped on the way to the restaurant.* He's added a knife emoji, but rarely do we have a texting conversation without one. The man has more knife jokes than anyone I've ever met, and I hate to say it, but I don't dislike them.

Leaving now, I say, not telling him that I got wrapped up in the edits on the Southern Roots cookbook. I've had them back for about a week, and some of the recipes need a tiny bit of tweaking. I work on them at home instead of in the kitchen at Saucebilites, because being married is more important to me than strawberry lemonade cupcakes. Plus, Alec can help me here at home, and we can be with our animals.

"Bacon," Peaches chirps as I move past her cage, my attention still on my phone. When I don't look up or answer her, she ding-dongs like the doorbell.

"Okay, Peachy," I say, throwing her a smile. "Your

daddy will be home soon." I open the door on her cage so she can come out. Alec only puts her away for me, and that makes me feel guilty too.

Callie's sent a couple of messages about the restaurant —*There's been a flood in the kitchen. We have to go somewhere else.*

Then she named a place.

Then took it back because it was too busy.

She's probably freaking out, and instead of using my slow thumbs to text her, I tap to call her. "Hey," I say when she answers. "I'm just leaving. Where did you end up?"

"I got tired of trying to decide," she says, and she sounds tired...and maybe one breath away from crying? It's hard to tell on the phone. She's been my best friend for so long, and I feel like I know her like I know myself.

"Well, it's not dark yet," I tease, though she's pointed out to me multiple times that serial killers can strike during daylight hours. "What about somewhere simple like Hotbox Café?"

"Oh, I'm close to that," she says. "I'll see you in a sec."

Hotbox is only a few minutes from my house, as Callie didn't want to go back downtown for our girl's night dinner. I don't know what Dawson's doing, but he and Lance play basketball in the evenings quite often. He's so busy at work too, and sometimes he puts in a full day at his marketing firm, and then spends a few hours in the swanky office on the top floor of the Fowler International building.

Callie doesn't like to be home alone after dark, and it's a miracle she made it into her thirties without getting married.

I find her standing outside the café, on her phone. She wipes her eyes and turns slightly away from me, but she hasn't seen me yet. There's something going on with her, but she hasn't told me what it is. She and Dawson have a lot going on in their professional lives, and the two of them have been on Lance like green on grass.

I think they're going to list her house in Sugar Creek for sale, and maybe that's making her emotional. She's been there a long time, and she worries about her declawed cat fitting in with other cats in the neighborhood. I smile at that, because it's such a Callie thing to care about. Claude Monet is a fun, chonky cat, but he does have some...issues. Blindness, no claws, likes to get magpies riled up and then blame them for dive-bombing him. At least according to Callie.

"Hey," I say as I approach.

She spins toward me, says, "Yes, she's here. I have to run, Ariel," and lowers her phone.

"How's your sister?"

"Good." She steps into me and hugs me tight, tight. That's nothing new, but there's so much emotion swirling around her. Callie's always been more...intense than I am. She loves cute clothes and shoes, makeup, hot tea and coffee, Skittles, rainbows, unicorns, and having everything in its place. I like that last one too, but I only buy new shoes when she insists I do.

I pull back and look at her. Really look. "What's going on with you?"

"Let's get food first," she says.

Fear grips me for the first time. I mean, I knew *some*thing was going on, but it's something that requires food for her to tell me? I don't move. "Tell me if you're moving to New York City. Right now, Callie Michaels." It's a possibility, no matter how many times she's told me it won't happen.

She blinks at me, her pink-painted lips finally curving upward. "First, it's Callie Houser now. Second, we're not moving to New York." She shakes her head and turns to open the door to Hotbox Café.

I relax as I follow her inside. "You've been acting weird," I say.

"I have not."

"Yes, you have," I say. "You don't order the double espresso anymore. You won't answer your phone after nine p.m. You and Dawson are all over Lance every time you're together."

She pauses at the corner of the line and looks at me, her eyebrows up. "You're moving," I say. "Maybe not to New York City, but you're moving."

"We're thinking about it," she says. "Yes." She continues toward the registers where we'll order, and I blow out my breath.

"I don't want to move," I say. "I need the space for the chickens."

"Your place is amazing," she says. "I wouldn't move if I lived there."

"Come over to Cottonhill," I say. "It's so great, Cal."

"We're looking everywhere," she says. It's her turn to order then, so she does that. I do the same, and we fill our soda cups and head to a table with our numbers.

"No Diet Coke?" I ask, then take a long draw on mine. "It's been a long week."

"It's Wednesday." She giggles and shakes her head, then sips her light lemonade. "I..." She studies her nails, then the tabletop, then the salt and pepper shakers between us.

"If you don't start talking, I'm going to lose my mind," I say.

"We don't have our food yet," she says, glancing toward the busy kitchen.

"Callie," I warn.

She meets my eye, and such a storm rages in her blue ones. "You're going to scream."

My heart pounds, the sound booming through my ears. "Good scream or bad scream?" I ask. I swallow and reach for my Diet Coke again.

Callie smiles. So a good scream. "Do you want to guess?"

"No," I say, though my mind is now moving five hundred miles a minute. "Just tell me."

"We've got a chicken sandwich," a man says, and both Callie and I look up at him. She raises her hand, and he puts the basket of food in front of her. "And butternut soup and roast beef." He slides that in front of me, and we both thank him.

She picks up the ketchup bottle for her sweet potato fries. I'd make a spicy garlic-barbecue-mayo dip for those, but I keep my mouth shut. I select my spoon from the bundle of silverware I got when I paid for my food and look at her with both eyebrows raised.

Pretending not to notice, she takes her sweet Southern time squeezing ketchup into her basket. "Callie," I bark.

She grins at me as she looks up. "Dawson and I are going to have a baby." She just states it. Lays it out there. Joy streams from her now, and I blink, my false eyelashes catching on themselves as I make sense of her words.

And then, Callie is one-hundred percent right. I scream. She bursts out laughing, and I nearly knock over the table as I get up to go hug her. Everyone's looking at us, but since we're not crying, they figure the screaming is good.

It is. Once I get back to my seat and settle down again, I ask, "When are you due?"

"End of January," she says.

More blinking. Alec tells me I have to do something else when I'm surprised, but I don't know what. A gaping fish mouth? How would that be better? "You're not very far along," I say.

"No," she says.

"Have you told your mom?"

"My parents, yes," she says. "Just last night. Ariel wasn't there, so I told her moments before you arrived." She takes a big bite of her chicken sandwich then, but even when she's not smiling, her happiness exhibits itself on her face and in her eyes.

And I'm happy for her, so the same joy flows through me.

"That's my news," she says. "How are things going for the Food and Wine Fest? Do you need any more taste-testers? Dawson says he's ready." She grins at me, and I giggle with her.

"I think we're ready," I say. "We leave in what? Three weeks." I shake my head, because it's come up so fast. "Should be fun."

"It's going to be *amazing*," she says. "Miami? With your hot husband? Food. Wine." She waves her chicken sandwich around like it's a magic wand. "And you'll win, of course." She takes another bite of her sandwich while I appreciate the vote of confidence.

"If we do win anything, it'll be because of Alec." The man's a genius of a chef.

"Mm." Callie shakes her head and wipes her mouth. After swallowing, she says, "No, Tara. Saucebilities is *all you*. That cookbook is *all you*."

"He helps with it," I say, hiding behind a spoonful of soup a moment later.

"Tara," Callie says in her mom-voice.

"I know," I say. "Okay? I know." I have a tiny self-confidence problem, and Alec *is* a good chef. But it doesn't mean I'm not.

"So you'll do great in Miami," Callie says, and I love her for how easily she moves on. She doesn't hound me to death about anything. She's going to be a great mom. "Oh! And then you can put that foily-sealy thing on the front cover of the cookbook!"

I laugh again, because I don't think they put "foily-sealy" things on the covers of cookbooks. "Carrie says I should have the cover soon," I say, picking up half of my roast beef sandwich. "Next week, maybe." I take a bite of my sandwich and moan at the salty beef, the creamy mayo, and the tart pickles. There is nothing as good as a roast beef sandwich from Hotbox.

"You have to show it to me the moment you have it," Callie says as if I won't.

"Yes, ma'am."

She reaches across the table and covers my hand with hers. "I love you, Tara." She tears up, and I tell myself that's because of her pregnancy hormones.

But I love her so very much too. "I love you too, Cal." My eyes tingle and burn, and I open them wide and blink-blink, blink-blink. After a deep breath, I make things light again. "So, are you hoping for a boy or a girl?"

"A girl, of course," she says. "I can barely handle Dawson. Can you imagine if I have two boys to take care of?" She laughs, and I join in. Alec and I have talked about kids, but I don't think either of us thinks now is a good time to have one. And if I was pregnant, I'm the opposite of Callie—I'd want a boy with Alec's deep, dark eyes and growly-bear voice.

"All right," she says. "Anything new going on with Jason and Bri? What about Coy and Macie?" She stabs a sweet potato fry at me. "I know there's something between them besides bad vibes. Anyone with eyes can see it."

"Except them," I say.

"Right." Callie eats her fry, her thinking-eyes on.

"Cal, you don't have enough energy to set them up," I warn.

She sighs and slumps back in her seat. "You're right. I don't." She laughs lightly, and I join in with her. "But hey, stranger things have happened. Look at Jason." She cocks one eyebrow, and I can admit my cousin has made huge strides this year.

He says it's because of me, but I don't like that pressure. It's because he's finally ready to settle down with someone he can be comfortable with, and I really hope he and Bri make it.

CHAPTER TWENTY-ONE

BRI

I STEP UP ONTO THE STOOL AND JAM THE CROWBAR behind the cabinetry. One good tug and down it comes. There's something so satisfying about ripping out old things to replace them with new ones. I feel like that's what I've been doing in my life for a few months now, and working on this house is a manifestation of that.

I've been here about a month now, and a twinge of guilt steals through me as the cabinet tumbles to the ground. I've got a new case at work, and Jason does too. I'm out in the country a bit now, and so is he.

We don't see each other as much as we used to, because we're nothing if not professional at work, and I've been devoting all of my spare time to my new house, Timber, and my romance novels. Even on weekends, we might only text.

I jam in the crowbar again, frustrated with myself. I

enjoy my time with Jason. He's adorable, and smart, and the man can kiss a woman and leave no doubts in her mind.

Another cabinet comes down, and I stand there and watch it. Then I get down and move the step-stool over a little bit. I've redone the guest bathroom off the foyer already, and I decided to go all-in on the kitchen next.

My doorbell rings as the third cabinet falls to the floor, which I've covered with a white painters sheet, and then plastic to protect the wood. "Yeah," I yell, expecting it to be Jason. He hasn't said he's coming today, but he's stopped by before, usually with food and something fruity-delicious to drink. "Come in."

The door opens, and I twist to see who it is.

It's not Jason.

But Nathan Hatters. He gives me a smile and holds up a to-go cup of coffee. "Macie said this is your favorite."

I practically leap off the stool, not sure why my heart is lodged up in my throat. "Nate," I say with surprise. He's never been here before. I don't recall giving him my address either. "What are you doing here?"

I look down at myself—I'm not properly covered. I'm wearing an old T-shirt from the college I attended in Montana and a pair of shorts that no one should ever see. I feel naked in front of him, and desperation claws up my throat.

"I thought we could chat about the case while you rip

out cabinets," he says, taking in the debris on my floor. "Wow, Bri, this is intense."

"Yeah." I pick up my phone and tap to get to Jason. I need him here, right now. The scent of Nate's cologne comes closer, and I look up. "Do you want to start to haul these out? Then we can start at the beginning."

His expression doesn't slip. "Sure." He bends to pick up the first item—a broken cabinet door. My thumbs fly across the screen as I text Jason. *Where are you and what are you doing this morning? I have a crisis at my house, and I need you here ASAP.*

I send the text and wait. He doesn't appear to have read it, and I tap to open our work email. He should be alerted when I text or message him. It's not super early, though I know he likes to sleep in on the weekends. "Come on," I mutter, glancing toward the back door, where Nate has gone. The coffee he brought waits on the counter, untouched. I'm not drinking that.

I send Jason an email, and then call him as Nate darkens the doorway. I park a smile on my face and say, "Got an email from Jason."

Nate has to know we're dating; everyone at the firm does. He nods and bends to pick up more rubble. Jason answers with a groggy, "Hello?"

I spin around and hunch my shoulders. "Hello? Are you still in bed?"

"I had a rough night." He sighs, something shifting and clicking on his end of the line. Or maybe mine. My service out at this house isn't as good as it was at my apartment. "Got in late. Remind me never to tell the Simmons I can go to dinner with them again."

Clients of his, and everyone knows Jason works hard to ensure his clients know he's on their side, especially in family cases with children.

"I need you here," I hiss. "Nate showed up, and he wants to 'chat about the case.'"

"He what?" Jason demands. "I'll be there in twenty minutes."

"Make it ten," I whisper as that cologne comes nearer. I lower my phone and step toward the fridge. I've bought soda and water for it, so Jason can't say I have nothing in it when he comes over. Of course, he hasn't been doing that a ton, so when I open it, there's plenty of Diet Dr. Pepper —his favorite—and a plethora of water bottles.

I bend and pick up two of them. "Something to drink?" I ask as I turn back to Nate. He's not far behind me, and he hasn't picked up another piece of cabinetry. I've had boyfriends before, and I'm exceptionally good at reading people. I'm not sure why he thinks I'd be interested in him, as I've been nothing but friendly and professional as we've gone over our new case.

"Nate," I say at the same time he says, "Bri."

I shake my head. "You didn't come to talk about the case." It's been thirty seconds since I hung up with Jason. I have to handle this on my own. "I'm not interested in you. I have a boyfriend."

"Jason Finch," he says, taking another step forward.

"That's right." I grip the water bottles, because I'm not above using them as weapons if I have to. I'm not sure what plastic water bottles can do to a man who stands several inches taller than me, but the crowbar lays on the counter too. Of course, Nate is between me and it, but I'm already calculating how I can get to it if necessary.

I offer him a water bottle, and he takes it. My heartbeat is doing weird cartwheels in my chest, and I step around the island and toward the more open living room. I've had to furnish this place myself, and while I'm a lawyer, I'm not rolling in money. So I've managed to buy a couch and a coffee table, a TV and a stand for it to sit on, and nothing else.

"Come on, Timber," I say. "Come get a treat." That perks up the big dog—who didn't even bark when Nate walked in—and he jumps down from the couch where he's been napping.

"He's huge," Nate says.

"Yep." I scrub the dog's ears. "Can you grab that bag of dried liver?" It's further down the counter, and as he moves that way, I circle around closer to the crowbar. He hands the bag to me, and I set down the bottle of water to take it, then open it to give Timber a snack. He's between me and Nate now, and I've never been so happy for my ability to connect to animals.

After a couple of treats, I look at Nate again. He sure doesn't look like he's going to leave. "Well, thanks for the coffee," I say, though I still haven't touched it. "But I think you should go."

He nods, his expression folding into a frown. He takes a step toward me, seems to think better of it, and goes around the island by the fridge instead. "See you Monday."

Unfortunately, I think, but I say, "Yep."

He leaves, and Timber sits, looking up at me expectantly. "Some guard dog you are," I say to him. "You bark your fool head off when I get home, but you let someone like him waltz right in?" I shake my head and give him another piece of liver. That's me, rewarding bad behavior.

I put the liver away, uncap the bottle of water, and take a drink. My hand shakes, and that tells me how unsettled I am at Nate dropping by. Timber trots back into the living room, and I've just picked up the crowbar when he sends a thunderous bark through the house.

"Timber," I chastise. But Nate walks right back into the house, and I dive for the nearly full bottle of water.

"Bri," he says. "I just have to—"

"No." I lift the water bottle like I might throw it at him. If he knew how terrible I am at sports, he'd laugh and come straight at me.

He holds up both hands and backs out of the house. My right arm trembles, and I realize I'm also holding up the crowbar. Well, that did the trick. I lower both weapons, seriously wondering what I can possibly do with a bottle of water, and take a deep breath.

I'm not sure how long I stand there, thinking. Or maybe I zone out. I'm not sure. Someone knocks on my door and it opens, and immediately, I grab the nearest object and raise it.

"Hey," I yell, and then Jason comes into view.

He pauses as Timber barks and dang near knocks over the coffee table to get to him, but even his dog doesn't distract him from me. "What's...going on?" He looks left and right, still not committing to coming in.

"I thought you might be Nate," I say. "Coming back."

"Coming back?" He scrubs Timber a couple of times and then comes inside. He closes—and wisely locks—the door and approaches me. "You can put the water bottle down, sweetheart." He smiles at me, and the man undoes all of my strongholds.

I do release my weapon, my arms suddenly too weak to hold it. Jason envelops me in his arms, and I hold on tightly to him. "I don't want to work with him on that case," I say. "How did he even get my address?"

"He's an employee on your legal team," Jason says. "Everything is shared once you're on a team together."

"I don't like it," I say. "He can show up unannounced whenever he wants." I look up at him. "That's insane when you think about it."

"Just put a case of water beside your bed," he teases. He taps the water bottle I had in my hand and it tips over. "What did you think this would do?" He starts to chuckle, and I can't believe I'd drank all of that water. I don't even remember doing it.

The crowbar lays next to it, dormant. "This isn't funny," I say, though me attempting to fend off an unwanted crush with an empty water bottle is slightly humorous. Slightly.

Jason sobers, and he removes the lid and crushes the plastic bottle with one hand, further testifying that I might have been able to tickle a would-be attacker with my "weapon."

"Do you want me to ask for a transfer of the case?"

I consider it, then think of the client. "No," I say. "We're going to arbitration this next week. Let's see how that goes first. It might be done then."

"I can talk to Nate," he says, something dark shuttering over his eyes for a moment.

"No," I say. "I handled it."

"Beautifully, I'm sure."

I meet his eyes, my curiosity piqued. "What gives you that idea? The empty water bottle I was using as a shield?"

"Just...you," he says, smiling at me. "I've missed you, Bri." He takes me into his arms and takes a deep breath. "Mm, I've missed you a lot."

"I know," I whisper into his shoulder. "It's been a busy month for both of us."

"Busier than a bee," he says.

"Oh, you can do better than that," I tease.

He cocks an eyebrow at me. Sexy. "Busier than a moth

in a sweater closet?" His eyes dance with light. "Your closet, Bri. You own more sweaters than everyone in Carolina."

I roll my eyes. "*Every*one in Carolina?"

"It's not a cold state, hon."

"A moth in a sweater closet is kind of lame." I step out of his arms and pick up my crowbar. "And I'm not wearing a sweater today."

He doesn't seem scared by my possession of the weapon. "What would you say?" he asks.

"Busier than..." I get back on the step-stool and jam the crowbar behind the cabinet still stuck to the wall. "Wal-mart on Black Friday."

He chuckles; I pull; the cabinet falls. I look at him triumphantly, and he grins back. "I find it fascinating that you can do this, but you can't boil eggs."

I give him my sweetest smile. "I don't need to boil eggs. I have you to bring me something to eat."

"Oh, I see how it is." He chuckles as he shakes his head and looks at his phone. "Wakes me up early, insults my clichés, then wants lunch."

"Just the fact that you put lunch in the same sentence with having to wake up early is wrong," I point out.

He yawns in what is so over-exaggerated, finishes on his phone, and says, "You would not *believe* what Karly Simmons requires of me." He turns away from the fallen cabinets. "I'm taking a nap until lunch gets here." Then he goes over to the couch, moves Timber—who just jumps back up once Jason has laid down—and proceeds to do exactly what he said he would.

I smile to myself, because it sure is nice having him here, even if all he does is sleep. I'm not sure what that means, but I'm glad I'm comfortable enough with him that we can do things like this. I do wonder what he finds attractive about me—and it can't be my wielding of water bottles—but I push aside those thoughts and focus on getting down the cabinets, each of them with Nate's face as I pry them loose and let them shatter on the floor.

"YES, just down at the end of the hall," Jason says, standing and stacking his papers. I do the same, smiling our potential clients out of the conference room. Neither Jason nor I say anything. We won't talk about them until we're sure they're out of the building.

The man leaves with his brother, and while I do my best not to predict the outcome of any case, I doubt they'll be able to get their niece away from their sister.

I meet his gaze, and we head for the door. I'm closer, so I enter the hallway first. Down at the end of it, I catch sight of Nate standing there. I suck in a breath, my feet growing roots. I've seen him around the firm, of course. We go to arbitration tomorrow, and we prepped all morning in the very room Jason and I just left.

"In here," Jason hisses, and he grabs my hand and pulls me further down the hall and into a room.

Except it's not a room. It's a supply closet, and as he brings the door closed, everything goes dark except for a strip along the floor.

"Jason," I say, confused.

He takes my briefcase bag from me with one hand and slides the other along my face. How he does that in the dark, I have no idea. He loosens my bun, and my hair cascades down around my face and across my shoulders.

My pulse pounds in my throat, because we've never done this at work before. He says nothing before he kisses me, and wow, this is a whole new level of excitement. Because it feels forbidden. Thrilling. Dangerous.

I can definitely get used to this, and I can't believe we haven't been sneaking off to random closets and doing this for the past few months. He's not knocking me into the shelves, and things aren't spilling. He's always very controlled in how he kisses me, and this is no exception.

There's passion and heat—maybe more than any other kiss—but still this sense that he's in absolute control of himself. And if I'm being honest, of me.

After several minutes, I pull away and say, "I should go."

"Mm, not yet." Jason brings his mouth back to mine and kisses me again. Something vibrates in his pocket, but he ignores it. I kiss him back, because I'm fairly certain I've fallen for him, though I'm doing everything in my power not to.

We haven't talked about children. No real discussions of our past dating history—especially him. I've asked him nothing. No talks about our future plans, dreams, none of it. In some ways, our relationship is still very new, and in others, it's not.

His phone rings again, and he sighs as he steps back. "I swear, if it's Vincent or Karly..." The threat hangs there as he pulls his phone out and looks at it. The blue light of it feels ultra-bright in the darkness. "Oh, I have to take this." His voice doesn't hold any of the venom of a moment ago, and he turns, swipes up his bag, and opens the door, all in the same second of time.

"Vi, darling," he says as he walks away. He laughs a moment later, and I've never heard that sound come out of him before. I stand in the doorway, feeling disheveled and set aside as he leaves, and I'm still standing there when his secretary, Brenda, says, "Miss Shadows, can I get you something out of that closet?"

"No," I say quickly. I retrieve my bag and flash her a smile. "Thank you, Brenda." I hurry back to my office, ready to dig into Jason's case files and figure out who this "Vi, darling" is.

CHAPTER TWENTY-TWO

JESSIE

I look up as Bri hands me a cup of tea. "Whoa," I say. "What's wrong with you?"

She slumps into the recliner perpendicular to me, and I take one more deep breath to clear my mind. There are so many letters and numbers in it still, and I left work a half-hour ago.

"Nothing," Bri says, but she's a bad liar.

"Callie will be here in ten minutes." I take a sip of my tea. "And I heard Tara isn't working today, so she'll probably be here too." Our eyes meet, and I can see clearly that Bri doesn't want to talk to them. She's friends with all of us, and I really like her—especially now that I found her a house that the sale went through on.

She was one of the first people I worked with when I started at Lance's real estate firm, and she has a special place in my heart because of that. She has a cool vibe, and she doesn't care what anyone thinks of her, and I really admire that.

"Of course they're going to be here." Bri takes off her glasses and wipes her eyes with both hands. "We're going to your dress fitting with you." She looks at me again, and I wonder how blind she is. Not blind enough to miss my obvious attempt to get her to talk.

"Something with Jason?" I ask, going right in this time.

"As a matter of fact, yes." She puts her glasses back on and sighs. At least she doesn't look like she's going to lead someone to their death now. She looks...disappointed with a capital D, as my fiancé would say.

I smile in my head at the thought of Lance. We're getting married next weekend, and my final dress fitting is tonight. I designed the dress, of course. I'm still sketching in my spare time, and I'm great behind a sewing machine. I've made a couple of dresses for girls in my neighborhood for their proms and dances, but summertime is extremely busy for real estate agents, and Lance is still training me for that too.

I did a lot of the preliminary piecing and sewing of my dress, then I took it to a tailor to make it perfect.

"Get talking then," I say.

"You knew him before," she says, and hope enters her gaze.

"Before what?" I lean forward and set my cup of tea on the table in front of me.

"Before he decided he wasn't going to flirt with every female he came across," she says.

"Ah." I nod. "I did indeed. Just before, I think." I don't believe I changed Jason at all—that was Tara and Alec. Seeing the two of them work through hard things, their jealousy, their jobs, their roles—it was inspiring for me too.

Alec has been my best friend for ages, and it's nice to see him so happy. More than nice. Awesome. Amazing. Outstanding. I want the same thing for myself, and I'm sure I'll have it with Lance. I told him we didn't have to get married super soon, because he's been burned a couple of times in the past.

He said he trusts me and loves me, and of course he doesn't want to wait forever. I was relieved, because every day we're not married is another day my mama is trying to break us up. Lance is beyond handsome, kind, and he has plenty of money. He's simply not Southern royalty, with a plantation and trees older than the hills. Therefore, he's not good enough for my mother.

"Is he doing that again?" I ask. Shock moves through me, because Jason and Bri are darling together. They share secret smiles, and he treats her like a queen. At least from what I've seen. In my head, they go together like bread and butter. She's more serious and as smart as a person can be. She tames Jason's playboy qualities, which has been fascinating to watch from my perspective. Even Tara says he's always needed someone like Bri, and that she hopes he doesn't mess up with her.

Bri forgives, but she doesn't forget, and if Jason has done something to upset her... He better be on his knees praying morning, noon, and night he can fix it.

"I don't know." Bri sighs again. "He's been talking to this woman for a few days, and I don't know who she is."

"Did you ask him?"

"I did. He says she's a client, but I'm his junior partner." Something that looks a bit like guilt crosses her expression. "I can see all of his cases. Present, past, all of them. There is no one with her name."

"Maybe she's in the witness protection program."

Bri cocks her head, a dry scoff leaving her mouth. "We work at a family law firm," she says. "We help people with custody issues for the most part."

"You were doing that criminal robbery case," I say. "That's not family law."

"Actually, it was the sister of the man accused of the robbery who hired us," she says. That case isn't anywhere near over, and Jason and I are still in the discovery phase even after months. The trial date isn't until November, so we have plenty of time still. "She wanted to sue for defamation." Bri takes a small sip of her coffee, the steam fogging her glasses for a moment.

I hate seeing her distressed, but I don't know how to help her. "I'm sorry." I reach over and touch her knee. "Do you really think he'd cheat on you?" I wasn't impressed with Jason—other than how drop-dead gorgeous he is— when we first met and he tried to cut in line, citing the reason as his grandmother needed a hot cup of coffee. Later, I'd found out his grandmother was dead.

He was a player then. I thought he'd changed. Since he started dating Bri, he's seemed so happy—they both have—and so...different. Like he just needed to find his One True Love, and then he'd settle down.

All of us think that person is Bri. Sure, they've only been dating for a few months, but everything with them sparkles and sings, even when she's brought his ginormous dog to the coffee shop or he's teasing her about her clothes.

They're *cute* together, and I hate seeing her so upset.

"No," Bri finally says. "I don't think he'd cheat on me."

"Then she's probably a client," I say. "A family acquaintance. Something like that."

"What if—?" She presses her lips together and shakes her head. "Never mind."

"No, you can say it." Our relationship started out professional, but Bri is a friend now. She and Jason spend just as much time with me and Lance as we do with Callie and Dawson and Tara and Alec. Out of everyone, Tara and Alec are the busiest, and they work at night so often, they don't drop by Legacy in the evenings the way the rest of us do.

But the six of us—Lance, me, Dawson, Callie, Jason, and Bri—we're here almost every night. Macie comes too, and she brought her boyfriend Andy last week too. He was...different, but I smiled and reminded myself that I'm not the one who has to date him.

I believe there's someone for everyone, and I'm into the tall, handsome, blond type as much as the next woman. But I want to be treated with respect, and Andy... He talked down to Macie a little bit—in my opinion. Lance said later that he didn't notice, and I'm sure it's just me and my issues.

"My sister is calling," Bri says as she stands. "I'm going to take it outside. Don't leave without me, okay?"

"Okay." I watch her go, noting that her shoulders are far stiffer today than they've been in the past. I've met and worked with this version of Sabrina Shadows before, and she is no picnic. I'm sure she has a reason for the way she puts up walls and keeps others out, but we haven't gotten that far in our friendship yet.

Macie knows her really well, and she comes into the shop the moment Bri leaves it. She's frowning as she faces me, and she hooks her thumb over her shoulder. "What's up with Bri?"

"I don't know," I say, not wanting to betray her confidence. "Something with work." That's almost true—she and Jason do work together—and I don't feel bad saying it. "Where's Andy?"

"I didn't think men were coming to the dress fitting." Macie sinks into the other end of the couch from where I'm sitting. "Are they?"

"No, good point." I take another sip of my tea. "Why does Bri keep everyone out?"

"What do you mean?"

"Oh, we were just talking." I shake my head and put down my tea again. "I'm pretty sure she made up a phone call from her sister to get out of continuing it."

Macie frowns again, then swipes her bangs off her forehead. "Must've been about men, then," she says. "Bri's had...a tough time with relationships in the past."

I nod, so many things clicking into place now. "She's a strong woman."

"That she is." Macie sighs and closes her eyes. "I'm exhausted."

"You don't have to come tonight," I say. I can't even imagine what time she has to get up to be here to open Legacy Brew by six a.m. With the coffees and teas bubbling and boiling hot. With all the pastries ready. It's an hour of the day I never see—and never want to.

"I want to," Macie says. "I haven't eaten at The Table, and if what Tara says is true, I don't want to miss it."

"Right?" I giggle and shake my head. "She makes it sound like we'll be translated simply from tasting the shrimp." We laugh, and it feels good. Lance and I have been extraordinarily busy this month, especially because of the upcoming wedding.

We'll be moving into his house, as my tiny space is nothing to be emulated. I'm fiercely proud of my basement apartment, but he has a great house, with multiple bedrooms, and a yard where Cha-Cha roams free.

I've already started taking some of my boxes over there, and we're trying to tie up some loose ends before my family comes into town early next week. I dread the thought, and I shove against it just as Callie and Tara enter the coffee shop.

"There they are," Macie says, getting to her feet. "Ready to go?"

"Bri's outside," I say, picking up my tea again. I'm not ready to go, and I take another sip. The spicy, hot liquid soothes me, and I look up at the other women.

"We don't want to be late," Macie insists. "Tara says they won't hold the reservation, and we won't get another one for six months."

"Six months?" Callie looks at Tara, her blonde waves swinging. "They're booked out for *six months?*"

"I told you the food was phenomenal," Tara says as if this is normal. "Saucebilities is booked out for four."

"Wow," I say. "I didn't know that."

Tara grins at me. "The husband-wife team is a real draw."

"I bet." I return the smile and fold my arms. "We're going to the dress shop first anyway," I say. "And my appointment isn't until five-thirty. We've got a couple of minutes."

Macie reluctantly sits down, and Tara eyes the line for coffee. "Do I have time to get a Frappuccino?"

"Yes," I say as Macie says, "No." I look at her, and she adds, "She doesn't. Mildred is on the frap, and she's slow." She doesn't even look behind her, but she probably knows.

"I'll get coffee then," Tara says, and she goes to join the

line. Callie asks Macie something about Legacy Brew and how things are going with the new marketing campaigns they're running. I guess Macie hired Dawson and Callie to do some things to get Legacy out there more, and I will say, they have been busier.

My alarm goes off before Tara or Bri return, and I get to my feet then. "Time to go," I say, glancing over to Tara. She's collecting her coffee now. Bri still hasn't come back in. She hasn't texted either, so I expect she'll be waiting on the sidewalk.

She is, and the five of us pile into one of Tara's catering vans. My stomach recoils against the tea, wanting either less liquid inside it or more food. I don't know which. Probably neither, as I'm really just nervous about the dress.

I've only shown sketches to my friends, and no one's seen the real thing yet. Tara wore one of my designs at her wedding too, and she was the Bride of the Century. I know I won't be more beautiful than her, but it's still a dress that means a lot to me.

Once at the shop, once we park, once we go inside and I say my name, we all wait near one of the huge dressing rooms for the attendant to retrieve the dress from the back room. I can't stop tapping my fingertips together, my eyes glued to the door the woman went through.

"Calm down," Callie says.

"What if they can't find it?" I ask. I'm getting married in nine days. There's no way I can re-sew my dress that fast. Not with Mama and Daddy coming into town in only five days and all the work Lance and I are trying to get done before we take off for a few weeks.

I thought we might go on a short honeymoon to the mountains or something, but no. Lance wants to do a whole tour of Newfoundland, and I wasn't going to say no to a two-week trip with my new husband. Away from the pressures of life, the office, phone calls, documents, files, and people.

With family coming into town early, and the wedding, we'll be gone for three full weeks from Finley & Frank, the real estate firm that Lance co-owns.

"Here she is," Callie says, and I blink my way back into the dress shop. She gasps. "Jessie. Is that your dress?"

"It's blue," Tara says as if she's in kindergarten and just learning colors. Gold star for her, because the dress is blue.

"His tie is orange," I say, not sure if they'll get it.

Callie whips her attention to me. "For Auburn? Tell me you are *not* letting him dictate the colors of your wedding because of where he went to college."

I only grin at her, then match my smile to that of the attendant. "This is a *gorgeous* dress," she says. "Where did you get it?"

"I made it," I say.

"In here." She guides me into a dressing room with a red velvet drape that closes, and I start to step out of my clothes so she can help me into the dress. "I love that it's so elegant. I think we could sell these here."

"You think so?" Our eyes meet in the mirror, and I tamp against the excitement building inside me. I love fashion and clothing, but my attempts at a career in that industry have not gone well. I mean, I've been talking to a designer in New York for a solid year.

Everything in my life seems to move a little slower than others. Lance and I were supposed to be married in the spring, but the venue I wanted was booked until the first week of August. There are still plenty of flowers in South Carolina in August, so I'd postponed. It turned out that I needed the extra time for my dress anyway, and Lance has gone along with every change and modification I've made.

"I definitely think so," the woman says. "We're always looking for something that's unique and different." She helps me into the dress, and it fits like a glove. I haven't tried to lose or gain any weight since I made it, and the finishing touches with the buttons and beading are beautiful.

With a capital B.

I sigh as I look at myself in the mirror, the blue of the dress mirroring the blue in my eyes and making them shine even deeper. I smooth down the front of the dress, bumping over the clear glass beads that will catch the light and reflect it. "I love it."

"I do too," the woman says in a hushed voice. "When I get married, will you make me a dress?"

"Absolutely," I say, wondering if that's what I do. Word of mouth wedding dresses. Unique. Custom. Hand-sewn. "Can I let in my friends?"

"Yes." She moves to open the curtain separating us, and I step out of the room, one hand on my hip.

"Well?"

Callie turns toward me and shrieks, just like I knew she would. Tara applauds in the always-more-reserved-than-Callie way she has. Bri's eyes widen, as does her smile. Macie puts her fingers in her mouth and whistles, and I feel like a million bucks.

"He's going to lose his mind," Callie says, rushing toward me. She hugs me, then starts examining every seam, strap, and stitch.

Tara circles me and says, "Jessie, I'm so glad I got married before you."

"Seriously," Bri says somewhat darkly. "The rest of us are going to look like old maids." She laughs afterward, so I know she's not really mad.

"I'll make you a dress," I say. "For when you and Jason get married."

That throws all eyes on her, and I instantly regret my statement. Bri simply smiles and shakes her head. "I don't know about that."

"What do you mean?" Tara asks.

Bri faces her, their connection and relationship unique. "Do you think he's the marrying type?"

"Before he met you, no," Tara says. "But now, yes."

"I agree," Callie says, still examining the beads. "Did you buy these, Jess?"

"I did," I say. "I got them from a great shop online. Then I had the seamstress here put them on."

Another whistle fills the air, and we all turn toward another woman. I grin at her, step away from my friends, and do a full twirl. "Look, Petra," I say. "*Look* at what you did."

I step into the brunette and hug her. "Thank you for making it perfect."

"It didn't need much," she says. "Your vision for it was perfect."

"But you did all the tiny stitches." I grin at the seamstress and add, "Did you get your invite?"

"Yep," she says. "Jaden and I will be there."

I nod and turn back to everyone else. "All right," I say. "It's perfect, and we have a reservation we can*not* miss. Someone help me out of this thing." I step back into the dressing room and take one more look at myself.

I really am gorgeous—stunningly gorgeous, Lance called me once—and I can't wait to walk down the aisle on my father's arm and marry Lance Byers.

CHAPTER TWENTY-THREE

LANCE

CHA-CHA WHINES BEFORE MY ALARM GOES OFF, BUT I'm already awake. Sunlight streams through the windows, because it's the middle of the summer, and I think we get like six hours of darkness at the moment.

"All right, girl," I drawl at the dog. She jumps off the bed and trots toward the door. I get up and pad after her to let her outside. I'm standing at the back door, waiting for her to take care of business and come back when I remember—"I'm getting married today."

The dog dress on the dining room table on my left suddenly makes sense.

Of course I haven't forgotten. My parents have been in town for two days. So has my sister, Ruth. Jessie's family has been here for longer than that, and a sigh flows through my whole body.

I'm so ready for this production to be over. Her

momma has been nice since their arrival, and that's more than she's been for the past several months. Our initial meeting went well, and I thought she'd accepted me. Turns out, she hadn't. But Jessie knows how to handle her momma, and I've done my best to support my fiancée.

Cha-Cha comes back up the steps, and I slide open the door for her. "Come on, Chachy," I say. "We've got to get ready and get going."

There's time, but I don't change into my running clothes like I do most other mornings. Instead, I shower, shave, check for all of my wedding clothes, get dressed, and start taking things out to my truck.

Jess named it Mammoth, and the name fits, that's for sure. Her car—Lucy—still plugs along, but I want to buy her a new one. She wouldn't let me for her birthday, but Christmas is coming up, and I've already started plotting ways I can help ease Lucy toward retirement. If she's missing a spark plug or something...

I've waited an extra two and a half months to marry Jess just so we could say "I do," at Bentley Farm. It was important to her, and whatever's important to her is important to me. She's the most important part of my life, and I dash back into the house to get the outfit she bought for Cha-Cha.

Jess wants everyone to be part of the wedding, and I'm not surprised to get a call from Dawson as I'm loading Cha-Cha into Mammoth. "Hey," I say, feeling rushed and winded.

"Are you on the way?" he asks, as if I need a father to make sure I show up at the church on time.

"Yes," I say.

"And you have the package?"

I swear inside my head, and say, "Yes," out loud, already looking back to the front porch.

Dawson laughs, because he's impossible to lie to, and we both know I didn't have the package. "I'm getting it," I say. "Right now."

"Tie? Tux? Shoes?" he asks.

"Yes," I say. "Check, check."

I jump behind the wheel and start the truck, so Cha-Cha won't suffocate while I'm inside the house, and then I run back inside. I should grab another stick of deodorant for all the running I'm doing.

The package sits on the mantle, and I grab it and turn around. "Got it."

"Callie says to drive safe. You're not late."

"Are you guys on the way?"

"Yes."

"Then I'm late," I say.

"We're going to stop for Skittles," Callie yells. "You're not late."

"Hear that?" Dawson asks with a chuckle.

"You probably have to check for serial killers too," I say, laughing with him. "So I'm good."

"You wouldn't believe what I have to check for,"

Dawson says under his breath, and that only makes me laugh harder. "Especially now."

"Now?" I ask, exiting my house and pulling the door closed behind me. "What does that mean?"

"Uh...nothing. We'll see you there." He ends the call quickly, and that makes my eyes narrow. Something is definitely going on there, and my mind churns as I get behind the wheel and get blasted by the powerful air conditioning. I yelp and reach to turn that down before my eyelids get turned inside-out.

That crisis averted, I get on the road. My pulse beats a little bit faster with every passing second and every mile I cross. The turn for Bentley Farm approaches, and I take it without throwing myself or Cha-Cha around.

Only a few cars wait in front of the building, and Jess told me to park at the west end of the lot and go in the door down there. I do that, scanning for Lucy. She's not here, which means Jess isn't here.

"No big deal," I say to myself, because Jess isn't going to stand me up at the altar. She's the third woman I've been engaged to, and this is it. If she's somehow been abducted by aliens and doesn't make it to our wedding, I am never dating again. Period. The end, with a capital T and E.

I go in the door and find a woman standing at a podium. "You must be our groom," she says like being a groom is the greatest thing a man can be.

"Yes," I tell her.

"Will you just check this list for who can come into the dressing room with you?" She hands me a list on a pristine, thick piece of paper, and I scan it. My father, Ruth's husband, Dawson, Jason, Alec, Peter Finley from work—my partner at the real estate firm we own together—Jessie's father, brother, and brother-in-law.

"Looks right," I say. I'd be surprised if Jess's family comes in, but she's put them on the list should they want to.

The woman takes the list back, her smile ever-present and bright. "Right this way."

I follow her down two doors and into a huge room with mirrors all along one side of it. Hooks and bars adorn the wall where the door sits, and one whole wall is windows looking out into the parking lot.

From here, once I'm dressed in my tuxedo and ready, I'll head outside to "the most amazing" barn. It doesn't have a roof, only rafters, and the moment Jessie saw it, she wanted to be married there.

Fine by me, as long as she shows up. I swallow my fears and hang my garment bag on a hook in the corner near the mirrors. On the opposite wall from the mirrors sit a couple of doors, and I go explore those. Two restrooms, right here in the groom's room. Between them stands a table which bears breakfast pastries, juice, milk, and water.

Jessie's family has money, and everything I look at testifies of that. She's included her momma in the planning of the wedding as much as possible, and I know she's ready for it to be over and done with too. Her momma loves parties, though, and we won't be out of here until late tonight. So late, I've booked us at a swanky hotel in Savannah before our flight to Canada tomorrow morning.

That's still a drive from here, and we'll be lucky if we get there by midnight. When her momma had found out we were flying out of Savannah for our honeymoon, she'd wanted to change the location of the wedding. Jessie had refused, so not everything had been sunshine and cotton candy during the wedding planning.

All of the Dunaway's fancy guests have come into town—and it's not that big of a deal. A two-hour drive for them. Jessie said a lot of them came into town last night, and I felt bad for two seconds. Then I remembered that they can afford a night in a hotel. They can probably *buy* the hotel, so it's not a big deal.

Their wealth does add to my nerves, though, and I pick up a chocolate croissant and take a bite. Flaky pastry and dark chocolate flood my mouth, and I suppose that if this is all I get today, it'll still be a good day.

I shake my head at the stupid thought—because I'm supposed to get married today. No way is a chocolate croissant better than that.

The door opens, and Dawson walks in. I breathe out, my shoulders falling. "Hey," he says, and no matter what happens today, I'll be fine. "Ooh, breakfast."

I step out of the way and say, "Help yourself." The Dunaways have paid for it; we might as well enjoy it.

More people start arriving then, and after they've all eaten a little something, I start getting changed. Dawson fixes my tie so it's just right. My dad puts on my cufflinks. Ruth's husband makes the tails on my jacket lay just right.

I feel important and special with all of them fussing over me, and while I've done interviews and been in newspapers and magazines, there's nothing like being the Man of the Day. So perhaps that woman was right to smile at me the way she did as she asked me if I was the groom today.

Alec and Jason stand back, both of them dressed to the nines too. They're part of the wedding party, as is Peter, who waits with them. As predicted, Jessie's brother, father, and brother-in-law haven't come in, but that's okay.

I have the people I need right here with me. Everyone finally stops fussing over me, and I look at myself in the mirror. "This is it," I say.

Dawson stands beside me, and I meet his eyes. "Can you believe I'm doing this?"

"I'm glad it's Jess, and not Hadley," he says, and my jaw only twitches for a moment.

"Me too," I say.

"I'd have supported you," he says. "Always."

I turn toward him and take him into a hug. He's been my best friend for my whole adult life, and there's no one better than Dawson Houser. "Thanks, brother," I whisper. We pull apart, and Dawson wears pure emotion on his face. "What's going on with you?"

"Callie's gonna have a baby," he whispers, and then he does something I've only seen him do once, a long time ago when he spoke about his father's death. He reaches up and swipes at his eyes, which have filled with tears.

"Wow," I say, genuinely happy for him. "That's so great, Dawson." I hug him again, clapping him heartily on the back. "Look at you, becoming the family man."

He chuckles and shakes his head. "It's wild, right?"

"A little," I say, stepping back. I grin at him. "But not surprising. It's...perfect."

"Don't tell Callie I told you." He pulls in a breath and straightens his own tie. "I guess we're not out of the first trimester yet, and you just don't tell people until you are."

"My lips are sealed," I say as my dad approaches.

"Ready?" he asks, and I step into him for a hug too. He taught me everything I know about the real estate market, and he sold me his half of the firm when he was ready to retire. I owe everything I am to him, and I have no way of expressing my gratitude other than this hug.

He seems to get the message, because he's semi-crying when I step back too. "Ready," I say.

"I think they want you out there then," he says, and I face the door, where the same woman who greeted me this morning is waiting.

I go with her, and I'm glad I have a guide as we make turn after turn in this building. She finally leads me outside, and I have no idea which direction I'm facing. I walk along the gravel path, taking in the sunshine, the scent of grass and dew, and the blue, blue sky. *It's a perfect day to get married*, I think.

The barn sits just ahead, and I can admit that it's one-of-a-kind. The old wood on the outside makes it rustic and charming at the same time, and the open rafters give it a huge feeling inside.

Chairs have been set up in rows, and nearly every one of them is full. Women wear fancy hats, and all the men have on their best suits. I feel like I've shown up to someone else's wedding, and I'm the most underdressed. It almost looks like the crowd you'd see at the rich-and-famous gala at the Kentucky Derby, with custom-made gowns, jewels that probably only see the light of day once a year, and plenty of glances around to see who's who, and who hasn't shown up, and who has that shouldn't have.

I ignore them all and head for my momma. She's wearing a dress the color of peaches that bears plenty of sequins. She looks elegant and comfortable at the same time, and I lift her off her feet as we embrace. She laughs, and I smile at her as I set her down.

"Look at you." She brushes something invisible from my lapel and controls the shake in her bottom lip as she meets my eyes.

"Thanks, Momma."

"She is so very lucky," she whispers. "Don't forget that."

"Okay," I say, though I feel like the lucky one. I turn to say hello to her family, letting my REA—real estate agent

—voice come out again. I've dealt with a lot of people, some with plenty of money like the Dunaways. Sure, they have fancy Southern names like Rutherford and Constance, but they're just people.

I shake hands, give hugs, and kiss cheeks until my face feels like it might crack. Then I take my spot at the altar, hoping it's almost time for Jess to walk toward me. Her daddy isn't here anymore, so I'm assuming it is.

As I look toward the huge barn doors I walked through a while ago, Dawson emerges from the left and Callie from the right. He's wearing an orange tie, and she's got on a blue dress. I start to laugh, because his tie was *not* the same as mine when I left him in the groom's room thirty minutes ago. And Jess told me the bridesmaid's dresses would be "in pastels."

Perhaps Callie is the only one wearing blue, but they take two steps and then separate to show the couple behind them.

Tara and Alec walk toward one another, and she's wearing the same robin's-egg-blue dress as Callie. Alec's tie is the bright Auburn orange as mine and Dawson's. They both wear smiles the size of Jupiter, and I keep chuckling at them.

They take two steps and fall into line behind Callie and Dawson. Then the four of them take two steps back into the middle of the aisle, then two more back toward the edges to reveal Bri and Jason meeting in the middle.

Another blue dress, another orange tie. The two of

them link arms, but there's something off between them I can feel all the way at the end of the altar. They both wear a smile though, and I think they're some of the best pretenders I've ever seen.

Jessie's sister and her husband join the procession, then her brother and his wife, then Ruth and her husband. With the last of them in the line, they proceed normally toward me, and I start another round of shaking hands and kissing cheeks.

With everyone in their proper position—women on the left of the altar, and men on the right—we all look down the aisle again, expecting to see Jessie there.

She's not there, and my heart tumbles to the soles of my most expensive pair of shoes.

The music changes, and her father comes out from the left, crosses the width of the barn doors, and disappears. I glance at Dawson, but he's still staring down the aisle, his smile stitched in place.

My feet shift, almost like I want to run, and then Rutherford Dunaway appears again, an absolute angel on his arm.

Jessie is wearing a blue wedding dress too, and I suck in a breath. No wonder her momma was so not happy about this wedding. A blue wedding dress?

Once I regain my senses, I can only stare as the most beautiful woman in the world takes one—step—at—a—time toward me. She's radiant with her hair piled on top of her head and jewels along her forehead and the corners of her eyes.

The dress is a deeper, richer blue than that which the bridesmaids wear, and I love her harder and deeper for what she's done. She looks like she's been poured into the dress, which has two straps—one wide and one paper thin —that go over her shoulders. The bodice is encrusted with gems, and rainbow-colored light gets thrown around the barn as the sunlight filters down and hits the stones.

The dress hugs her hips and thighs and only widens at her knees into layer upon layer of ruffles. I'm speechless, because I know Jessie designed this and sewed most of it herself. It encapsulates everything about her, from her fun personality to her soaring spirit to how very hard she works at absolutely everything she does.

Her determination, her wit, her intellect—it's all there in the dress.

They reach me, and I take Jessie's arm from her father, lean down, and whisper, "You are my favorite person in the whole world. ILY."

She gives a light giggle, and says, "I love you too, Lance."

Then we face the pastor, both of us ready to take the next step into our future...together.

CHAPTER TWENTY-FOUR

JASON

The last wedding I attended with Bri actually went better than this one currently is. Tara and Alec's affair had been a bit simpler, and while Bri and I weren't dating at the time, we'd had fun. At least I had.

Looking at her from the other side of the altar, I can just see there's something on her mind. She's denied it for a couple of weeks now, but I'm not stupid. She knows I'm not stupid, and I don't know how to knock down this wall and get her to talk to me.

Frankly, I'm tired of trying. If the woman wants to have barriers between us, who am I to *force* her to remove them?

Maybe it's just distance, I tell myself for the tenth time just that day. It's more than that, though, and I know it. I've been busy at work before and maintained a relationship. *Not with another lawyer*, is the excuse I keep coming back to.

I'm usually the busy one in a relationship, but now there are two of us with extraordinarily busy schedules. Since Bri moved into her house and started tearing it down cabinet by cabinet and brick by brick, we haven't seen each other as much. Still, the closet-kissing has been pretty hot, and I can't figure out what's changed outside of her move.

Lance and Jessie are the most amazing couple on the planet, but I remember thinking that about Tara and Alec too. There's some sort of magic gloss that comes over people on the day they get married. I usually don't mind it. It reminds me of how amazing love is, and while I stood at Tara's wedding, that was the first time I realized I wanted that kind of love, that type of relationship, that closeness to another person.

I look at Bri again and catch her looking at me. A smile flashes to my face, because she's wearing a blue dress today that makes her dark hair and tan skin stand out. She's so beautiful, it almost hurts to look at her, and I want her to know that.

She looks away, and I only saw her for ten seconds before we had to walk down the aisle together, so I didn't have time to talk to her then either.

There's time, I think, but her glance away feels like a rejection. I study her, knowing she can feel my eyes and won't be happy about the staring. I just can't look away.

The blue dress shows her shoulders, which I've only seen on the yacht, once. She's wearing a bright white diamond necklace around her throat, just like all the other women, but hers makes my pulse leap and bound through my body.

The dress falls in straight layers past her hips and over her legs, unfortunately, to the ground. She's wearing a pair of white heels, and I've never seen her wear shoes like that. Her step had been a tiny bit wobbly as we'd come down the aisle, but that could've been from the cement floor here in the historic barn.

"I do," Jessie says, and I tear my eyes from my girl-friend. I've missed most of the ceremony, and I wish I felt worse about that than I do.

The pastor turns slightly to Lance and asks him all the traditional questions. "I do," he answers in a big, loud voice, and the pastor announces them husband and wife.

I start to clap and cheer along with everyone else, and Lance takes Jessie into his arms and kisses her while they both seem to laugh. They face the crowd, and since I'm not really important in this wedding, I don't rush toward them to hug and congratulate them. I already did that for Lance inside anyway.

I just want to talk to Bri. Maybe we can sneak away, but one look at her, and I know that won't be happening. She's closed off today, and I hate that there's nothing I can do about it.

When I get to Jessie, I grin at her with everything I

have, employing some of my more recent meditation studies. *I'm happy for her,* I tell myself. *May she have all the
happiness in the world.*

We hug; she laughs, and I say, "I'm so glad you found
Lance."

She pulls back and looks at me, something keen in
those blue eyes. "Thanks, Jason."

I turn to tell Lance he's lucky and congratulations, and
then I duck away from the altar. Once, I never thought I'd
want to be standing there, waiting for a woman to walk
toward me. But now that I've been to three weddings in
just about a year, something inside me has definitely
shifted.

I catch Bri's arm, and say, "Hey, are you okay?" She
swipes at her eyes and nods. If she's not talking, she's not
okay. I know her better than she thinks I do.

"A penny for your thoughts?" I ask, taking her hand in
mine. She lets me, which is great. I'm not sure I have
anything to worry about, but my gut says I do, and my
heart is telling me not to let her get away without telling
me what it is. Then my brain can figure out where I went
wrong and how to fix it.

"Really?" She squeezes my hand like she's trying to get
it to pop off. "I get paid two hundred and fifty dollars an
hour for my thoughts."

I laugh, because she's not wrong. "You can charge it as
a billable hour if you want." I lead her down the aisle the
way we came and outside. After taking a deep breath—

every time I open my meditation app, it tells me to do that —I tilt my head back and look up into the sky. "It's nice here."

"Yeah? Would you get married here?"

"Maybe," I say, leveling my gaze at her. "Would you?"

"I'm more of an indoor person." She wipes her forehead. "Especially at the end of July, in the South."

I'm practically melting, so I understand what she's saying. "The luncheon is inside."

"There's a whole day of activities here," she says. "Are you going to change?"

"We're supposed to change?" I look down at my dark black suit. "I missed that memo."

Bri giggles. "It was a little card in your invitation," she says. "For a lawyer, you miss the most important details."

"Hey," I say. "They're lucky I knew what day it was on." Bentley Farm isn't that far from my house, and I could run home and get whatever I need. "What kind of activities?"

"It's a farm," she said. "There was some honey tasting that I remember. An apiary visit. Wine tasting. Then, inside, they're doing some yoga, line dancing, and something else. There's hatchet throwing and archery somewhere." She scans the grounds in front of us as if there will be targets there. "We could do that."

"You're the pro at that," I agree. Maybe I've been imagining her mood. Maybe she's stressed dealing with Nate. Or another case, though we meet all the time about those. Something gnaws at my gut, and when a dog barks, the hair on the back of my neck stands up. "Bri..."

"I didn't want to leave him home," she says.

"You can't bring a Great Dane to a wedding." I can't believe her. "This is Jessie Dunaway. Her family is super-rich."

"I asked Jessie, and she said I could bring him," she says. "He's out with the other dogs here. He's fine."

I shake my head, my nerves firing even harder now. "I have a bad feeling about this."

"Take him home then," she says. "You can get different clothes and find me by the hatchet targets."

"So you can throw a sharp object at me?" I'm teasing, but Bri doesn't laugh. I draw in another deep breath, trying to concentrate on the top of my head. I've been to a couple of classes at the spa next door to Dawson's office, and I actually like them.

In my earlier days, I could've met a lot of women there, but now, I'm more focused on my mental health than scoring my next date. I'm actually proud of myself for that, and I give myself a mental pat on the back.

"What kind of clothes?" I ask.

"It's only thirty minutes until the luncheon," she says. "Then the whole day is activities. Then dinner and dancing tonight. You can wear your suit, but I brought a separate party dress." She does give me a smile then. "It's not blue, so I'm excited about that."

"You look great in blue."

"Do I?" She reaches to open the door, and I let her. My mama wouldn't be happy with my poor manners, but she's not here, and Bri's a strong woman. "I don't like this color of blue."

"You like navy," I say at the same time she says, "I like navy blue, though."

Our eyes meet, and there's definitely something nervous in hers. I swallow and seize the moment by the horns. Or whatever that cliché is. A bull? Something. "What's wrong?" I ask her. "With us. I know there's something, and I can't fix it until you tell me what it is."

She blinks, her anxiety replaced with surprise. "We're at a wedding."

"Yes, I know." I reach up and run my hand through my hair. "I know we've both been busy. I'll come sit at your house every night, and you can boss me around about whatever you want. Take that trash out. Knock out that window. I don't care."

She shakes her head and moves out of the doorway as another couple comes up behind us. The hall here is wide, with plenty of room for people to move in and out. "It's not that."

"I don't like how we don't see each other as much. There's three new places in town we haven't eaten at yet."

She gives me a soft smile and half rolls her eyes. "Wow, three," she says.

"You'd think for someone who doesn't cook, you'd want new places."

"I'm willing to go with you, as long as I don't have to eat foods I didn't know were foods."

"Kimchi is a totally normal food." I laugh, glad she seems more normal now. But I know what I saw, and there *is* something between us. I take a step closer to her and lightly touch her hair where she's pulled it up. "Bri, I..." I swallow and employ my bravery along with my new meditation techniques.

"I'm falling in love with you, and I know—I *know*—there's something you're not telling me." I move my gaze from her hair to her eyes. "Your hair is really pretty for this wedding." I lean down and touch my lips to hers, semi-expecting her to lightly push me away or protest about kissing her in public.

Instead, an inferno spirals between us, and she latches onto my collar with both hands and pulls me closer. The kiss is frantic almost, and I've never felt anything like that from Bri. It only lasts a few moments, and then she pulls away.

Her eyes are dark and filled with danger. "I don't want to make a scene at Jessie's wedding. Can we table this discussion until tomorrow?"

"Yes," I say, my voice scratching on the way out. "Tomorrow, when tomorrow? Brunch? Breakfast? Lunch? I can do dinner." For some reason, my mind is scrambling, and I say, "My house? Yours?" before I force myself to stop talking.

"In the library, it was Mister Green, with the

revolver," she says, and I cock my head at her. Bri laughs, and it's a beautiful laugh, but I wish it wasn't coming from her right now. The Clue reference makes me think murder, and my pulse stutter-steps through my chest.

"Your house," she says. "I'll bring breakfast about nine if you can be up by then."

"I'm always up by nine."

"Except when you're out partying with clients." She cocks her eyebrows—a double-cock—and then slips away from me, easily attaching herself to Macie and Andy as they walk by. The timing that took... I marvel at Bri, just as I always have.

Only now, I'm a little bit afraid of tomorrow at nine o'clock too. Thankfully, I have no clients in town. Heck, I probably won't even be able to sleep tonight. If it's something Bri wants to tell me that might cause a scene?

I lick my lips, glance around, and then head in the same direction as everyone else. After all, Jessie's family is wealthy, and the food at this wedding should be something spectacular.

———

THE FOLLOWING DAY, I've run four miles on the treadmill, done my online banking, grocery shopping, and swept my floor before eight a.m. Bri still has an hour to get here, so I open my meditation app, find a comfortable position, and dive into my next lesson.

I'm still sitting on the floor when Timber barks, when the front door opens, when I hear the scratching of dog claws against my hardwood floor. I have a hard time opening my eyes, so the canine is on me before I'm fully aware.

I laugh as his tongue lashes my face. "All right," I say. "Okay, yes, I'm here."

Bri comes down the hall, her arms laden with bags. "What are you doing on the floor?" She's wearing something I've never seen her wear—a pair of black leggings that look suspiciously like workout pants.

I can't get up, because Timber is on top of me, and I fall backward when that's the opposite direction than where I want to go. "Stop it," I say to him, but because I'm laughing, he doesn't quit anything.

Bri continues toward the island in my kitchen, saying, "There's more in the car."

"I'll get it." I manage to push Timber away and get to my feet. I'm not wearing shoes or socks, because Jillian at the spa told me I'd feel more connected to the earth if I didn't. Instead of going outside, I walk over to Bri. "You look pretty today."

She looks up at me, and I'm not sure what kind of scene there will be, because she smiles. "Thanks, Jason." No return compliment, but I haven't showered since my run, so maybe I stink.

I turn to go get the rest of the food, and when I return,

Bri is setting up a breakfast buffet. "Wow," I say. "This looks amazing. Where did you go?"

"This is from my sister," she says.

I whip my attention to her and set the last couple of bags on the counter. "Your sister is in town?"

"She got here yesterday," she says.

"And you stayed at the wedding all day long?"

Bri nods, pressing her lips together. "She knew I had the wedding when she decided to come. She said she could spend the day filling my fridge and freezer, so I don't have to eat out so much or buy so many convenience foods."

I blink, not sure how to answer. "Will I get to meet her?"

She reaches into the last couple of bags and takes out the remaining items—some whipped butter and three kinds of syrups. "Maybe," she says.

"Maybe?"

She fiddles with the positioning of some things on the counter, then looks directly at me, and asks, "Who's Vi?"

I scrunch up my face, my mind moving a mile a minute. "Vi? Vi who?"

"That's what I'd like to know," she says. She picks up a plate and starts putting food on it. Sausages, eggs, hashbrowns. "I've asked you about her before, and I didn't like your answer. So I'm asking again."

I watch her, realizing who she's talking about. I start to laugh, but I cut off when she throws me the sharpest glare

I've ever seen. "Do not make fun of me, Jason. This is important to me."

"Do you think I'm cheating on you?"

"I don't know what to think." She sighs as she squirts ketchup all over everything. I don't say anything, though I've teased her about that before too. Her sister is a good cook; she should at least *try* the eggs before making them taste like sugared tomatoes.

A sting starts in my chest. She doesn't know what to think. Her voice sinks into my ears. She thinks I'm cheating on her. She one-hundred percent does.

Though my mouth waters, I don't pick up a plate. I can't eat, not when the woman I've been steadily falling for—and might already be in love with—thinks I'm a cheater.

She walks around the counter and sits at the bar. "Are you going to eat?"

I shake my head. "No." I breathe in through my nose and try to find my center. I have no idea where it is, and I'm too new at meditation not to be horribly, raging upset. I'm literally seeing red, and I don't care if that's a cliché.

CHAPTER TWENTY-FIVE

BRI

I DON'T DARE TAKE A BITE OF MY BREAKFAST EITHER. Chelsea went to so much work, and I've laid it all out. "I just want to know who 'Vi, darling' is." I can't help the way my voice drawls into a British accent over the name. "You've talked to her a lot the past couple of weeks, and don't—" I stab the fork in his direction. "Say she's a client. I know she's not a client. I'm your junior partner, and I can see all of your cases."

"I can't believe you think I'm cheating on you." He reaches up with both hands and runs them down his face. "For probably one of the very first times in my life, I have a single girlfriend in a long-term commitment—who I'm crazy for, by the way—and I'm *not* cheating, and I *still* get accused of cheating."

His eyes flash dangerously, and while I've worked with Jason for a while, I've not seen him truly upset. Even when Vincent called me into his office and I found out I couldn't be on the legal team with Jason after my stellar performance in court, he hadn't been this upset.

"I'm sorry," I say, then immediately regret it. "You know what? I'm not sorry. I've asked you about her. You said she was a client, and she's not. What am I supposed to think?"

"You don't think anything," he says. "I'm not a liar."

I snort and push my potatoes around. "All lawyers are liars."

"Then so are you," he shoots back at me.

Who I'm crazy for, by the way.

Those words won't stop ringing in my ears. My stomach tightens, and I feel sick, sick, sick. Worse than I've felt before, even when I've had to run body-stew out to the Dumpster and when I've had to forfeit my security deposit because of egg yolks embedded in plaster.

This is so much worse.

Maybe I made a mistake, but I have to trust my gut, and she's still saying that he hasn't told me who "Vi, darling" is.

"Come on, Timber," he says, and then he's walking away. I watch him, somewhat stupefied. Come on? Where are they going?

Jason strides past his dog and down the hall to his master suite. I know, because I once looked at this house to buy it. He hired Jessie to sell it, then decided against it. I'm glad he hasn't sold, because this place is amazing, and I always feel better coming here.

Usually, I amend. I *usually* feel better when I come here.

Today, not so much.

He returns with sneakers on his feet, and Timber trots after him as he moves toward the front door. The dog stops, obviously torn between me and his real owner. Or maybe Jason and the food, though I'd like to think it's me and not the chorizo. But let's face it, Chelsea is an amazing cook, and it's probably the sausage.

"Come," Jason barks, and Timber turns and heads toward him. They leave, and I'm left sitting there. Just sitting there, a full plate of food in front of me. The breakfast works. I look down at the scrambled eggs, which I watched my sister make. She added just a touch of cream to them, and I marveled that she didn't measure anything.

She laughs when I ask her about measuring, and as tears fill my eyes, I get to my feet. "Shouldn't have said anything," I say to the empty house. It doesn't feel the same without Jason here, though I see him everywhere I look.

Family picture on the wall. His keys hung on a hook beside the refrigerator. An old record player on the antique desk in the corner. He loves old things—except for clothes and electronics. Then he wants the latest and greatest. He dresses like he has money, because he does.

I start to clean up the food, wondering how I'm going

to explain it to Chelsea when I return in only a few minutes.

He broke up with me.

Those words filter through my head, and while he hasn't said those words, him leaving his own house with a full spread of delectable food in front of him is more than a good hint. It's the truth.

I sniffle, because I didn't want him to break up with me. I didn't want to break up with him. I just want to know who that woman is that keeps calling him—and she's *not* a client.

With my determination and resolve back in place, I haul all the food back out to my car. His SUV is gone, and when I get behind the wheel, I realize he's taken one of my good friends from me too.

Timber.

The tears slide down my face then, which is so freaking ridiculous, I want to scream. I can't be in love with a man because of his dog. I can't stay with a man because of his dog. I can't be with Jason if he won't tell me the truth.

That street goes both ways.

The words lodge in my throat, but they scream in my head. My daddy used to say that to me whenever I'd get upset that Annika didn't call me. He'd say, "The phone lines work both ways, Bri. Call her."

I hate that I'm thinking in clichés or idioms or whatever they are. It's something Jason would do, and I push him and the fact that I can call him and spill everything to him just as easily as he can me.

On the way back to my new, old house, I think about Max. My gut had gonged at me several times during that relationship, and I'd ignored it. "I will not do that again," I tell myself, though I know for a fact that Jason doesn't have a wife and kids somewhere.

How do you know that for a fact? Those traitorous words whisper through my mind, and I can't shake them. Because I don't know that for sure. This Vi-woman could be his wife, living somewhere like Kansas or Arizona. I'd never know. How would I?

The reasonable part of my brain tells me that Jason hasn't traveled to Kansas or Arizona or anywhere else in months and months, if ever. Last year, about eighteen months ago, he went to New York City for a training, where he did brag at the office about having two girl-friends up there.

I learned then that the word "girlfriend" doesn't mean the same thing to him as it does most people. But that was the Jason-Before. The Playboy version of himself. Not the man I've been dating for the past few months.

I pull into my driveway and park behind my sister's rental. I sit there, not wanting to go inside. But Chelsea has never let me get away with being silent and sneaky. Just like she flew across the country because I'd stopped texting her, she comes out onto the front porch and then down the steps when she sees it is me who's returned.

She pulls open the passenger door and gets in. "What happened?"

I look at her, and a fresh wave of tears fall down my face. "I think we broke up."

"Oh, no." Chelsea takes me into her arms, and even across the console, she comforts me. She's always been able to, and I feel like a rotten, no-good monster for letting my jealousy and inability to be happy for her come between us.

I sob for what feels like forever but is probably only a few seconds, and then she says, "Let's get inside. Then we can talk about everything."

That's the last thing I want, but as my dark-haired sister gets out of the car and retrieves the food she labored over, I know I can't avoid it. She won't allow me to, and maybe for the first time since I moved to South Carolina, I admit that I need to get some things out of my head for others to examine and help me with.

So I follow her inside.

She lets me eat in a robotic way while she cleans up in the kitchen. With my stomach full and the house as clean as it's going to get, she parks me on the couch and drapes a blanket over my legs. "Start at the beginning."

I look at her. "I'm so sorry about ignoring you."

Chelsea's dark eyes study mine, and I love that we look so much alike. She's so sweet, though, and I swear it's because I took all of the salt and spice before she was born.

I hate that she's younger than me and so put together, with everything I want.

At the same time, I should be glad she has those things and isn't suffering the way I am.

"It's okay," she says.

I shake my head. "It's not okay. I'm jealous of you, Chels. You're just so perfect, and you have this perfect life, and I *want* it. I want it so badly, and you know what's even stupider? I thought I might could have it with Jason. That he'd really changed." I reach for a tissue and wipe my nose. "I don't know if he has or not."

"I'm still not sure why we needed a thirteen-course breakfast for your boyfriend," Chelsea says. "I really do need you to start at the beginning. The last I heard, we really liked Jason, and—and I quote—how he made your bones melt with a simple look." She grins at me, but I don't deserve it.

Before I can speak, she glances around. "Wait. Where's your dog?"

"He's not my dog." I hiccup and realize how far back I need to go. My eyes brim with tears again as I look at her. "He's Jason's, and he took him." I can't believe I'm crying over a dog, and even more unbelievable is that I'm weeping over losing Jason. Not that long ago, I was imagining carving out his heart with one of the hatchets I like to throw.

Now...now I miss him already, after a good solid six weeks of miserable distance between us caused by this house. I can't seem to do anything halfway, and it's either all-in or all-out for me. No wonder I can't get and keep a boyfriend. My attention span is that of a gnat.

I shake my head, trying to get my negative self-talk to silence.

"The beginning," Chelsea says as she stands. "And we'll need hot chocolate for this."

"It's at least ninety-five degrees out there." I watch her walk back into the kitchen, undeterred.

"But what did you make me when Bruce and I broke up the first time?" Chelsea flashes me a smile

I'd forgotten completely about that, but the memory of us sipping hot chocolate while she told me what had happened between her and her now-husband rushes into my mind. It had been a terrible thing, how heartbroken she'd been, but they'd fixed it.

Maybe I can fix what's broken between me and Jason too.

———

"YOU LOOK like someone spit in your tea." Macie flops onto the couch next to me, a question in there somewhere.

I feel like I'm moving through quicksand as I turn toward her. "What?"

"You haven't touched your tea." She indicates the delicate cup sitting in front of me. I have no idea what time it is, or how long I've been sitting here. I know I finished with a meeting close to here, and I didn't have to go back to the firm. Oolong sounded good, and here I am.

"I forgot about it." I reach for the cup, but it's stone-cold. I'm not drinking that, and I set it back down. I lean back into the cushions on the couch and close my eyes. My breath leaks out of my body, and I'm glad Macie doesn't ask another question.

It's a bit unusual for her, but I can barely function right now. It's been a terrible week at work, even though Jason canceled our meetings, and I didn't have to work with Nate. I've basically been confined to my office, sifting through documents and papers and eating far too much chocolate.

Macie sighs, and I clue into that. "What's up with you?" Things at Legacy Brew have been going well, at least according to me—and I've been in a fog for the past five days. Last night, I ate the last of Chelsea's food, and tonight... Well, I have no idea what I'm going to eat tonight.

My stomach growls as if the thought of my sister's food has reminded it that we haven't eaten anything of substance for a while. I should've drunk my tea, but it's too cold now. If it's not one thing, it's another.

A cliché.

I shake my head, and I realize Macie is doing it too. "What?" I ask her. "Talk to me."

"Oh, like you've been so open about what's going on

with you and Jason?" She gives me the stink-eye, but I just shrug.

"I told Chelsea," I say. "I don't want to relive it a thousand times."

"One more time," she says.

"I'll tell you, if you tell me," I say.

She draws in a deep breath, and I watch her chest rise, then fall. "I'm not sure, but I think..." She trails off, then a smile fills her whole face. "I think Andy might be asking me to marry him soon."

I suck in a breath in a very Callie-like move. "What? Really?"

"We've been talking about diamond rings," Macie says, turning fully toward me. "And tonight, he said he has an 'appointment' and he can't tell me what it is." She looks like she's swallowed sunbeams, and I tell myself to be happy for her.

"That's great," I say.

"A couple of weeks ago, he told me about how his brother asked his now-wife to marry him after taking her to Pretty Little Things, and they only do ring-buying...by *appointment*." Macie glows, and I grin at her.

"Oh, that's so happening."

"You think so?"

"I have no idea," I say, grinning. "But you seem like you know."

She sighs and gazes up at the ceiling. "I don't know. I

just know it's a late appointment, and we're going after dinner at Southern Grill."

"You need a reservation there at least a month in advance," I say, and I only know because Jason's taken me there before. "And it's great food."

"A month," Macie repeats, and she's floating somewhere in the clouds. I am too, but mine are dark and stormy and filled with the threat of lightning.

The bell on the door rings, and it catches my attention. In walk Callie and Dawson, followed by Alec. Tara's not with them, and that might be my saving grace. Either way, it's time for me to leave.

I stand up, leaving my tea on the table. "I'll be up late," I tell Macie. "I want to be the first person you call if you get engaged tonight." I mean it too, and Macie nods as she grins.

"Not a word to them," she says in a loud whisper. "I don't want to have to explain it a 'thousand times' if he doesn't ask."

I roll my eyes while she giggles, and then I head for the door.

"Bri," Callie calls, but I hold up my phone as if I have a call. I feel like a liar—exactly what Jason called me the last time we spoke face-to-face—and that I'm a thief sneaking away from a crime scene.

Still, I go, because I'm too big of a chicken to face my friends and answer questions about Jason. Tara might as well name me Yellow Custard and add me to her flock of hens for how cowardly I am.

I slip out the door and take two steps before I smell something completely recognizable. I come to a complete halt as I see Jason standing in front of the coffee shop. "Oh."

"You're leaving?" he asks, leaning away from me. He doesn't smile, and it looks like he was peering through the window to see if I was there before he came in.

"Yes," I say. "I have a meeting in a few minutes." He doesn't have to know it's with my latest book boyfriend, my recliner, and the pizza delivery guy. I nod at Jason, because while he makes every cell in my body vibrate in a new and exciting way, I don't know how to bridge the gap between us.

He doesn't seem to be able to either, because he nods, pulls open the door on the opposite side of the shop from where I exited, and goes inside Legacy Brew.

I watch him, because I want to amend my thought from before. I don't know how to bridge the gap between us. "Yet," I say out loud.

Maybe I'll get an idea in my romance novel, and I head home to get started on that.

CHAPTER TWENTY-SIX

MACIE

I CHECK MY MAKEUP FOR THE FIFTH TIME. IT'S harder than people think to make everything look good when you have red hair. I actually color my hair to keep it redder and shinier and full of light. It's got highlights in it that are peach, and I think it looks amazing.

But there are colors you can't wear when you're a redhead, and I'm really careful to make sure every piece goes together. I have to, especially now that I own half of Legacy Brew. I smile at myself, then flinch when the doorbell rings.

My dogs go nuts, and I step out of the bathroom while saying, "Hush, it's just Andy." My heels click as I hurry to get the door. I imagine him with a huge bouquet of red roses, dressed like a true gentleman in a dark blue suit, his tie bright pink, and his shoes shining like stars.

My heartbeat speeds as I turn the corner and walk

along the back of the couch. I nearly trip over Justice, my little chihuahua who can't stand to be left out of anything. When I pull open the door, she shouts at Andy, who is the one standing there.

"Shush, Justice," I tell her, trying to toe her back with my shiny black heel. It doesn't work, and she doesn't bolt, so I leave her. My French bulldog is a bit more unpredictable, and while he has a loud bark, he's a complete wimp. So he's standing behind me at the corner, eyeing the danger instead of doing anything about it.

Andy grins at me, but it feels...dim. "Hey, Macie." He's not wearing a designer suit, shiny shoes, or a tie. He's got on a pair of blue jeans and a polo. No flowers are in sight.

I'm wearing a slinky black dress I ordered online last week. Jessie said she'd help me alter it when she gets back from her honeymoon, but I couldn't wait to wear it. I thought I might be getting a proposal tonight, but now... I doubt it.

I hitch a smile in place and pick up my clutch. "Hey, Andy." Hey? We've been dating for almost four months. Why are we talking like we're high school friends going out for the first time?

Something is definitely off, and it might be me. I'm a little... Well, Bri would say I live in a fantasy world filled with coffee and unicorns. I haven't argued with her in a while, because that's about my life. Coffee, tea, quick breads and muffins, managing people and money. When

I'm not doing that, I like to imagine my life as one where I tromp through the jungle to find rubies and diamonds. A real adventure, though I've never left South Carolina for longer than a vacation.

We walk down my sidewalk to his car, and he's chivalrous as he opens the door. I slide in and adjust my skirt so it's covering me properly. No need to show more leg than necessary. Tension hangs in the air, and I don't know why. I *hate* that I don't know why.

Andy gets behind the wheel, and I look over to him. "So...Southern Grill for dinner?"

He shakes his head, and my heart falls into my stomach. "I was only on the wait-list," he says. "They don't have a table tonight."

"Oh." I grip my clutch as he pulls out of the driveway. I take a breath, but it catches in my throat, and I end up coughing. Choking on my own air, then spit. Humiliation fills me, and I'm sure my face is as bright red as my hair. I manage to find a breath that goes down right, and Andy looks at me.

"You okay?" He smiles, but again, it's not the megawatt grin I've seen before.

"Yes." I clear my throat and take a deep breath. Thankfully, my body cooperates with me this time, and the air gets where it needs to go smoothly.

He pulls into the parking lot at the Sundowner, and horror strikes me behind my ribcage. My heartbeat shorts out. "Sundowner?" I ask. It's a steakhouse-slash-buffet, and they see their biggest crowds before five p.m. as all the senior citizens come for the early bird specials. They definitely don't need a reservation, and I'm overdressed by at least ten levels.

"They're fast," he says.

"Fast?" I look at him. Since when do we need to dine fast?

He gets out without saying anything, and I do a quick survey of his car. It's always been clean—Andy's house is like a museum—and tonight is no exception. There's nothing in the back seat, not even a scrap of an errant receipt. An empty water bottle or can of soda. Nothing. It's like he's scrubbed it clean before leaving his house that evening.

He opens my door, but I'm not sure what to do. I get out, but I don't take a step toward the entrance of the Sundowner. "Why do we need to eat fast?" I ask.

Andy sighs, and it is one motherlode of a sigh, let me tell you. I've worked with a lot of people. I've sat with them on the couches at Legacy Brew and listened to them talk about work, about their mother, about their husband, boyfriend, girlfriend, boss. Anything and everything. I've heard it all. Therefore, I can categorize sighs better than anyone in the world.

And that one? That one is him about to tell me something he doesn't want to tell me.

That's a break-up sigh.

I brace myself by putting one hand on the wind-

shield of his car. He won't look at me—break-up sign
number two. I've seen *countless* couples break-up at the
coffee shop. Sometimes there's tears. Sometimes shout-
ing. Sometimes just angry silence until one of them
stalks out.

Legacy Brew has given me a real show over the years.
Real-life observations that I hate I can see in my own life
right now.

"I'm moving, Macie."

"Moving?" Whatever I expected him to say, it wasn't
that. "Where? When?"

"I've, uh…" He runs his hand up the back of his neck,
something I used to find oh-so-adorable when he did it in
line at the coffee shop. It showed his nerves, and I liked
that he was nervous to talk to me. "I've already moved. I'm
up in Philly now."

I stare at him, my false eyelashes creating a curtain
every other nanosecond as I blink-blink-blink at him.
"What?" I mean, I heard him, but I can't comprehend.

"A job came up," he says feebly.

"When? Why didn't you say anything to me?"

"You'd just bought Legacy," he says. "I knew you
wouldn't come with me. So…" He shrugs, and my mind
goes nuts filling in words after that stupid-casual "So…"

So I thought I'd just lead you on for a while longer.

*So I thought I'd keep kissing you without saying
anything.*

So I thought it would be a good idea for me to keep this

secret, because I'm a double-douche-bag-coward who can't face you.

So I'm an idiot who cares more about my job than you.

So I thought I'd make my own decisions without even asking you what you might want to do.

I scoff in an attempt to get my mind to stop. It needs to stop, because I am going to lose something if it doesn't. Probably my dignity, but standing in front of the Sundowner in a slinky black dress meant for a fancy rooftop restaurant, that's already gone.

"Okay." I turn away from him and take my phone from my clutch. I'm not stranded here. I can get a Carry to anywhere. I tap the app and call the car while Andy sputters behind me.

"Macie." He jogs up to me. "You don't want to eat?'

"With you?" I glare at him out of the corner of my eye. I do want to eat with him. I don't want him to move to Philly. If he'd have asked me to marry him, I'd have said yes. I don't get how I could've been that far off in how things were going in our relationship.

Tears fill my eyes, and I keep walking. I can't go faster than him, because hello tight dress and high heels.

"Macie," he says again, falling behind a little.

I whirl around to face him. "Go," I say. "You're already gone." I shake my head. "What a joke."

"What's a joke?"

I roll my eyes. "You're not this dumb, Andy. We've been dating for a few months now. I thought we were getting along really well. You've literally never said a word about a job transfer."

"I got promoted."

"Or a promotion!" I'm aware my voice is inching up in volume and pitch, and I don't need the cops to come to the Sundowner. What a downer that would be. "I'm dressed up like we're going to Southern Grill, and you look like you'll be on an airplane in an hour."

My stomach hollows out in that moment. "Fried green tomatoes," I say. "You *will* be on a plane in an hour. That's your appointment."

He doesn't deny it, and I want to pick up a handful of dirt and throw it in his eyes. "You're cute when you swear in Southern food," he says.

"Don't you dare," I say, my voice deathly quiet now. I take the four steps back to him, our faces only inches apart. "I thought you had this romantic dinner date planned. Fancy restaurant. An appointment to look at diamond rings. Why'd you even bring up wedding rings a couple of weeks ago?"

"*I* didn't bring it up," he says. "*You* did."

"You went with it."

"I always go with you," he says, his eyes flashing now too. "That's how you are, Macie. You're like this huge hurricane out at sea, gaining strength. No one can stop you."

I don't know what to say. Maybe I'm a little bossy sometimes. Maybe my mouth runs away from me. Maybe

I am riding through the rain forest on my unicorn. I certainly don't need him to point it out to me.

"Did you really think I was going to ask you to marry me?" He chuckles, and I have the strong urge to punch him in the nose. Thankfully, my app chimes at me as the soft rumble of a car engine pulls up to the curb.

I turn away from him before he can see me cry. He has no right to discard me so easily. Almost four months. He's already moved to Phila-freaking-delphia.

I get in the car, and since I've already put in my destination, I don't have to speak. I keep my head turned away from Andy as I reach to close the door, and I ignore him as he says, "Macie, come on."

No, I will not come on. He lied to me. He misled me. He should've been strong enough to rope the storm and calm her down.

Tears slide down my face, ruining my perfect-for-redheads makeup, as my Carry driver takes me to Legacy Brew.

Yeah, that's the destination I put in. Not home.

This is home—and if that makes me pathetic, then that's what I am. The car starts to slow, and I ask, "Can you go around to the back, please?" I don't have my key for the front doors, but the back one has an electronic lock with a code.

The driver does, and I slip out of the car and into the narrow alley with a, "Thanks." He can tell I'm upset, and he waits while I tap in the code and disengage the lock. I go into the kitchen at the back of the coffee shop and press the door closed so I can be alone faster.

It clicks, and that's when I really start to sob. Great, heaving emotion moves through me, making my chest hitch and pitch and stitch.

I kick off my heels right there inside the back door and walk on bare feet to my office. It's locked too, and I don't have a key for it. Of course. I sink into the chair outside the door, thankful I keep it there for people waiting to interview with me.

Then I remember that there's a whole coffee shop out front. We're closed, and no one will be here until morning. Early morning, but still morning.

I get up and push through the swinging door into the barista area of the shop. I can make coffee in my sleep. Heck, I bet I could make coffees and teas after I'm dead, and as it brews, I go grab the nearest thing to the door in the walk-in fridge.

It happens to be a half-loaf of cinnamon bread, and I take a bite of it like a Neanderthal as I walk back out front. No knives needed. Not here. Not tonight. I'm a cavewoman in my party dress, ready for a rager.

I don't drink anything stronger than coffee, but tonight I wish I did. Instead of alcohol, I pour in a lot of sugar and cream—my momma says anything can be fixed with sugar and cream—and go right over the counter in my dress. It bunches up around my hips, but who's there to see?

No one, that's who.

I put my coffee cup on the table and lay down on the couch and take another cavewoman-style bite of the bread and stare at the ceiling. Bri wanted me to call her after my date, but there's no way in Hades that's happening.

Nope. I'm just going to lay right here, chomp on my bread loaf, and contemplate how utterly messed up it is to move seven hundred miles away from your girlfriend and not say a Phila-freaking-delphia-word about it.

———

"MACIE?"

I twitch at the sound of my name. The voice is familiar, but I'm still swimming toward the surface of consciousness. A hand touches my forearm, and my eyes jerk open. I blink, wondering why the light is so bright and why Coy Cochran is looking at me with such concern in his eyes.

I sit straight up, almost knocking skulls with Coy. Only his ninja-like moves spare us that agony as he pulls back like a whip. "Whoa," he says.

I twist my hips so my legs are over the edge of the couch, and that's when I realize I'm not wearing pants. Or even my skirt. Not really. I look down at my bare legs, then up at Coy. He's staring at my legs too, his face growing redder with every microsecond that passes.

He clears his throat and yanks his eyes back to mine. "What are you doing here?"

"Andy moved." I cradle my head in my hands, wishing it didn't pound so hard. My heart races too, and that's probably from the cupful of sugar I ingested at who-knows-what-time. I don't know what time it is now.

"What?" Coy asks.

"To Philadelphia." I look up. "Am I that bad? I'm so bad—so stormy and so noisy and so bossy—that you can't talk to me?"

Coy's face blanks, and then he says, "No."

"Yeah, I know I'm not." I *know*. "So why'd he do that?"

Coy sinks onto the couch next to me, his sigh the kind that says he didn't sign up for this. No, he didn't. Still, I've known him for a decade, and he knows me.

I perk up at that. This man knows me. Andy doesn't. Not really.

"He said he just went along with whatever I say," I say. "I hate that." I turn and look at Coy. "You're not doing that, are you?"

"Doing whatever you say?" He scoffs and vaguely gestures toward the kitchen area. "We fight every day, Macie. About everything. How is that me going along with everything you say?"

"You didn't want to hire Dawson and Callie for the marketing campaign," I say. "But you said I could." Maybe he's been doing it too. Maybe everyone has, and a new pit opens in my stomach.

"I said you could, because I wanted to see if it would

work too." Coy shakes his head. "Not because you told me I had to. And it's working."

"It is working."

"Sales are up twenty-four percent."

"Yes, they are."

"That's because you won't take no for an answer." He kicks a sexy grin in my direction, and I find myself returning it. Another round of horror hits me, just as strongly as eating at the Sundowner. Sexy grin? On Coy?

I laugh right out loud. No, he is not sexy, though he does tick a lot of my boxes. Dark hair. Rugged jawline. Beautiful eyes. Big, strong hands. Dedicated to family and this shop. Employed. Handsome. Hard-working.

I stop myself there, because jeez. So he ticks all of my boxes. Big deal. Like he said, we fight all day, every day.

"I take no for an answer," I say as I sober. "Besides, that's what I was just asking you, and you said no, I'm not so bossy that you can't talk to me about things."

Silence joins us, and I realize it's a bit chilly in the coffee shop. Probably because I'm half-naked. Sitting on the couch in the middle of the night, half-naked, with Coy Cochran at my side.

So not how I saw tonight happening.

And when he reaches over and takes my hand in his? I still completely, only my eyes watching the way his thumb traces an unseen pattern on the back of my hand. "I think you're a smart woman," he whispers. "And Andrew Watters is a stupid, stupid man for letting you go." He nods like he's proclaimed it to the world, and therefore it will be so.

"Coy," I say, not sure what comes next.

He lifts his eyes and so do I, and we look at one another. The moment is soft, not filled with challenge, tension, and loud voices. There is no competition between us. None at all.

He offers me a quiet, soft smile. "You've been crying." With his free hand, he traces his fingertip down my face, right where my tears have left tracks. My skin sizzles and pops, everything inside me telling me to get closer to this man.

This can't be happening.

This is *Coy*.

I don't like Coy. I barely tolerate Coy. Coy is my nemesis in every way.

Except tonight.

"A little," I say.

"Over Andy?" He shakes his head. "He's not worth crying over."

Irritation flares in me, but it's short-lived and gone after only a moment. "Probably not." I sink back into the couch, and Coy goes with me. Our shoulders touch, and after fighting it for a second, I lean into him and lay my head against his shoulder.

"What are you doing here?"

"Couldn't sleep," he murmurs. "Nearly killed myself on some high heels inside the back door."

I giggle quietly while he chuckles in the same low voice. "Sorry," I say. "I didn't know where else to go."

"How about home?"

"You're not home either." I lift up and look at him. Again, more energy than is needed to light Charleston for a month flows between us. His hand in mine tightens, and he cradles my face in his other hand. He's caring, and kind, and gentle, and I didn't know Coy could be those things.

I see things in his eyes he's never showed me before, and the next thing I know, I'm leaning down, and he's raising up.

Then, he's kissing me.

And I don't hate it. I don't hate it at all.

CHAPTER TWENTY-SEVEN

JASON

I PULL UP TO THE HOUSE WHERE I GREW UP, A BIG slippery sigh sliding from my mouth. In the way-back of my SUV, Timber barks. "I know," I tell him, but I make no move to get out. He's been cramped back there for an hour, and he probably needs to find a good patch of grass to take care of his business.

When I still don't move, the dog gives another half-bark, and that propels me out of my seat. I move to the back and open the hatch, and Timber leaps down. He's off and running, as if I've caged him for days instead of sixty minutes.

I feel caged, I know that. Nothing has gone right since I left Bri sitting in my house. Of course she wasn't there when I got back. It had been hours, number one, and the old adage of actions speak louder than words is absolutely right.

I'd left. Walked out. Sayonara. Good-bye.

She'd picked up what I put down.

"Enough," I mutter to myself. Clichés used to be funny. Living one…is not so fun or funny.

Bri and I will have to meet soon, and I figure we can do it. Maybe. Maybe she can. I feel like someone's taken my skin off, shredded it, and then tried to glue it back together on my bones. Just the fact that I came to visit my parents this weekend shows that.

It's been two weeks since I walked out of my own house, and Bri and I have spoken once face-to-face. Last weekend, she'd been leaving the coffee shop as I'd arrived. Jessie and Lance will be home from their honeymoon on Monday, and they've already started a group chat and invited everyone to their place to see all their marvelous pictures.

I roll my eyes as I start toward my parents' house. Of course, I wouldn't feel like this if Bri and I were still together. I'd want to go to Lance's house and bask in their life-giving love. Wouldn't I?

I honestly don't know. I know I'm not happy to be alone again, and I'm especially not happy that it's Bri who's gone. Tara's been to the farmhouse a couple of times, always bearing so much food I can eat for a week. So she's due to come again soon.

She's worried about me, I can tell. I've tried to blow this break-up off like it's nothing, but that's the real stickler. It's something, when nothing before ever has been.

Even Tara can see it, and she told me earlier this week, "Do something, Jason. Go talk to her. Text her. Send her a new cardigan. Something."

I'm still stewing over what that something could be. I asked Tara, but she always comes back to food and flowers for make-up gifts. They work for her. Or a chicken, as I'm pretty sure Alec just gifted her with a half-dozen new chicks after he messed something up in the kitchen where they work.

Bri isn't the type of woman to be bought with flowers or food. Well, maybe food, as she can't cook. But I'm not sending some poor delivery guy over there to be abused. I won't do that. And knowing Bri, she'll refuse the order and squint her eyes as she demands to know who sent the Alfredo pizza with her favorite toppings—ham and asparagus.

"She'll know it's you," I tell myself as I head up the steps at the sprawling mansion house. Fine, it's not a mansion. It just feels like one, because it was huge when Connor and I grew up here, and now it's just Mama and Daddy.

Bri didn't date in Charleston, and she hadn't been to Pie Squared before I took her, so she'll definitely know the pizza is from me if I send it. I'm not going to send it.

What can I do? I wonder.

I ring the doorbell and stand back like a visitor. I hear distant barking and remember I have a dog. "Shoot." After whistling through my teeth, the front door opens and Mama's butler stands there.

Yes, a butler. A legit man to open the door and bring her the mail and tell her what's on the menu that night. My parents are a little bit rich, and they live out in the wealthy suburbs, with a gate around their community and plenty of green space.

Timber crashes through the bushes, his doggy face so, so happy. "Come on, bud," I say, then I turn toward Hector. "I brought my dog."

"Delightful," he says, his tone even and his smile cemented—absolutely cemented—in place.

"Is my mother home?"

"She's in the library."

Which means she's sitting in the front formal room she had built-in bookcases installed in last year. Before that, it was Daddy's office, and before that, Connor and I used the space as a toy room.

Library.

Mental scoff.

The good news is I don't have to go far to trek to the library. The last thing anyone needs is Timber tearing up the house. I clip his leash to his collar, and that's a signal for him. He calms, and he walks at my side as we squeeze past Hector and enter the foyer.

A huge vase of fresh flowers sits on the front table, as if Mama was expecting grand company like the President of the United States. I veer left around it and enter the library, which is the first door on this side of the house, before the staircase goes up, up, up.

"Mama," I say upon entering. I hate how formal my voice is, and I force my shoulders down. I'm so tense, and being in this house does that to me. But for some reason, I need to be here.

Someone coughs, drawing my attention to the front windows, only a pace or two away. Mama rises from a chair there, only to wobble a little bit on her feet. She grasps the arm of the chair, and I rush toward her. "Hey, are you all right?" I drop the leash along the way, because my mother is more important than Timber.

"Yes," she says, and her voice is weaker than I remember. "I'm just not feeling well today. Tired is all."

She looks more than tired, but I don't say so. Quips like that used to earn me sharp looks and extra chores about the property. Mama can come up with some wicked punishments, and just because I'm in my thirties doesn't mean I'm immune.

"Sit back down," I say. "I'm just here to chit-chat."

She sits, and I retrieve the leash. Timber curls into himself beside the chair I sit in, and my mother and I look at one another. "You haven't visited for a while," she says.

"Excuse me, ma'am," Hector says, saving me from saying the first thing that comes to mind. I mirror Mama and look up at him. "Would either of you like tea? Coffee? Shelley left those pudding cookies as well."

"Yes," Mama says. "To all of it." She looks at me, and I nod too.

"I'll take coffee," I say. "No tea, but I never say no to cookies." I flash Hector a smile, who returns it. He leaves the library then, and I lean my head back into the soft cushions of the wingback chair.

I look out the window, noticing the amazing view Mama's been enjoying. It's interesting to just see the woods, the flower garden, and the rolling waves of grass and not the driveway. Not the pillars on the front of the house. Not the road leading up to it. It almost creates a brand new scene that I knew existed, but that I've never seen in quite this way.

"Bri broke up with me," I say, my voice hardly my own. "Or I broke up with her. Something. We're not seeing each other anymore."

Mama makes no noise, and I'm not looking at her to see her reaction. I'm sure it'll be disappointment. That's all I've ever really brought to her. She was thrilled when I said I wanted to be a lawyer, but she wanted me to go to Washington D.C. or New York City and be a big corporate lawyer. Mostly family law at the local law firm isn't what she had in mind.

I'm not married, no kids, and that basically means I have no worth to Mama.

"You don't seem happy, Jason," she says.

"I'm not happy." I move my eyes to her, and it feels like I'm doing everything underwater. These big estates out here have a way of making things seem slower. Of forcing life to just be, instead of it rushing and zipping around the way it does in the city. That's one reason I bought my farmhouse further out, and the main reason I decided not to sell it earlier this year.

"Do you love her?" Mama isn't asking to then make fun of me. To her, nothing is as serious as love and marriage. I've been in the house when she's wept and wailed and asked where she'd gone wrong in my upbringing to make me think being thirty and single was okay. Connor got the message; I didn't; Mama must've done something wrong.

Truth be told, I'd walked out on her then too. Apparently that's something I like to do when things get too hard.

Which doesn't make me proud or feel better about myself.

I blink, trying to find the answer.

"Oh," Mama says, a smile touching her lips. Her face almost looks gray, and there's definitely more going on here than not sleeping well last night. "I can see you do." She reaches for the book on the table, folds down the corner, and tucks it against her leg. "What are you going to do?"

"I don't know," I say with another pathetic sigh. I return my attention out the window. "What would you do?"

She remains silent as Hector returns with a tray of

cookies, a cup of tea and coffee for Mama and just coffee for me. He sets everything on the table, removing the little pitcher of cream and the sugar bowl one by one until it's all laid out. "Anything else?" He looks from Mama to me.

"No, thank you," I say as graciously as I can.

"Thank you, Hector." Mama places her hand on his arm, and then he leaves.

I stare at her. "Mama."

"What?" She reaches for her spoon and stirs her tea, lifting the bag out of the cup by the string. She looks up at me.

"You and Hector?"

She gives a short, barking laugh. "Heavens, no." She flicks a look in the direction Hector went. "He's been extremely attentive while your father's been gone this time, that's all."

"Attentive to what?"

"Don't make it sound scandalous."

"Well, it sounds that way whether I make it sound that way or not," I say.

"I've been ill." She lifts the cup to her mouth and takes a sip. "He hasn't left once, which is a good thing. I passed out last night, alone, in the study. He heard me and found me, or I might still be there."

"Mama." I watch her closely, trying to see beneath the layers she's put up between herself and everyone else. I've seen her do it for decades, and I'm able to peel them back easily. I think that's why I was able to see through some of

Bri's prickly layers too. I recognize them from dealing with my mother.

"Are you hurt?" I ask.

"No," she says. "A bit of stiffness in my neck."

"Why did you pass out?"

"Verne came by and checked on me," she says, referencing the family doctor who lives down the street. He has to be eighty if he's a day, and I narrow my eyes. "I'm fine. He thinks it was probably exhaustion combined with not eating."

"Why aren't you eating?"

"I've been under the weather." She takes another sip of tea. "Your daddy's back tonight, and I've promised him I'll eat even if I don't feel like it." She sends me a ghost of a smile. "I'm fine. Let's talk about how you can get Bri back."

I freshen up my coffee then, because Mama's gonna say what Mama wants to say. I might as well get some sugar and caffeine out of it. She waits until I lift my cup and settle back into the chair again, and then she says, "I've never seen you like this."

"I told you I'd changed."

"Yes, you did," she says slowly. "I suppose I didn't believe it."

"Thanks for the vote of confidence." My tone is akin to a desert, but seriously? She doesn't believe I can change? Not what a son wants to hear from his mother.

"Forgive me," she says, and I wave my free hand to mean *already forgiven. Don't worry about it.*

We sip in silence, and finally she says, "We forgive each other, don't we, Jace?"

"Yes," I say quietly.

"Why do you think we do?"

I tear my gaze from the gently waving branches outside to focus on her again. "I don't know. We're family."

"We love each other, even if it doesn't seem like it sometimes."

"Yes," I say. "That's accurate."

She nods, her smile turning up into prideful points. "Bri will forgive you."

"How do you know?"

"You're family."

I shake my head. "No, Mama, we're not. We work at the same firm. That's not family."

"She loves you."

"No." I look out the window again. "I don't think she does."

"But you love her."

"Is one-sided love enough?" I challenge. Our eyes meet again, and I've all but admitted to being in love with Sabrina Shadows. I said it to her too, and it didn't matter. She still found me capable of cheating on her, and she still let me walk away.

I can't pin that on her, so I shake my head to get rid of the thought. *I* walked away. She didn't let me. *I* did it. *I* chose, and *I* left.

"Sometimes," Mama says simply, and the conversation

falls back into silence. I'm not sure how long we sit there, but it's companionable and comfortable, and I don't feel the itching urge to leave the way I have in the past.

I think my meditation has helped quiet my mind. Not trying to live life at four hundred miles an hour has too. Dating Bri definitely has.

"Oh, Tara's here," Mama says, and I look up.

I look away from the yard. I'm not even sure what I was looking at. "She is?"

"Coming in hot." Mama gives me a smile and takes a sip of her tea. "Isn't that what you guys say?"

The doorbell rings before I can answer, and Tara doesn't wait for Hector to come to the door. Timber barks, only quieting a smidge before she calls, "Hello? Aunt Cynthia? Jason? Are you here?"

I get to my feet, and Timber does too. He looks up at me for guidance, and I tell him to "Stay here," before I stride for the door. My heart pounds in my chest as I enter the foyer. "I'm right here. What's going on? Why did you drive out here?"

She studies my face, panic on hers. Tara looks over my shoulder, but Mama won't be there. She could barely stand a while ago. Timber's claws click against the wood as he emerges from the library, and he speeds into a trot.

Tara strokes his head absently as she says, "I called you four times, and you didn't answer. So I checked your pin, and you were here. I figured...something bad must've happened."

"Just visiting," I say. Anything is better than sitting home on a Saturday afternoon, alone. Even my farmhouse reminds me of Bri. She's probably doing the opposite of what I am. She's likely torn out her whole house in the past two weeks, barely stopping to sleep, eat, or breathe. I've seen her do that before. When she's stressed, she works more, not less.

"Why did you call?" I gesture to the library. "Do you want to come in and visit?"

Tara looks past me again, then shakes her head. "Alec and I have extra tickets to the symphony tonight. I thought you might want to come."

"You drove an hour out here to tell me about the symphony?" I cock my head, trying to read between the lines. Suddenly, it all makes sense. "You invited Bri."

"No." Tara reaches up and pulls her ultra-tight ponytail tighter. "Okay, fine, yes. She loves music."

"Yes, she does."

"You're trying to be more cultured."

"You want to get me and Bri back together."

"I mean, someone has to—"

"That's not how it works, Tara." I shake my head. "I'm not going to the symphony. Mama isn't doing well, and I'm going to hang out here until Daddy gets home."

Tara's eyes widen, and she blinks like she's trying to win the world record for the most blinks in a single second. "Jason."

"I'm fine, Tara."

"You are not. You need to do something."

"I know I need to do something." I turn around to go back into the library, and Mama's standing there. "Mama, let's go sit back down."

"Your cousin is right." She looks past me and smiles. "Hello, Tara, dear."

"Hello, Aunt Cyndi." She moves past me and kisses Mama on both cheeks.

"Would you like some tea or coffee?" Hector asks.

"Yes, please," Tara says kindly. "Tea would be lovely." She takes Mama by the arm and eases her back into the library.

"Tea would be lovely?" I echo, but neither Tara nor Mama look back at me. Once again, I'm left out in the cold, with that stupid piece of glass between me and everyone else.

I hate that, but I'm not sure how to shatter it and get myself into the places I want to be. Bless Tara, she doesn't take my chair, and she brings me right into the midst of her and Mama again. That's what she's always done—include me. She never forgets about me, she feeds me, and she's always accepted me just how I am.

There is no glass between me and Tara. She pulls up another chair while I make room on the table for her saucer and teacup Hector's bringing. "Pudding cookies," I say, nudging that plate closer to my cousin as she sits.

"Thanks."

Hector brings the tea, and Tara drinks and eats, and

the moment the first cookie is gone, she says, "All right, let's hear your ideas for how you can talk to Bri."

"He works with her," Mama says. "They have to talk."

My face must have a neon sign on it, saying I haven't spoken to her at work in two weeks, because Mama says, "Jason Blakely."

"She's got her cases; I have mine." I pick up another cookie and shove the whole thing in my mouth. They're the size of half of my palm, so it's not a crime.

"She's your partner," Mama says.

"She's at the coffee shop sometimes," Tara says. "How are you two avoiding each other?"

"We're extraordinary people." I lift my chin and dare either of them to defy me.

"Jace." Mama leans forward and takes a cookie too. "What else does she like to do?"

"Renovate her old house," I say. "Go out to eat. She loves Italian ice, and she stops by the hatchet throwing arena once a week." An idea starts to form in my head, but I really don't know if I can put myself in the same small space as Bri while she's holding a sharp weapon.

"Hatchet throwing," Tara says, and I meet her eye. We can have whole conversations without speaking, and I don't even have to ask her if she'll make me something sweet and delectable to take to the hatchet throwing arena.

"She likes dips," I say.

Tara's face lights up, and she nods. She sets down her teacup. "She likes you."

"We'll see."

"No, we won't," Tara says. "I know she does. In fact, I think she loves you." She grins at me, but I can only shake my head. I can't think like that right now. Otherwise, my stupid heart will grow wings and start to soar.

"He loves her," Mama says. "He'll get her back."

"Mama."

"Do you, Jason?" Tara asks, suddenly earnest. Her dark eyes bore into me, and I can't really meet her gaze.

I watch the breeze outside as it tickles the rose bushes. I don't need to deny how I feel about Bri, not to my mama and my cousin.

"Yeah," I say. "I'm in love with her."

Tara deafens me with a screech, and then I'm knocked sideways as she wraps her arms around my neck. Or tries to, as I'm seated and it doesn't really work. "Tara," I chastise.

"This is *huge*," she says, and she's now perched on the edge of the table. "Jason, you're in love with someone."

"Who's not myself," I quip.

Tara's smile doesn't falter, but she shakes her head. "I knew you were human."

I do the head-shaking now, and I shoo her out of the way so I can get another cookie. "It still doesn't matter if she doesn't love me."

"She does," Tara said with conviction. "You just need to be in the same space as her and ease all of her fears."

"What about my fears?" I ask.

Tara laughs and shakes her head. "What fears?"

I throw a look at Mama. "She wants to know who Vi is."

Tara sobers, and she looks at Mama too. "You're still talking to Vi?"

Mama holds up both hands. "She doesn't call me."

"She calls me," I say. "I'm doing the best I can to keep her at bay. I don't want her to know about Bri, and she thinks I'm cheating."

Tara does the rapid-blink again. "Jason, you have to tell Bri about her. What are you going to do when you're married and the crazy woman shows up on your doorstep?"

"I would've told her," I fire back, immediately on edge again. "If she hadn't accused me of cheating, like that's the first—and most obvious—answer to when a female non-client calls."

"She was once your client," Tara says.

"Off the record." I shake my head, because I'm not perfect, and the moment I tell Bri about Vi, she'll know. *She already knows*, I think, and she does.

Now, it's up to me to let myself be imperfect and vulnerable in front of her. While she holds a weapon and I offer chips and dips.

Doesn't seem like a fair fight, but my heart insists I do it, so I'll probably do it.

CHAPTER TWENTY-EIGHT

BRI

MACIE STANDS IN MY KITCHEN, SOMETHING FRYING on the stove in front of her. I haven't used the appliance since I bought the house, so I'm glad someone is giving it a trial run. "Smells good." I lift the coffee pot from the burner and pour myself a cup. Having Macie here with me is better than I anticipated.

She's gone early in the morning, and she scopes out the coffee shop in the evening to let me know if Jason is there or not. If he is, I head to throw hatchets. If he's not, I join everyone on the couches at Legacy Brew. No matter where I go and who I'm with, I feel the same.

Lonely and alone. Upset with myself for jumping to conclusions and pinning guilt on someone before they have a chance to lay out their case. Isn't that what good lawyers do? Listen to everything and then make a judgment on best how to proceed?

He didn't give you a chance, I tell myself for probably the hundredth time. I still don't know who Vi is, because Jason hasn't volunteered that information. He simply got upset that I thought he'd cheated on me, took his dog, and left.

Macie looks at me, her eyebrows up. "You in there?"

"Yes," I say. "Sorry, I was thinking."

"About Jason or a case?" Macie goes back to stirring whatever's in the pan.

I don't need to hide anything from Macie. She's been staying with me for the past eight or ten days, because Andy didn't propose. Instead, he's left Charleston for a new position at his job in Pennsylvania. She said she just can't face sleeping in a house alone, and since I've stayed with her multiple times, I immediately said she should come stay with me.

It's been good for both of us.

"Jason," I say. "I miss him."

"And you want to know how Vi is."

"Of course I do."

"Sit," Macie says. "This is ham hash, and it's going to blow your mind." She gives me a smile, and nods to the counter behind me. I do what she says, because I'm hungry.

"Why aren't you at work this morning?"

Macie doesn't face me as she says, "Coy says I don't need to work seven days a week at five a.m. He's good to go in sometimes."

"That's nice of him."

"Yeah." Macie's voice sounds a bit false, and it probably kills her to admit that Coy is nice. They've always rubbed each other the wrong way, and I think it's a miracle they've managed to make this partnership work at Legacy Brew. It's been a couple of months since Macie bought into the coffee shop, and neither of them has died yet.

The barstool scratches on the floor, and I still expect Timber to bark like a bad man is approaching the house. The only sound is the sizzling of the hash, and then Macie's feet as she turns and puts the pan on the countertop.

"I'll let you know if he's there tonight," Macie says. "But maybe you should just come anyway. Maybe if you two talk to one another, things will get worked out." She serves me a plate of ham hash, with a side of a smile.

"Not tonight," I say, feeling a bit like a chicken. "I've got an appointment tonight."

"An appointment?" Macie cocks her hip. "Really, Bri? You're just going to throw a hatchet."

"Sorry," I say, ducking my head and picking up my fork. "I shouldn't have said that." Her ex-boyfriend had told her he had an appointment on the last night they were together. It was really a flight out of Charleston for the last time.

Macie puts some hash on her plate and joins me. "It's okay. I know you didn't mean anything by it."

We eat for several minutes, and when I finish, I stand

up to take my plate to the dishwasher. I look out the window at the perfect late-summer morning, and I want to talk to Jason.

"Would it be horrible if I just walked into his office and told him I don't think he cheated on me, and I want to try again?"

"No," Macie says quietly. "It wouldn't be horrible."

In my head, it would be pretty great. I won't have to tiptoe around at work. I won't have to jump every time my phone goes off with the sound assigned to his texts and emails. I won't have to wonder when Vincent is going to call the two of us into his office and demand to know what's going on.

I have to fix things between us before that happens. I take a deep breath and turn from the window. "Well, I have to go. Another week at the firm."

"Good luck," Macie says. "I'll follow you out. Give Coy a break." She does just that, and I glance into my rearview mirror as she makes the turn to go to Legacy and I continue toward the parking garage for Farmer, Buhler, and Cason.

"Good morning," I say to Cheryl as I stop at her desk. "Morning, Orion."

"Hello, Miss Shadows," they chorus together. Cheryl hands me several slips of paper—the calls I've missed. Sometimes she simply has Jason's schedule on a few of them, so I won't run into him.

Today, there's a green slip of paper that says, *Jason is out of the office today.*

I look up, and our eyes meet. I turn the green note toward her. "Really?"

"Sick," she says.

My mind buzzes, because I'm not sure I believe that Jason is sick. "Thank you." I head down the hall to my office, a plan forming in my head. At my desk, with the door closed, I pick up my desk phone and check the internal extensions to make sure I get the right one.

The line rings, and then Brenda says, "Good morning, Jason Finch for Farmer, Buhler, and Cason."

"Brenda, hi." I clear my throat. "It's Bri. I'm wondering if Mister Finch has any slots in his schedule today."

"Hey, Bri." A squeak comes through the line, and it's probably her chair. "Jason's not coming in until later."

"Oh," I say, a bit confused because of the differing messages. "Could you give him a message from me when he does come in?"

"Sure thing."

I take a deep breath, because if I say this, it'll be like me hurling the ball at Jason and inviting him to play with me again. What if he doesn't? What if he won't?

"What's the message?" Brenda asks.

"Uh, can you tell him that I have an appointment with Ben at five-thirty, and I'd like him to be there?"

"Meeting with Ben..." Brenda repeats. "Where? In your office? A conference room in our hall?"

"Same place we've met before," I say, and hopefully she won't ask more questions. Lawyers can be a secretive bunch, and Brenda's been Jason's secretary for a while now. She doesn't ask for more than that, and she says she'll let Jason know.

The call ends, and I simply sit at my desk, numb. When I come back to my senses, I hurry to get my cellphone from my briefcase. I have one more call to make, and I get that job done with shaking fingers.

———

AT FIVE-THIRTY, I'm about to lose my mind. "Have fun, Bri," Jasper says, and I take the bin of weapons from him. It'll have enough tomahawks and hatchets for three people, as I've reserved a trio of lanes. One for me, one for Jason, and one for Ben—who won't be coming.

As I find the assigned section and start unpacking the weapons, I'm very aware of time passing. If Jason's coming, he's late. And Jason Finch is never late.

My chest vibrates in a strange way, and I suck back on a round of tears. I don't need to cry; I can throw a sharp object and hit the bullseye. I used to imagine Jason's face on the huge wooden target in front of him, but the past couple of weeks, it's been my face in front of me.

I don't mistrust Jason. I believe I got so jealous that I

lost my mind, and I can't let myself act like that again. Jason isn't going to get uglier, and there will always be women who want to be with him. If I'm going to be with him for longer than a few months, I have to learn how to trust him and trust myself.

The real problem is that I don't trust myself...or him. At least I didn't until the past couple of weeks. But I think I'm ready now.

I open the bin and start unpacking the tomahawks. Even though I've thrown here lots of times, I always start with the tomahawks. They're lighter, and they kick on my muscle memory so I can hit the target easier with the heavier, harder to rotate, hatchets. Not only that, but the hatchet has to hit either on the top tip or the bottom tip in order to stick, and the tomahawks have a pointed blade that sticks if it hits at all.

I glance toward the door, don't see Jason, and tell myself not to look again. Either he'll come or he won't. I go through the motions with the tomahawks, and when the third one sticks, I think, *Maybe Brenda wasn't able to tell Jason about this meeting.*

I dismiss that, because I feel like she'd have called me and told me if she wasn't able to communicate with him. Professional courtesy and all that.

I check the lanes, and of course, there's no one else there. So I'm free to retrieve my tomahawks, and I head down to collect them. I turn around, don't see Jason, and retake my position a couple of inches behind the line.

Three throws, and three hits. I go get the tomahawks, turn, and stumble over my own feet. I start to go down, and I'm scared I'm going to impale myself with the tomahawks or throw them at Jason.

He's standing several feet away, a box of something in his hands. "Bri," he says, but I can't stop myself now. I'm going to fall.

A yelp comes out of my mouth, and I toss away the tomahawks. Thankfully, not in Jason's direction. My knees hit the ground at the same time the tomahawks do, and that creates a strange sensation in my legs that doesn't go with the sound of the metal on concrete.

I throw my hands out in front of me, but then Jason's there to catch me. "I got you," he says, and he's right in front of me. No scrapes on my hands, no jolt up my arms as I catch myself.

There's just Jason.

We come to a pause, and I blink and look into his eyes. "I'm sorry," I say at the exact moment he does.

He smiles first, and I'm still too stunned that he showed up to do much more than involuntary bodily functions. "I threw the dip to save you, so we might have to go to dinner instead."

He strokes his hands down my arms and back up. One hand goes up into my hair and releases my bun, and he's gazing at me with what I can only describe as joy. Light, and love, and just...joy.

"I've missed you so much," he says.

"Me too," I say, finally finding my voice. "I trust you. I do." I swallow. "I know you're not cheating on me with some woman named Vi. I *know* that."

"I'm not," he says. He groans and shifts. "Can we get up? I'm too old to be on my knees this long." He gets to his feet, and then helps me to mine. We turn and sure enough, the box he was holding rests off to the side. Some delicious-looking dip has been splooshed all over the side of it, and I'm sure those chips and crackers were arranged neatly at one point.

He retrieves the box, looks down into it, and says, "We will never tell Tara of this." Our eyes meet, and I physically cross my heart with my pointer finger. He grins and says, "She made this corn and bacon dip, because I told her you love chips and dips." He nods with his chin. "This one with a jalapeño and hot chicken dip. Really nice with corn chips."

"Wow," I say.

"And the last one was—is—a pistachio hummus. She said it sounds weird but is the most amazing thing we'll ever eat."

I lick my lips, thinking of something else that is the most amazing thing I'll ever taste. And it's not pistachio hummus.

"You got my message from your secretary?"

"Yes," he says. "That was after I called Cheryl to find out when your next hatchet throwing appointment was."

"So everyone knows," I say, not that I care.

"About." He moves over to the small table where some people keep track of their points. He sets down the box of snacks and faces me again. "I was late, because Tara was still arranging things. I would've texted, but it felt like I should come in as a surprise."

"You're not late," I say. "I've only thrown a few times."

He nods, clearly still nervous. I know I am. "I really am sorry," I say.

"Don't," he says. "I'm the one who walked out and left you in my house, no explanation."

"You were upset."

"Yes, I was."

I give him what I hope is a flirtatious smile. "At least I know you're not perfect now."

He chuckles and shakes his head. "We've known that all along."

"Not me."

"Bri."

"Jace."

His eyes burn at me, and I know what he's going to say before he says it. "I love you," he says. "I thought I could move on, like I've done a bunch of times before. But...I can't. I can't, because I want to be yours—and only yours. I want you to be mine—and only mine."

My stupid tears are back, and I take a step toward him, my pulse choking me. "I love you too."

"Do you really?" He seems so boyish then. So open and so vulnerable. He's nothing like the man I started working with a couple of years ago, and I fall for him even more in that moment.

"Yes," I whisper. "I really do."

He receives me easily in his arms, and he lowers his head toward me. "Should I kiss you first, or do you want to know about Vi first?"

"You better kiss me," I whisper. I don't care that we're standing in the hatchet throwing arena, with *thunk, thunk, thunk* going on around us. I don't care if Jasper comes over and yells at us. I don't care all that much about Vi.

I simply want Jason to kiss me.

He does, and just like the first time, the world shifts. This time, my mind moves too, and I find myself in a brand-new place with Jason. One where he cherishes me, and loves me, and will bring me dips every day of the week until we're married.

He pulls away without taking things into gross PDA territory. "I've waited for a long time to feel like this about someone," he whispers. "I'm so glad it's you."

I keep my eyes closed and pressed to his collarbone. I listen to him breathe, and match my inhale to his. "I have a hard time trusting men," I say. I open my eyes and look at him. "But I trust you, Jason."

"Thank you," he murmurs.

We separate, and it's far too cold in the arena without him wrapping me up. "We have to have some of the dips," he says. "Tara's going to ask me about it."

"I'm sure she will." I step over to the table and pick out

a chip and try the hot chicken dip. It's spicy, and creamy, and warm, and I nod enthusiastically at him while I chew and swallow. "Mm, yes, this is great."

Jason finishes tapping on his phone and turns it toward me. A woman probably a decade older than us sits there. She looks benign, with bleach-blonde hair, perfectly applied makeup, and a smile that could charm snakes and gators alike.

"This is Vi," he says.

I don't know what to say.

"I helped her with a legal issue about five years ago," he says. "Not on the record. Nowhere at Farmer, Buhler, and Cason. She lived out by my parents, and she had some tenant issues."

"Okay."

He tucks his phone away into his pocket. "She was married, but she still wanted a relationship with me. I wasn't down with that, and things got a little...nasty."

I simply watch him and listen, good lawyer-like.

"She started, uh, going over to my mama's place a lot," he says. "She escalated quickly, and now when she calls me, I play into her hand, calm her down, and move on. Then I won't hear from her for months or even years."

"Wow," I say. "Is she still in the area?"

He shakes his head and dips a cracker in the hummus. "Fortunately, no. When she called a few weeks ago, she was in California."

"That's good," I say.

"She might show up at some point," he says. "I was going to tell you about her, because I will have to deal with her again, I know that. You deserve to know that."

I reach back and gather my hair into a bun. "I can handle Vi."

He watches me put up my hair, a light entering his eyes. "In your battle-mode-bun, yes you can." He smiles at me, and I smile back at him. I want to kiss him again, so I move right into his personal space and do that.

I probably catch him by surprise, and then the inferno ignites between us, and I'm afraid we do fall into the gross PDA type of kissing. Thankfully, I remember we're in public, and I end the kiss pretty soon after it starts.

Jason takes a deep breath and asks, "How committed to you are throwing tonight?"

"Not at all," I say.

"Wanna get out of here and, I don't know. Kiss me some more?" He gives me his sly, Playboy-Jason look, but I know there's something deeper behind it now.

"Yes," I say without hesitation.

"Great. I'll get the dip. You get the weapons."

I gather up the fallen tomahawks and pack them back in the bin, a new giddiness prancing through me. Then I go with my person out of the arena and to his SUV, where he presses me against the car and kisses me again.

He says he's waited a long time to fall in love with someone like me, and I can easily say the same thing about him. I break the kiss and hold his face in my hands. "I'm glad I get to be me with you," I whisper. "That I'm just okay being me, and you're okay being you, and we're comfortable being us."

"I'm glad for that too, sweetheart." He smiles at me again and reaches to open my door. "Now, I'm pretty sure you're dying to see Timber, so let's go see how he's doing."

"Yes, good idea." I have missed his dog these past couple of weeks.

"He's probably torn my couch to shreds," he says dryly.

"Oh, he has not." I push against his chest. "He's a good dog."

Jason catches my hand. "You like me more than him, though, right?"

"Mm..." I look up into the sky as if really considering it. "Yeah, I think so." I laugh with him and then kiss him again so he knows for absolute certain that I prefer him to his dog.

CHAPTER TWENTY-NINE

JASON

I DON'T KNOW WHAT WE'RE GOING TO SEE IN COURT today. As a general rule, I never walk into a courtroom blind. I always know what questions the other side will ask, and I know how they're going to lay out their case. I have my case locked down tight, with maybe a deviation here and there. But not often.

Bri looks at me, her grim face in place. Her bun is tight, her glasses perched just-so. She makes my blood so dang hot, and that's only increased over the past few months since we slopped dip around at the hatchet throwing arena, then went back to my place so she could be reunited with Timber and I could kiss her until neither of us could breathe.

We've been working together and dating since, and we've survived one major holiday already. She came to my parents' house for Thanksgiving dinner, and with Connor and his wife and baby there, I didn't even want to hurt anyone.

"Are you nervous?" she asks as we step onto the elevator to go up to the fifth floor courtrooms.

"Yes," I admit. I told her as much last night too. We'd spread out the case across the new twelve-foot island in her house, and we'd gone through it step by step. By step. No one's getting anything past me today—and that's doubly true because Bri is at my side.

She's not been in the courtroom since last summer, because she's so good at negotiating terms outside of a trial. That's the dream for a lot of lawyers, because they win without having to fight. Bri's good at both, but the firm makes more money when we aren't tied up in long court proceedings.

Bri's done so well this year that I nominated her for a full partnership position at Farmer, Buhler, and Cason, and I have every confidence that she'll get it. Maybe not this year, because she's only been a junior partner for nine months. But she's not junior partner material, and anyone who looks at her caseload, her ratings online, her customer evaluation forms, and her win-rate knows that.

I reach over and take her hand. "Dinner tonight? I got a reservation at Southern Grill."

"You did? During the holidays?"

"I called like four months ago," I say. "The day after we got back together."

"How'd you know we'd be in court today?"

I lift her hand to my mouth and kiss the back of it. "I didn't. Lucky coincidence."

She narrows her eyes at me. "Hmm. I don't think there are any lucky coincidences with you, Mister Finch."

I laugh, because Bri's always telling me I have the Midas touch. Whatever I do turns to gold. She's wrong, but I kinda like that she's got me up on a pedestal. I certainly have her up pretty high, and she never ceases to amaze me.

The elevator dings, and we get off on our floor. By the crowd in the wide, windowed lobby, the courtroom isn't open yet. I tug Bri off to the side to stand near the windows, in the sunlight.

"Vincent called me this morning," she says, not looking at me.

My heartbeat bumps wildly against my breastbone. "Oh?"

"Someone nominated me for a full partnership."

"That's fantastic." I smile at her, and she shakes her head. "What? You don't want to be a partner?" It's better money, higher status, bigger office—one with windows.

"I don't know," she says. "What about if we have a family?"

Ah, kids. I nod, trying to find the right thing to say. We've talked about marriage a few times now. I'm not in a hurry to get engaged or married, because I sense Bri isn't. But maybe...maybe she is.

"Did you want kids right after we get married?" I ask,

and now I'm the one who can't look at her. I don't want to influence her either way. "I mean, I haven't even asked you to marry me yet." We haven't looked at rings. I don't even know what *kind* of ring to get for Bri.

"I'm aware," she says dryly. She waits for me to look at her. "Why is that, Jace?" She turns toward me fully. "Are you waiting to buy a ring? Or...?"

Oh, so we're being bold today. I suppose we have to be in order to face our opposition in court. Frankly, I'm already nervous about that, and talking about marriage and babies isn't helping. Or maybe it is. I don't feel rattled or afraid.

"I don't know," I say. "I thought we were...going slow. Still learning about one another. Still deciding if you should get a dog and we'll have two when we move in together." I give her a grin, hoping she'll know I'm kidding.

"Macie has a dog who needs a home," she says. "I might take her."

"Great." I watch the crowd move as more people pile out of the elevators. I swallow and say, "I'm nervous."

"You know the case forward and backward," she says.

"About buying you a ring," I say. "And asking you to marry me."

"Why?" When I don't look at her, she steps in front of me. I don't have anywhere else to look now. Her dark eyes hold compassion and love. "It's me, Jace. There's nothing to be afraid of."

"Things will change," I say, swallowing again. "Like

you said, what if you make partner? Will we be too busy to get married when we want to? What if there's a big case we're working on? What if you then get pregnant? I mean, Callie and Dawson weren't married very long before they got pregnant."

I'm aware of the rambling, and I take a big breath to calm it. "I just want you to be happy."

"I'm happy with you," she says. "I think—" She reaches up to touch her bun. "I think life is unpredictable. I can't write out a script for when things will happen and what else will be going on. If people could do that, there would be no indecision. No choice to be made. Life wouldn't be interesting at all."

"So maybe you'll become a partner, and we'll get married, and you can have babies."

"Maybe." She takes a step closer to me, glancing around as people start to move. They've opened the doors to the courtroom. We don't need to be first inside, and she has something to say to me. I wait. She waits. With a bit more breathing room around us, she finally says, "I don't want things in that order, Jason."

"Things?"

"I don't want to be made partner before I become your wife." She cocks an eyebrow at me, bends to pick up her briefcase, and turns toward the courtroom.

I stare after her. They announce partnerships on April first. She wants to be married before then? It's almost Christmas as it is.

Better get the job done, then, Finch, I tell myself as I hurry after her. "After dinner tonight, do you want to look at diamonds?" I whisper.

"No," she whispers back. "We better go before dinner, or everywhere will be closed." She gives me a smile, and we enter the courtroom together. I have a great feeling about today, and it has everything to do with Sabrina Shadows.

I OPEN the door to the coffee shop, my smile so wide it actually hurts. "What about when Palmer said, 'I honestly don't know, Your Honor.'" I laugh, and Bri chimes in with me as she goes past. I enter behind her, and the moment I step inside, an enormous round of cheering begins.

Tara jumps to her feet, obviously clapping the loudest. Everyone's gathered there—Dawson and Callie, Alec and Tara, Lance and Jessie, Macie and her partner, Coy. My secretary, Brenda, and my across-the-hall lawyer pal, Benedict. Bri's secretary Cheryl, and her pod partner, Orion and his lawyer Aaron. Even Vincent Buhler is there, and a good kind of embarrassed heat rushes into my face.

Bri joins them as if she wasn't a huge, major driving force behind the single-day win in court today. She's clapping among the hooting and whooping and whistling, and I hate that she's not at my side. Even regular customers who don't know me shine smiles in my direction, and plenty of them applaud too.

"All right," I say, lifting one hand. I'm still wearing my ultra-expensive designer suit—I own just one, no matter how many Bri teases me that I have—and I'm actually ready to get out of it. The collar is a bit too tight, and I only wear it for really special occasions.

They keep cheering, and I yell, "Okay," to get them to stop.

"Speech!" Tara cries, her face alight with joy.

"Yeah," Callie calls. "Tell everyone here why we're cheering for you."

I look around, seeing a lot of familiar faces. So much friendship and camaraderie. I belong, and there's no glass between me and anyone else. I've never felt like this before, even when I've been the life of the party. The man of the hour at some nightclub or hotel bar.

But having real friends is fifty times better than that life.

I still can't stop smiling, and I say, "We won the United Methodist School robbery case today!"

More cheering, and I move away from the door and join my friends. Tara hugs me first, and then I get passed around to everyone. I finally end up next to Bri—right where I want to be—and I call, "I didn't do it alone. Sabrina Shadows was the one who blew the case open several months ago, and without her brilliant mind, we'd still be prosecuting the wrong man."

"Not true," she says, but it's not loud enough for anyone to hear.

"It is true," I tell her, beaming down at her.

"Two Frappuccinos over here," Macie calls, and the crowd starts to settle. Tara makes room for me and Bri on the couch with her and Alec, and we cram into the small space.

"Tell me everything," Tara says. "I got a few all-capped words is all."

"We don't have time to tell everything," I say, accepting a Frappuccino from a barista. I take a sip and lower it, my cheeks aching from the smiling. "Bri and I are going ring shopping tonight."

"You're what?" Tara screeches and begins to bounce up and down on the couch cushions.

"Baby," Alec complains as his coffee sloshes over the side of his cup. "Can you stop it?" He frowns at her, and Tara doesn't stop. She gets to her feet and perches on the edge of the table to tell our news to Callie and Macie.

They all look our way, and Bri says, "Good job, Jace," like I've done something horrible.

"Oh, come on," I say. "Tell me you don't want to go over there and gossip with them about your wedding ring."

She give me a grin. "Fine, I do."

"Oh, honey, the I-do comes later. At the wedding."

She shakes her head as she giggles, then gets up to join her friends. I watch her and sip my coffee, basking in the vibes of a really, really great day.

Dawson takes the middle seat on the couch and looks from Alec to me. "So," he says. "How are you going to ask her to marry you?"

Lance crowds in on my left, and I look at him. He looks real serious. "Um, I don't know. I haven't gotten that far yet."

"Oh, bro," Lance says. "You've got to have a plan."

"Agreed," Alec says. "A good plan."

"He's a lawyer, guys," Dawson says. "He'll have an amazing plan."

The three of them look at me, and the high from an amazing day in court and all the cheering fades to nothing. Because I have no plan to ask Bri to marry me, and she wants the whole she-bang done by the end of March.

I swallow, feeling like I'm marching to an open grave. "Yeah, and she wants to get married fast."

"Oh, so you're going to come up with an idea tonight," Dawson says. "Got it." He pats my knee as he stands up. "You have my number if you want to run it by me."

"You should definitely run it by all of us," Lance says. "You don't want to have the worst proposal in the group."

"Are there rankings?" I ask.

"Not among us," Alec says, and all of us look over the group of women with their heads bent together. "But with them?" He doesn't have to say anything else, and while I've experienced fear before, it's nothing like the chill moving through my blood right now.

CHAPTER THIRTY

BRI

JASON KEEPS FIDGETING WITH HIS TIE, AND HIS anxiety bleeds into me. I want to slap his hand away from his neck, but I don't. One, that's demeaning. Two, it's rude. Three, he's allowed to be nervous to meet my parents.

Heck, I'm nervous for him to meet them.

"Almost there," I murmur. A moment later, his GPS directs him where to turn, and he does. We're in the home stretch now, and I sit on my hands so I won't adjust my clothes too. It's fine. I'm fine. Everything is fine.

He pulls up to my parents' house just over a minute later and parks behind Chelsea and Bruce's obvious rental. "Okay." I blow out my breath and twist to get the boxed cake from the back.

"I'll get it, hon," Jason says, and he's out before I can

reach for the box. From the backseat, he adds, "I don't want you to drop it."

"Then we won't have anything." I face the house again, unbuckle, and get out of the SUV. We didn't bring Timber, and Tara's watching him for the next couple of days while we're in Savannah for Christmas.

Jason carries the Babycakes box, with the bag swinging from his arm with the cream we need to whip. I'm certain we'll be able to whip it here when we couldn't at my place the first time we got this cake. I glance over at him. That night was our first true kiss, and magical things seem to happen whenever we get a double-chocolate cake from Babycakes.

Maybe something amazing will happen tonight too.

I don't stop to knock or ring the doorbell, but push down the latch and enter the house. "Mama!" I call. "Daddy. Chelsea, we're here."

"Oh, they're here," Mama says from somewhere in the back of the house I can't see. The living room takes up the front part of the house, and there's a wall that runs parallel to the front of the house, dividing the living room from the kitchen and dining room. Everything here is sectioned off into its own little room, and if it were me, I'd be knocking down walls left and right.

I'm really good at that now, both physically and emotionally.

Mama comes around the corner from the kitchen and Chelsea swarms through the doorway leading from the dining room. I'm glad I don't have the cake, because I'd have dropped it to hug them both simultaneously.

I have time to take in my sister's big baby belly before she and Mama arrive in front of me. The three of us hug, all of us laughing and talking at the same time. The excitement lasts for a few seconds, and then they step back to give me room to introduce Jason.

"Where's Daddy?" I ask, falling to Jason's side.

"He's out in the backyard with Bruce," Mama's eyes are stuck to Jason. "They're checking on the pig."

"All right." I'll have to do introductions twice, but that's fine. Not ideal, but fine. "Mama, Chelsea, this is my boyfriend, Jason Finch. Jason, my mama, Josephine, and my sister, Chelsea."

"It's so wonderful to meet you," Mama says, rushing forward and taking Jason's hand in both of hers. She pumps too hard, and I want to tell her to calm down. Of course, I haven't brought a man home in, oh, ever, so she probably has a right to be excited.

"Mama," Chelsea warns, and I'm glad she says it and not me. Mama extracts her hands and steps back, patting her hair as she does. Jason is handsome, and apparently the age of the woman he influences doesn't matter.

Chelsea steps over to him and hugs him tightly. "It's great to meet you in person," she says kindly.

"You too," he says, and he's so genuine.

She holds his shoulders as she moves back. "Maybe

you'll get to taste my food this time." She flicks me a glance, and I scowl at her.

"Thanks for that reminder," I say.

Jason brings me into his side, and I look up at him. He's relaxed and smiling, so there's nothing to be upset about. He once banned me from using the word nothing, and I love all of my memories with him. "Can we go check out the pig?"

"Definitely," Mama says. "Come with me." She leads the way into the kitchen and then through the utility room to the back door. It screeches like the unholy dead, and I cringe. We all go out onto the deck, and then down a couple of steps and across a patio to the fire pit.

Both Bruce and Daddy are there, watching the pig rotate on the spit. I have a flash of embarrassment for a reason I can't name. Jason is more used to city living, and while my parents live in a city now, they're really country folk.

"Wow," Jason says. "This is fantastic."

"Daddy," I say. "Bruce, this is Jason Finch. Jace, my dad Arnold."

"Great to meet you, son," Daddy says as if I'm eighteen and about to elope with my high school boyfriend. I roll my eyes as Bruce laughs.

He takes me into a hug, and while I'm pressed against his shoulder, he says, "You look so happy, Bri."

I am happy, but I don't have time to say it. Bruce and Daddy switch, and I hug my father hello while

Bruce shakes Jason's hand and welcomes him to the family.

"He's not part of the family yet," Mama says with plenty of suggestion in her voice.

"Mama," I warn.

Everyone looks around at one another, and Jason finally clears his throat. "Josie, would you mind if we did it now?"

Surprise covers Mama's face for only half a second. "Absolutely not."

"Do what?" I ask as Mama scampers for the door that leads into the garage. Daddy picks up a poker and stokes the fire beneath the pig, and Bruce whistles through his teeth.

I stand there, the feeling that something big is happening descending upon me.

Sure enough, a massive, black-and-white Great Dane comes bounding toward us from around the side of the shed.

"It's Timber," I say in disbelief.

I look at Jason, but he's not standing at my side. He's on the deck, and he tears off his tie and tosses it to the side as music begins to play. Not just any music, but the theme song for a popular superhero movie.

Chelsea stands on the step above him, and she whips a bright blue cape around his neck and fastens it. Daddy leads a now-leashed Timber to Jason's side, and I don't know which direction to look.

So many things are happening, and they're all *planned*. Jason *planned* this.

My heart warms, and I smile at him, my love for him becoming bottomless.

Daddy leaves me standing on the gravel, and he crosses the patio and hands something to Jason. "Got it all?"

"Yes, sir," he says.

Daddy returns to my side, and Chelsea and Bruce take up a flanking position too. Mama holds a boom box—a legit tape deck from the eighties—that blares out the music. She's grinning from ear to ear, and the five of us look at Jason.

The breeze decides now is the perfect time to kick up, and his cape flutters behind him, then ripples like a flag. Like he's really flying.

"Sabrina," he says, his voice loud and booming. "Before I met you, I thought I could do anything. I was so wrong. But with you in my life, I feel like a true hero. You make me a better man. You make me so happy. You make me want to slay in court and come to your rescue when another lawyer steps out of line. You are the wonderful woman I want at my side forever."

He drops to both knees, and I sniff back tears. "I never expected to find love at a law firm."

And there's the cliché. I don't even care, and in fact, his proposal won't be complete without at least one.

"Will you marry me?"

I don't have to think. I don't have to weigh my options. I simply say, "Yes," in the loudest voice I can muster at the moment. Thankfully, it's loud enough for everyone to hear, and Mama cuts the music as Chelsea starts to cheer.

I rush across the patio to Jason, who slips a gorgeous diamond ring on my finger. He looks up at me. "I love you with my whole soul."

"I guess I found love when I wasn't looking for it," I say, grinning at him and then the diamond on my finger. It's similar to the ones I said I liked a week or so ago when we went shopping together after our win in court.

"That's a cliché," he whispers as he wraps his arms around me.

"I love you," I say, because that's not.

"I love you too." He kisses me, and cliché or not, I'm glad I got out of my own way so I can be Jason Finch's wife one day. Soon.

I pull back. "We can get married fast, right?" I ask.

"I believe your mama already has it on the calendar," Jason says. He gets to his feet as Chelsea and Mama crowd in around me to see the ring.

"He gave it to Daddy," Chelsea says. "And he wouldn't show us." She holds my hand and beams at it. "It's *gorgeous*, Bri."

Mama actually holds a paper calendar. "I've got the wedding on March twenty-second, Bri. Jason says he has access to your calendar, and that works for both of you." She looks at me with raised eyebrows to confirm.

I look at Jason, still standing there in his superhero cape, and reach for his hand. He joins me on the patio. "If he says that day works, then that day works."

He presses a kiss to my temple, but I want more. I turn in his arms and kiss him again, another time when I don't care who's watching—because I'm kissing the man I love and will marry in only three months.

———

Read on for a sneak peek at the next book in the Southern Roots Romcom series, **JUST HIS BARISTA.**

SNEAK PEEK – JUST HIS BARISTA
CHAPTER ONE: MACIE

I JOG BACK TOWARD BRI, WISHING I'D GRABBED A jacket before we left her house. "How's that one?"

"Good." Sabrina Shadows hands me back my phone so I can see the video we've been working on for the past half-hour. She's honestly a saint for coming out here with me on this overcast, windy late-January day.

It's her wedding I need a date to, so I think she feels bad. I've told her not to a hundred times. It's not like I've never been to a wedding before. Not hers, and we have gotten really close since she moved to Charleston.

Of course, now she's a fancy lawyer, with a super-hot boyfriend—oops, fiancé—and she's getting married in less than two months. My last boyfriend moved to Philadelphia without telling me.

I watch myself do the stupid dance, but I look like I'm

having fun. "Ugh, I messed up the end," I say, handing the phone back to her.

She frowns at me, fumbling my device with hers. She shivers. Actually shivers. "I don't see why you can't come to the wedding with Coy."

"Coy?" My voice goes straight into super-sonic atmospheric range. "Why would I go with Coy?"

Bri gives me a dry look—you can't get drier than the scathing, piercing, half-eye-roll she tosses at me before she goes back to her phone. "Please."

"Please, what?'

"Everyone knows you two have something going on."

"Yeah," I say. "We own a coffee shop together." And, I might add, it's doing amazingly well since I added my funds and brain power to the mix. Even Coy has said so several times.

I haven't told Bri—or anyone else—about The Kissing Incident between me and Coy. It was a one-night thing, and I was so upset, and he was so nice...

Trust me, he's not always that nice. And I'm not always very upset.

The idea of having to go to Bri's wedding alone, when everyone I hang out with is married or engaged—that upsets me.

"I need a date," I say, the desperation clawing its way up my throat. A particularly nasty gust of wind comes off the ocean, and Bri starts striding toward the parking lot.

"It's too cold for another take," she says. "Jason's leaving work right now, and I have to get Timber home before I meet him." She looks over her shoulder and whistles, calling the giant black-and-white Great Dane out of the water.

He bounds toward her, barking at a plastic bag flying through the air. I go with her, because she drove us here, and I don't have a choice. She has helped me a lot the past few months, but the street goes both ways between us. She's stayed with me a couple of times now.

She won't again, I think as I boost myself up into her new truck. She bought it specifically so she could put Timber in the back of it, and she pounds the tailgate behind me. The dog woofs again as he jumps into the back, and then Bri joins me in the cab.

She looks over to me, and I can't turn away fast enough. I know she sees something on my face, but I don't know what. I'm not like her, and I can't hide how I'm feeling as easily. She's always been able to box up everything, stow it away until later, and then deal with it privately.

I kiss my co-owner on the couch in the coffee shop we own together after something bad happens. Then I tell him it was a huge mistake, and we can't do that again. He agrees, and it's awkward between us for a few weeks, and now we're back to normal.

And "normal" for Coy and I is silent death glares, arguing, and eventual peace agreements. It's not walking through the park, all sunshiny and blue skies, laughing with a dog beside us.

I own *two* dogs, and Coy's pets are reptiles. I think. He said something about them once, but I honestly wasn't paying attention. He'd also just said I was as stubborn as one of them, so that kind of clogged my ears.

As Bri drives, I edit the video. I can't really do anything about the end. I can't reshoot it, because the lighting and location will be different. I decide to cut it off a second too soon, and I add on text, a sticker or two, and post.

Then I tuck my phone under my leg, determined not to look at my social media until I'm home, safe and sound and alone. Hopefully, I'll have my pick of gorgeous men waiting in my inbox, all of them mad for me already and falling over themselves to take me to Bri and Jason's wedding.

I know a lot of people in Charleston. Okay, "know" is a bit of a stretch. I'm acquaintances with a lot of people in Charleston. The ones who come into the shop in the morning. I know their names; they know mine. I have their coffee orders memorized. I know what they do for a living.

They come in, and go out. All day long. Some of them move on after a while, and I don't see them anymore. Some come in once and never come back. Everything at Legacy Brew feels fluid and full of movement, motion, and magic.

And I'm stuck.

I go nowhere.

Home. The coffee shop. Home. The coffee shop. Day in and day out. Heck, I go to the coffee shop, then home, then back again twice in the same day. I get off at two o'clock in the afternoon, but my friends have real day jobs that keep them in offices or kitchens until evening. We congregate most evenings on the couches and chairs at Legacy Brew, a real-life version of the TV show, *Friends*.

Except they were all single, and I'm the only single one left.

My mind wanders to Coy as Bri navigates the suburbs and then goes out a little further. The live oaks thicken, and then she turns down a street where her house sits. I won't get out of the truck at all, because she'll just put Timber in the backyard and then come back to the truck.

"Be right back," she says.

"Yep." The need to look at my phone is strong, but I resist it. Even more horrifying than going to the wedding with Coy would be not having anyone respond to my desperate plea for a date in seven weeks.

As Bri jogs around the side of the house, Timber in front of her, I remember something specific: She went to Tara and Alec's wedding with Jason. They were just friends at the time, and I think that's being generous. They weren't friends at all. She could barely stand him.

But they'd been hanging out with the same people for a while, and they both needed a date...

She tells me now that she's always found him attractive. Anyone looking at Jason would say he's attractive. *Men* everywhere can admit it, straight or not.

I fiddle with the ends of my hair, something I do when I have thoughts I don't want to face. Right now, they're all about how good-looking Coy is. I've admitted it before, but I duck my head and brush my fingers along the ends of my hair, looking for dead-ends. I just got my hair cut and colored, so I don't have many.

My stomach growls, and man, what I wouldn't give for a dinner date tonight. As it is, after Bri drops me off at my house, I'll probably heat up a frozen pizza or call for take-out. The oh-so-glamorous life of a single small-business owner.

I sigh and sag into the passenger window as I wait. The thing is, I was perfectly happy in my life until everyone started getting married. With Callie, I cheered the loudest, because she's the nicest person on the planet.

She and Dawson should be having their baby any day now, and I close my eyes and try to find the happiness center inside myself. My mama always taught me that it's good to be happy for other people. Even if you don't think there's anything to be happy about. Even if you're so miserable and want what they have so much.

I miss my mama sometimes. In times like these, I would've called her and talked her ear off, going over and over and over everything in my head. Then she'd say, "Macie-Mae. God put you on this earth to spread sunshine, and you best figure out how to get out from underneath those storm clouds so he can use your positivity."

Macie-Mae.

No one's called me that since she died. Four years now, and I still go see Daddy, and I have two brothers who watch out for me. But none of them will tolerate an hour-long call where I whine about my lackluster love life.

Coy pops back into my head, and I can still clearly see the desire in his eyes. I can feel the tender touch of his hand as it slides down the side of my face. He kissed me good, and sweet, and long, and I sigh again just thinking about it.

He has feelings for me. No man can kiss a woman the way he kissed me and not. He didn't confess anything, and he let me put him in his place again. I'm not sure why I did it. Maybe because I'm afraid of him flying off to another city one night, and leaving me with a snake's nest of problems at Legacy Brew.

"He won't do that," I tell myself. He loves Legacy more than I do. His daddy owned it, and his granddaddy before that. The Cochrans built Legacy from the ground up, and the only reason Coy allowed me to buy in to the company was because he was about to go bankrupt.

Things are doing so much better now, and I know I'm a big part of that. But so is Coy. He swallowed his pride, and he listens to me now, and we work together...for the most part. I don't work against him, at least. He doesn't sabotage me.

When he can't sleep, I find him in the kitchen at Legacy. When I'm restless, I go there too, and he wakes me up from where I've fallen asleep on the orange couch out front. We both have extra clothes in our offices—his is twice as big as mine—and we both have keys to all the doors.

He runs everything administrative, and I run the front of the house, just like I did before I bought into the shop. I also do most of the marketing thinking, and that takes a lot of time and energy. I'm the public face of the coffee shop, and he makes sure all the nuts and bolts stay oiled and operational.

Bri comes running back to the truck, and she practically leaps into it like she's swallowed something radioactive and is now superhuman. She's always been superhuman to me, as she went to college, then law school, and became a junior partner by age thirty-four. She was nominated for full partner this year, but she won't find out until April.

She and Jason are planning an exquisite vacation to Tahiti for their honeymoon, and I wonder what it would be like to travel like that. I grew up in Georgia, but I've either been there or here in Charleston for my whole life. I've never *wanted* to go anywhere else, and I'm not sure what type of bug bit me or how long this itch will stay.

"Did anyone bite on your video?" she asks.

"I don't know." I swing my attention to her. "I determined not to look until I get home." I give her a smile, and she returns it.

"There are some single men at the firm," she says.

"Sure," I say. "That guy who hit on you while you were dating Jason? No, thanks."

"He's actually nice," Bri says, kneading the wheel. "Just a little...eager."

"I don't mind eager."

"I know, that's why I mentioned him." She pulls out of her driveway and starts to head back toward the city.

I live in Summerwood, which is further south, and I love my little house. I love my job. I am a girl-boss now. I don't need a boyfriend to make my life complete.

I just need a date, so I don't have to go to a wedding by myself.

———

LATER THAT NIGHT, as I'm easing myself into the bathtub, I remember the video. I still haven't checked the comments on my post, because Daddy called me right as Bri dropped me off. He needed help with his air fryer, and that had turned into a screaming match where I finally said, "Daddy! Unplug it! Just unplug the darn thing!"

He'd been resisting that action, because he didn't want to have to reprogram it. "Reprogram it to do what?" I kept asking him, but my daddy is a little bit deaf and a little bit old, and honestly, his default should be to unplug anything with a cord, count to thirty, and try again.

The beeping had stopped, at least. I haven't heard if he got his corndog heated up to his liking or not, which means he probably did. After that, my pets meowed and whined for dinner, so I went through the motions of preparing that for them.

They're seriously so spoiled, and I barely had a warm meal in front of them before my pizza arrived. The cats—Lizzie and Emma—make do with their wet cat food, but Darcy and Susan—the dogs I got in honor of my mother after she passed—want their kibble softened with warm water, a can of green beans—with the liquid, thank you very much—and three squirts of salmon oil.

And they know if you only put in two pumps, let me tell you. Susan often looks like I'm trying to poison her if the water isn't heated to exactly ninety-five degrees or Darcy gets an extra green bean than her.

Honestly.

I make them a special breakfast and a special dinner every night, and I don't eat better than them. No pet on the planet does.

Then, I'd just wanted to wash away this day. It was my day off—I take them now instead of working seven days a week—but tomorrow, I'll have to be at the coffee shop by five-thirty to get things open by six.

Our bakers work all day so we don't have to have someone come in at three a.m. Because if I had to go over to that shop and unlock the back door for someone to make pistachio muffins that early in the morning? There's be a cot in my office and probably a head hanging from the rafters.

I'm a morning person, but come on. Three a.m. is *not* morning. It's insane.

I've already tucked my hair into a low ponytail and then covered it with a shower cap. With the red color, I try not to wash it for several days after going to the salon. I use dry shampoo and hardly any products to keep it clean and strong, so it's fine.

I'm careful not to put my hands into the water so I can handle my device. I have a tub caddy over the water, and I've already placed my phone there. Sometimes I stream music from my tablet, or put on the latest reality TV show I'm watching. The tub is my one sanctuary. The place I can shut out the world and be who I am and who I want to be.

I can be upset. I can be jealous. I can be the dark storm cloud my mama didn't want me to be.

I don't go straight to my phone, because I have a ritual for my meditation and unwinding in my evening bath. First, I light my grapefruit candle. It has a hint of vanilla and mint in it too, but it's the citrus that helps me the most. Then I crush a few petals of lavender and add them to the hot water. They drift around, though I've already filled the tub. Water is always moving too, and there's something dynamic and alive about it that I really like.

I brought in a glass of sweet tea with me, and it rests in the divot specifically for it. A few bars of my milk soaps wait too, and on the tablet stand with my tablet is a book I started last week. Bri's a fiction-reader, but I like non-fiction. This particular story is about a man who got trapped behind enemy lines in a foreign country and his journey to get home.

One more thing... I spritz my eucalyptus spray toward my feet once, twice, three times, and then replace the bottle next to the soaps.

Now I'm ready.

I pick up my phone, and I swipe, tap, and swipe some more. I'm almost afraid to go to my messages. I arrive in the app, and my eyes go straight to the envelope at the top. I see a twenty-one—praise the heavens, though about half of those will be creepers—before a text rolls down from the top of my phone.

It's Coy, and I see the beginning of his message before it pops back to the top.

Hey, Macie, I saw you left—

My heartbeat bangs against my ribs. What did I leave at Legacy Brew that he found? I pull down the notification bar and tap his text.

Hey, Macie, I saw you left off the end of that video on SnapShot. I can never get the end of that one right either. At least you posted.

I wrinkle my brow. "What?" I say to my scented candle and rising eucalyptus mist. I have no idea how to answer this. Coy Cochran is on SnapShot? That's the best my mind can come up with, honestly.

Another text comes in, right below his first. *I'd love to go to Bri's wedding with you. Do you still need a date?*

My eyes widen. My blood burns through my veins. My mind screams *yes! Tell him yes!*

I make a yelping sound and drop my phone right into the lavender-scented bathwater.

I STARE AT MY PHONE FOR ANOTHER MOMENT, THEN throw it onto the table in front of me. "You're so stupid," I say to myself. Across the room, Elmer and Orion bask in their blue light. I give them that right before bedtime, and I'd be embarrassed if anyone ever found my color-coded Post-it notes for their incandescent heat lamp and the full spectrum of their fluorescent bulbs.

I swear, I've kept GE in business just with two bearded dragons.

My phone doesn't buzz or chime, which means Macie hasn't answered me. She's glued to her phone, so I'm sure she's seen the messages. The first one can only be categorized as creepy—I don't have a single posted video on SnapShot—and the second?

"I'm categorically insane." I get up and run my hands through my hair. It's too long and in desperate need of a trim. I take better care of my beard, and it's sculpted and neat. I pace away from the couch where I've been watching Macie dance with the wind for the past hour.

I need a life outside of this house, those two bearded dragons, and Legacy Brew. Oh, and Macie Wilheim.

Maybe if I get on the rowing machine, I can get myself away from the thoughts of the redhead who follows me into my dreams. I row for ten minutes, then twenty, then thirty. My lungs burn, and the bench actually starts to squeak.

I finally allow myself to stop, and I reach for a nearby towel. I mop the sweat off my face and forehead and get to my feet. My calves ache, but it's nothing compared to my shoulders and neck. I really can't push myself like that.

I'm not in college—or even my twenties—anymore, and there are no medals to be won. I toss the towel into the hamper on my way out of the spare bedroom where I keep my workout equipment, and I move into my bedroom, then the shower. Maybe if I stand there for long enough, my humiliation will wash down the drain.

Unfortunately, it doesn't, and I'm left with the bitter taste of it in my mouth as I get dressed and head back into the kitchen and living room. The bearded dragons haven't moved, and it's dark enough now that I step over and turn off their blue light. "Night, night, guys."

I'm eternally grateful no one's there to hear me say, "Night, night," to my freaking reptiles. I glare at my phone and leave it on the table. It's face-down, so I really have no idea if Macie or anyone else has texted or called.

"She won't call." I head into the kitchen and pick up the half-drunk can of soda I opened earlier. I don't remember drinking it, but the snap-pop-hiss of opening it is in my memory. Macie doesn't like to talk on the phone, and for once, that serves me well.

The night is young yet, and I can't stay here and pine after Macie. I'm not super-friends with Sabrina Shadows and Jason Finch, but Macie is. I see her hanging out with them almost every evening, and they all seem to get along really well.

There's four couples now, plus Macie. I've stepped over to say something to her a time or two, and I can see myself integrating into that group. Then there would be five couples, and I could hold Macie's hand and drive her home after we go to dinner.

I swallow and turn around, new determination flowing through my blood. She has to know how I feel about her. I kissed her like a lovesick teenager several months ago and brought her coffee the next morning.

She put a stop to that before taking the first sip, and I let her.

I'm tired of letting her.

I snatch my phone from the table. There are no messages or missed calls. Anger mingles with my embarrassment, and I tap-stab to call Macie. The line rings and rings...and rings. She doesn't pick up, and I swear under my breath and hang up before her voicemail can pick up.

My phone rings a moment later, which is a good thing, or I may have thrown it through the window. It's not Macie. It's not anyone I have in my contacts, and I take a deep breath as I debate answering the call.

It's probably someone who wants to give me money for my recent car accident. It might also be my only chance at human conversation tonight, so I swipe on the call. "Hello?" I turn toward the window above the kitchen sink and look out into the quickening dusk.

"Coy," a woman says, and I frown. I do know this voice, but it's not lodging in my head right. "It's Macie. Macie Wilheim?"

Everything connects in my brain, and I say, "Oh, Macie. I thought that was you, but you're not calling from your phone."

"Yeah, I uh, dropped it."

"Oh."

"Shh," she says, and I cock my head. "I've got this." She's not talking to me, and I simply wait. Macie can do about fifteen-point-seven things at the same time, so I shouldn't be surprised she's calling me and talking to someone else.

She clears her throat and says, "I'm going to have to get a new phone, but I'm borrowing my neighbor's for tonight."

"Okay."

"I thought I'd let you know, in case you need to get in touch with me."

"So this is your new number just for tonight?"

"Yeah," she says. "It's an old phone of her son's."

"Okay," I say, and I want to know if she got my messages before she broke her phone. It took a lot of the courage I possess to send those messages, and while I had another surge that drove me to my phone to call her, all I feel now is nerves.

She says nothing, and I take a breath. "Listen, I sent you a couple of messages, maybe an hour ago? Did you get those, or did you drop your phone before that?"

"I got them," she says slowly.

"Oh." I need to eliminate that word from my vocabulary.

"I was in the...backyard, and I, uh...then panicked about my phone, and then one of my dogs threw...uh, herself a toy, and I...couldn't find my keys, so I had to walk to my neighbor's house."

I blink, trying to fill in the right words in the blanks in her sentences. I start to laugh, and she'll probably yell at me about that. She has before, but tonight, she giggles with me. "I think you're a liar, Miss Wilheim," I say, heavy on the Southern drawl. I grew up here in Charleston, and I can be a gentleman if necessary.

"Maybe some parts of that story aren't true."

"Which dog threw up?" I ask, leaning against the counter behind me.

"Guess," she says dryly.

"Darcy."

"She's a diva," she says. "She does it to punish me when she thinks I've withheld something in her dinner."

"Or she ate a rabbit earlier," I say.

She laughs again. "That too."

There's another pause, and I exhale everything out of my lungs. "So...what do you think? I own a nice suit, and I can dance."

I don't like the hesitation, and I actually roll my eyes. This woman pushes all my buttons, and I can't decide if they're the good ones or the bad ones.

"I want to say yes," Macie says. "But Coy..."

"It's okay," I say, my heart heavy but her first sentence still registering in my ears. *I want to say yes.* She wants to say yes? Why can't she say yes? I hate the word "but."

"No," she says. "Let me talk."

"All right," I say. "Talk."

"It's my best friend's wedding," she says, and I can imagine her standing up for the conversation. Macie doesn't like to sit during meetings. She says it makes her nervous. "And there will be a lot of eyes on me. My family will be there. A lot of my friends."

I say nothing, because I've learned that Macie likes to take a moment between thoughts. She'll continue, and I'm not surprised it's only a breath later.

"So...I want to go with you, but I don't want that to be the next time we go out."

My muscles twitch. "What?"

"Are you seriously going to make me say it again?"

"Are *you* seriously saying you want to go out with me *before* the wedding?"

"Yes."

I smile, and I swear it's the first time I've done so in a year. A real smile. True happiness. "Have you eaten dinner?" I ask.

"I ordered pizza a while ago," she says, her tone turning flirty at the end of her sentence. I know, because I've heard her flirt with a ton of men. That sounds bad, but it's not. I've simply had a crush on her for the better part of five years, and she's had several boyfriends in that time. She's a fun, bright person, and I'm about the opposite of that.

"But there's always room for dessert," she says.

"Indeed," I say.

She laughs and mocks me when she says, "Indeed," but in a British accent.

"Do you know the best place for dessert in the city?" I ask, and maybe I'm flirting too. It's been so long since I flirted with a woman, I'm not sure.

But Macie makes me do things outside my comfort zone, and since that kiss on that orange couch... My pulse speeds just thinking about it. It's a throb I have to have again. I had a taste, and it was just as good as I'd imagined.

I want more.

I want to see if we can make a relationship work, and not the business kind. The personal kind.

"No," she says all coyly. "Do you?"

"I do," I say in all seriousness now. "Are you up for an adventure, Macie?"

"I think so."

"Great," I say. "Tell me where you live, and I'll tell you how long it'll take me to get there."

"I'm not ready to go," she says. "I didn't even drain my tub before I got out."

"I—your tub?"

"I mean—I need a few minutes to get ready," she says, but I've already started laughing. She was in the bathtub when I texted her, and she dropped her phone in the water, probably out of pure surprise.

Everything makes sense now—except she can't be that surprised that I asked her out. I laid down far too many cards when I kissed her in the coffee shop.

"An hour?" I ask.

"Yes," she says. "I can be ready in an hour."

"Great," I say. "Text me your address, and I'll see you in an hour."

———

Just His Barista **is now available!**

BOOKS IN THE SOUTHERN ROOTS SWEET ROMCOM SERIES

Just His Secretary, Book 1: She's just his secretary...until he needs someone on his arm to convince his mother that he can take over the family business. Then Callie becomes Dawson's girlfriend—but just in his text messages...but maybe she'll start to worm her way into his shriveled heart too.

Just His Boss, Book 2: She's just his boss, especially since Tara just barely hired Alec. But when things heat up in the kitchen, Tara will have to decide where Alec is needed more —on her arm or behind the stove.

Just His Assistant, Book 3: She's just his assistant, which is exactly how this Southern belle wants it. No spotlight. Not anymore. But as she struggles to learn her new role in his office—especially because Lance is the surliest boss imaginable—Jessie might

just have to open her heart to show him everyone has a past they're running from.

Just His Partner, Book 4: She's just his partner, because she's seen the number of women he parades through his life.

No amount of charm and good looks is worth being played...until Sabra witnesses Jason take the blame for someone else at the law office where they both work.

Just His Barista, Book 5: She's just his barista...until she buys into Legacy Brew as a co-owner. Then she's Coy's business partner *and* the source of his five-year-long crush. But after they share a kiss one night, Macie's seriously considering mixing business and pleasure.

A Very Terrible Text, Book 1: Sometimes the thumbs slip...

She's finally joined the dating app everyone in Cider Cove is raving about...when she accidentally sends a message about wanting to meet up for a first date to her enemy.

A Very Bad Bet, Book 2: *Sometimes a wager only makes things more fun...*

She's got seniority over the obnoxious grump next door, and she's determined to beat him out for the top job in their charming hometown. But a bold bet spins their rivalry into a flirty attraction that could change everything.

ABOUT ELANA

Elana Johnson is a USA Today bestselling and Kindle All-Star author of dozens of clean and wholesome contemporary romance novels. She lives in Utah, where she mothers two fur babies, works with her husband full-time, and eats a lot of veggies while writing. Find her on her website at feelgoodfictionbooks.com.